THE DANGEROUS EDGE

'The master of espionage . . . as tense a thriller as any.'

Oxford Times

'Ted Allbeury at his best, an intriguing story very well told.'

Woman and Home

'Regular Allbeury . . . long, interesting flashbacks of the war . . . you keep turning the pages.'

Daily Telegraph

* * * * *

'A writer of espionage novels that soar above the genre.'

New Yorker

'No one since le Carré has mapped the lonely lunar landscape of espionage better than Allbeury.'

Observer

'The best, the most authentic and skilled spy novelist in a very crowded business.'

Toronto Sun

'The one that other thriller writers point to as the finest craftsman among them.'

Guardian

TED ALLBEURY

THE DANGEROUS EDGE

NEW ENGLISH LIBRARY
Hodder and Stoughton

British Library C.I.P.
Allbeury, Ted
The dangerous edge.
I. Title
823[F]

ISBN 0–450–56640–4

Printed and bound in Great Britain for
Hodder and Stoughton Paperbacks, a
division of Hodder and Stoughton Ltd,
Mill Road, Dunton Green, Sevenoaks,
Kent TN13 2YA (Editorial Office: 47
Bedford Square, London WC1B 3DP)
by Clays Ltd, St Ives plc. Typeset
by Hewer Text Composition Services,
Edinburgh.

*This is for Prof McIntyre
of the Royal Free Hospital, London*

Our interest's in the dangerous edge of things,
The honest thief, the tender murderer,
The superstitious atheist.

Robert Browning

1

Copies of all that day's papers were spread over the long oak table. Toby Young stood looking out of the window. It had been a long but mild winter and now the pessimists who had said 'we'll pay for it later' could claim that they were being proved right. It was half-way through April and it was snowing. Large, lazy flakes were settling on the outside window ledges, and the roofs of the buildings across from Century House looked like an old-fashioned Christmas card. When he turned to look at Mike Daley he said, 'You've met Fogarty – do you reckon he knows something or is he just fishing?'

Daley shrugged. 'Probably a bit of both.'

'There isn't a single fact in that piece he's written. Not a name, not even a hint – just the same old rubbish about ex-Nazis running around loose. In the States, in South America, in Europe – and here. Why now – over forty years later? Most of the bastards are long dead.'

'So why are we talking about it?'

Young frowned. 'Don't be a smart-arse, Michael. You know bloody well why we're talking about it.'

'There's only three we know of where they could pin anything on SIS, and like you said, it was all a long time ago.'

'They can still make a story out of it – no facts and every claim carefully covered by "it's alleged that . . ." And there's no other scandal at the moment for them to latch on to. The other papers will pick it up and then the Opposition will start demanding statements or judicial enquiries – anything to stir the pot.'

'What's the most they could say, Toby, that would mean real trouble?'

'That when the Germans surrendered, SIS employed ex-war criminals for intelligence work, gave them protection and enabled them to avoid trials as war-criminals.'

'But everybody did it, not just us. The Russians did. The Americans took over Gehlen and his whole organisation. Lock, stock and barrel.'

Young shook his head. 'Gehlen wasn't accused of being a war criminal at any time.'

'CIC used plenty of others who were.'

'The difference is that the American public would support them. They're patriots, not back-biters like our lot.'

'Have you mentioned it to the DG?'

'Very briefly.'

'What was his reaction?'

'Very wary.'

Daley smiled. 'Probably worried about his "K".'

Young barely concealed his anger at Daley's flip comment. His anger made worse because the same thought had gone through his own mind. It was routine for every new Director General to get his knighthood early on. He sighed, a rather obvious sigh, as he said, 'Your head's as likely to roll as anybody's.'

Daley grinned. 'That's wishful thinking, Toby. Why me?'

'Because the DG wants you to arrange for one of your people to trace the three guys who worry us.'

Daley shrugged. 'So what's the problem?'

'The problem is that if any one of them is still alive it means trouble – like what do we do about him.'

'So why trouble for me?'

'Because – as you well know – there are folk around here who still think it's a good idea to put the messenger's eyes out when he brings bad news.'

Daley shook his head slowly. 'Not this messenger, buddy.' But he wasn't smiling.

'Who are you going to put on it?'

'I'll think about it. Probably Mallory.'

'Why Mallory?'

'He's bright, and he's too young to be interested in the outcome – whatever it is. He wasn't even born when these things were going on.'

When Daley had left, Toby Young walked over to the table and gathered the newspapers into a neat pile, the tabloid that had worried them on top. Slowly and carefully he tore out the offending page and, sitting on one of the straight-backed chairs, he read it again. Maybe Mallory's first move should be to contact the journalist, Fogarty, and try and find out what he knew. Then his mind went back to Daley. They had been recruited into SIS at the same time. Had been in the same training group, and Daley had proved himself a very competent field officer. Bold, imaginative and a good leader. And now he was in charge of the most successful group concerned with covert operations. But it looked as if that was the end of the line for him. And he knew it. For further promotion he would have to get behind a desk and Daley didn't want that. He wouldn't be good at it either. Field officers needed quick decisions; desk-men were where the buck stopped, and that meant reflection and evaluation, not instant action.

Young often found Daley's attitude vaguely irritating. He admired the man but found his constant cynicism both juvenile and intentionally subversive. And it was a pose that juniors could find attractive. The cynical man of action. He guessed too that Daley resented having him as his controller. But he had done his own stint in the field and then opted for admin against action. And at least it meant that he understood the pressures on field officers. The tension, the loneliness and the resentment when legal or political factors precluded positive action. Knights, rooks and bishops on the intelligence chessboard thwarted by desk-bound pawns who were controlled in turn by a stubborn king. Of course it would never enter Daley's mind that one of his, Toby Young's, duties was to be concerned and sympathetic to the likes of Daley himself.

3

He looked at his watch and reached for the phone to tell Penny that he would be late for dinner. Again.

Daley phoned for Mallory but was told that he was on the small-arms course at Hythe and wouldn't be back for two days. Daley told them to get Mallory back for a meeting with him the next day and then went to the small conference room where his section's weekly meeting was just coming to an end.

He took his vacant seat at the head of the table and listened to Harris explaining the procedure for using the software that allowed the computer to convert high-speed Morse to standard characters. The equipment was laid out on the table with long leads from the mains sockets to the monitor and the computer. A separate lead ran from the Torch disc drive. Daley smiled to himself as Harris did his presentation of the new equipment with all the showmanship of Paul Daniels and his Magic Show.

Harris held up the floppy disc. 'You switch on the computer and then insert the disc into the disc drive like this. You press "shift" and "break" together.' He pointed. 'Now you've got the screen asking for a command. You tap in LAMTOR on the computer and it comes up on the screen. You press the on/off switch on this – the Kantronics converter.' He reached over to the Kenwood R-5000 and switched on. 'Now you tune the radio to the frequency you're monitoring. Let's try 5208 megs – that's a main Interpol frequency.' He paused. 'A couple of seconds for the software to lock on and then – there it goes.' He peered forward. 'That's from Wiesbaden to all Interpol receivers in Europe and the Med and the Morse in clear language on the monitor.' He waited until they had read the message. 'Right. Now one last thing. Never – repeat – never – switch off the disc drive with the disc still inside. You'll almost certainly crash the disc. OK?' There were nods and then Harris said, 'Any questions?'

Mailer always asked questions and true to form said, 'What happens if one does crash the disc?'

Harris hated people who said 'one' even when it was grammatically correct. 'One will get a right royal rollicking from Signals section, and second you've wasted about four man-hours while a new disc is being formatted.'

Daley interrupted. 'Before I forget. What happened about the missing Smith & Wesson?'

Williams said quietly, 'It's OK, chief. We dealt with it earlier in the meeting. It never went missing. Logan had handed it in to the armourer a month ago for a check on the alignment and he'd not had it back.' He smiled. 'He forgot that he'd handed it in. I went with him to his rooms and found the receipt in one of his jackets.'

'Tell him I want to see him tomorrow morning at nine sharp. What's next?'

'Nothing, skipper. That's the last item.'

Daley stood up. 'Let's go to the pub for a pint.'

The sergeant-instructor at Hythe was a dark-haired Welshman who gave his lectures in a lilting brogue that sounded uncannily like Dylan Thomas doing his poet's voice bit. It was quite the thing these days for army instructors to adopt a laid-back attitude rather than the old formal rituals that had always had such a soporific effect on most listeners.

On the long blackboard behind him were blown-up illustrations of a field-stripped gun and on the army issue table in front of him were two Russian assault rifles.

'This, gentlemen . . .' he said, pointing at one of the guns, '. . . is the AK47 – the 7.62 mm Automat Kalashnikov named after its designer. They are often referred to as submachine guns but that is incorrect. A submachine gun, like the Sten or the Uzi, fires pistol cartridges. The AK47 is an assault rifle and fires rifle-type cartridges.

'The AK47 is still a Soviet issue but has been replaced in many units by the AKM assault rifle. They are both excellent weapons and you will be having practical experience with both of them.

5

'The differences between them are mainly in manufacture and are easily recognised. The AKM stock and fore-end are made out of laminated wood, not the usual beech or birch used on the AK. The bolt and carrier of the AKM are parkerised instead of bright steel. The gas relief holes in the AKM gas cylinder tube are semi-circular cut-outs . . .' He stopped talking as the class-room door opened and the adjutant of the Small Arms School came in. He nodded to the instructor. 'Forgive my interruption, sergeant. Is Mr Mallory here – ah yes. The CO has a message for you. I gather it's urgent.'

Mallory left his desk and nodded his apology to the instructor as he closed the door behind him.

It was well after midnight when Daley got back to his rooms at Putney Bridge. He sat looking at the news on CNN and thought about Toby Young. He had never been sure why he disliked him. At one time he'd thought it was because of the filmstar handsome face. The iron-grey hair, the clear grey eyes, the tanned skin. He looked like the chap in *Dynasty*. Listening, working out how to respond so that he always came out clean and right. But he knew in his heart that what he really disliked was that they had started level and now, although their grades were the same, Young was the man he reported to. And what made it worse, he knew because he was a professional that Toby Young did his job well. The charm wasn't faked, it was real. And it worked, even with him.

2

Mallory drove the Healey 3000 through the winding Kent roads from Hythe to Ashford, turned on to the main Maidstone road and then turned left to the inconspicuous road that seemed to be leading to a small huddle of council houses and drew up at the guard-room of Templer Barracks, the HQ of the Intelligence Corps. He was wearing civilian clothes and they checked his ID carefully and then checked the Healey, lifting the bonnet and searching the boot. When they had looked through the contents of his canvas bag they directed him to a parking space on the parade ground. After locking the car he walked to the Officers' Mess and signed in, then went in to the bar. He ordered a tomato juice and looked around. The others, about a dozen men, were all in uniform, their 'pips' and 'crowns' with the green cloth bases that signified that their wearers were officers of the I Corps.

As Mallory picked up his glass a captain walked over to him, hand outstretched. 'Hi, Charlie, what are you doing here?'

Mallory smiled. 'Just checking on what you boys are up to.' He paused. 'I've been down at Hythe, learning how to play with Uzis and AK47s. Thought I'd pop in for a quick bite on the way home.'

You didn't ask fellow officers what they were doing. That would not only be bad security but bad form too, and no trained officer would tell you the truth anyway. But Mallory was an ex-officer, a civilian now. The I Corps was a pool of specialists that was frequently fished by SIS and other secret intelligence organisations. But those who crossed over tended to keep a foot in both camps.

Captain Mason smiled. 'Let's go in and eat then. Friday – so it's curry day.'

As they sat with their coffees after the meal Mason said casually, 'Are you glad they pulled you out?'

Mallory shrugged. 'It's hard to say, Joe. It's an altogether different world.' He smiled. 'A bit like our time in Berlin. More political. You can't take it for granted that your colleagues are on your side. I miss the comradeship we had here. But I guess it suits me.'

'Changing the subject – are you still knocking around with that girl you brought down here on Corps Day?'

'Yes.'

'She's really something that one. Everyone was asking about her.' He grinned. 'You moved in with her yet?'

Mallory laughed softly. 'No. She moved in with me.'

'You jammy bastard. She gonna marry you?'

'Who knows? Just have to wait and see.'

Mallory stood up.

'See you again soon, Joe. Take care.'

As Mallory drove on to London he wondered what Joe Mason would think if he knew about his relationship with Debbie Harper. Debbie was twenty years old, from a good West-country family. Stunningly pretty, an ex-convent girl and both amoral and immoral. Given the choice of the two descriptions she would have unhesitatingly chosen the latter. She said she couldn't understand what being amoral was, and anyway being immoral was fun. Maybe not always fun, but a girl had to earn a living one way or another hadn't she? When she asked why he thought she was amoral as well, he'd raised the question of lying about almost everything. She had laughed and shrugged and claimed that that was just her defence mechanism. If you told lies you could change your mind and alter the scenario. But if you told the truth that was it. You were stuck with it. But his analysis wasn't fair and he knew it.

She was affectionate, generous and lively; and kept a lot of people happy. In the twenties she would have been just one more flapper. In the sixties she would have been the first swinger. She'd once made him admit that being immoral her way made nobody unhappy. What was the harm in having a cuddle? They were both naked on his bed at the time, and when Debbie Harper was naked no man was going to devote much of his thinking to the precise definition of moral standpoints. But he could say quite honestly that it wasn't just the sex. He liked her. The warm, eager, optimistic outgoing personality and he was touched by her vulnerability. A vulnerability that she wasn't even aware of.

It was beginning to drizzle as Mallory got to Battersea Bridge and he stopped to put up the hood of the convertible. As he got back in he reached for the towel and put it on the passenger seat. If it turned to rain he'd need to drape it across his lap to keep the leaks off his clothes. But by the time he got to Chelsea the sun was shining.

He parked the car off Sloane Street and walked with his bag to the flat in King's Road above one of the few original, individual shops that had survived the swingeing rent increases in King's Road, Chelsea. He had lived there for four years at a reasonable rent due to the good offices of one of his father's grateful clients.

There were two messages on the answering machine. The first was from the Century House duty officer. His appointment with Daley the next day was at 11 a.m. The second message was from Debbie. She'd be at the club if he wanted her.

Mallory wondered why Mike Daley wanted to see him so urgently. But everything was always urgent to Mike Daley.

He unpacked slowly, throwing his soiled clothes into a heap for the washing machine, putting his shaving kit and brushes on the bathroom shelf, and finally he took out his note-books and the tape recorder and placed them on the small desk in the bow window. He walked over to the phone and dialled the number of the Crossfire Club. It was a man who answered and when he asked for Debbie the man said, 'Who's asking?'

'Tell her it's Charlie.'

'She's busy. I'll tell her you called.'

'Tell her now and don't bugger about.'

'Or what?'

'Don't bullshit, Louis. Tell her I want to speak to her now.'

'How d'you know my name?'

'Because I was going to the club when you were still back-up driver for Hymie's lot.'

'Ah yes. I recognise your voice now. It's Charlie, ain't it? Charlie Mallory.' He laughed. 'The Honourable Charlie Mallory. Look, she went out about an hour ago. Havin' her hair done.'

'When will she be back?'

'Jesus God, two hours, three – who knows?'

'Tell her I'll be there about nine tonight.'

'OK, squire.'

Mallory hung up. They were such creeps. They thought that an Italian name made people think they were Mafiosi. It worked well enough with the middle-class businessmen who came to the club looking for a girl. Paying outrageous prices for fake drinks while the girls promised anything they wanted for just one more drink of champagne. And the sight of Louis and Tony looming over the table was enough to make them pay up. But face them down and they collapsed like punctured balloons. They called him 'The Honourable' because he didn't speak with a Cockney accent and they still weren't sure whether he slept with Debbie or not.

He looked at his watch. There wasn't time to see his father before he went to the club. It would take some time talking to the old man and he wouldn't be able to tell him much. But just talking to him would help.

It was only in the last few years that he had really been aware of how much he owed to the large, amiable man who had given so much of himself and his time and wisdom to a fifteen-year-old boy shocked by his mother's sudden departure with another man to a new life in California. Patient explanations that human beings were sometimes driven by forces that were beyond their controlling. Never a word of criticism of the pretty woman they had both loved in their different ways. He wondered now if the fact that his father was a barrister specialising in divorce and family matters was what gave him that patience and understanding. There must have been times when his father had been lonely and unhappy but he had never shown it. Always that ready smile and some amusing anecdote about what went on in the courts.

His father had been disappointed that he had left university after only one year and had joined the army, but he had been pleased when he was commissioned and transferred to the Intelligence Corps; although he had been shocked when he told him later that he had joined SIS. It seemed that his father had once acted for an ex-SIS officer who had fallen foul of the establishment and in the course of the action his father assessed SIS as being both devious and totally untrustworthy. Mallory had explained to his father that there were many layers to the SIS cake and his client had probably deserved what he got. His father would have none of it and fulminated against SIS whenever they were mentioned. His advice to his son was never to trust them no matter what they said.

Oddly enough his father had taken to Debbie the first time he met her. She was used to being all things to all men and knew how to captivate judges let alone mere barristers. A fleeting mention of the Ursuline convent school and long dark eyelashes on a modest cheek were enough, and as they were leaving she made sure that his father could hear her say to Mallory, 'Your father really is a darling.' The old man had taken her to Ascot and had been the envy of his contemporaries. There had been four she recognised and eyes that avoided hers as their owners glanced furtively at her escort.

3

Daley signalled to Mallory to sit down as he went on talking on the telephone. His eyes scanned through the litter of paper on his desk and finally he used one finger to slide the page from the offending tabloid across his desk, turning it so that Mallory could read it. The piece was marked off by orange highlighter and Mallory read it, aware of Daley's mounting anger as he talked on the phone. Finally Daley hung up and crashed the receiver back on to its cradle.

'That was Berlin. Can you believe it, they pick up two guys in Savigny Platz last night. One's a pusher and they hand him over with a fat packet of heroin to the Kripo. They asked for a holding charge on the other bastard as an accessory, while they double-check his identity. When they go back to the Kripo *they've* released him on bail. He was the one we wanted. KGB up to his eyes. Those Krauts believe more in *perestroika* than the Russians do.' He sniffed. 'You read that stuff, yes?'

'Yes.'

'Well I've got a real crappy job for you this time, Charlie.'

'Thanks.' He smiled. 'What is it?'

'That piece in the paper about ex-Nazis floating around. Could be a problem for SIS. Only an outside chance but it's possible.' Daley leaned back in his chair. 'When the Germans surrendered it was chaos. For our chaps as well as them. Our people were supposed to be rounding up the Gestapo, the Sicherheitsdienst, the Abwehr, the Party brass and on top of that they had to carry out the

12

de-Nazification of our zone of Germany.' He shrugged. 'So people had to cut corners, and one of the best ways of cutting corners was turning some of the poachers into game-keepers.'

'What's that mean?'

'Using Nazis to catch Nazis.'

'So what's wrong with that? As long as they deliver.'

'Well some of them could have been war criminals. SS guys. People who'd sent off thousands of people to the Nazi camps. God knows what they'd done. It got swept under the carpet. But, now it's long over, the birds are coming home to roost. People want to accuse us of protecting war criminals. Letting them off the hook. Letting them go down the line to South America.'

'So that's South America's problem, surely.'

'Not always. A few are still possibly in the UK. We've got three names. We want you to find them and give us a background picture.'

'But that's Special Branch and MI5, not us.'

Daley sighed. 'Don't say that. Don't even think it. Can you imagine how Five would rub their hands to pin it all back on to SIS? We've got a reasonable relationship right now but the temptation would be too much for them. Just a word in the ear of some MP and a hint to a journalist and there'd be a special programme on *Panorama* in no time.'

'But it was over forty years ago and anyway Labour were in power when all that was happening.'

'Look, Charlie, you don't understand. They'd make it out that we and the Government had been covering up. If we *didn't* know it was happening they'd say we were incompetent. If we *did* know it was happening, then it was a criminal act and those who are in charge should be either sacked or indicted. All I want you to do is let me know the facts.'

'And there's only these three to check on?'

'So far as we know. There may be others but these are survivors and the only ones we're aware of that could embarrass us.'

13

'Do I get any help?'

'All the facilities but no bodies.'

'And when do I start?'

'Now.'

'How urgent is it?'

'Results are more important than speed.' Daley paused. 'Toby Young thought you might sniff around this chap Fogarty who wrote that piece.'

'No way. That would just alert him. How often do you want a report?'

'Weekly will do unless it's something really crucial.'

'Can I ask you something, Mike?'

'Sure. Go ahead.'

'Why are you sticking this on me? Have I done something?'

'How old are you, fella?'

'Thirty-two.'

'That's part of why you landed this. You weren't part of those days and – ' Daley smiled ' – and I can trust you. Is that enough?'

Mallory smiled as he stood up. 'I guess so. Who's got the file on those three people?'

Daley grinned and handed Mallory two pages of type. 'File there ain't. All we've got is there.'

Mallory looked briefly at both pages then looked at Daley. 'What about photographs?'

'We don't have any. They wouldn't be much use anyway. They'd be forty years older now. If they're alive that is.'

For a moment Mallory opened his mouth to speak, then changed his mind and walked slowly to the door.

As Mallory walked towards the bank of elevators he wondered what he hadn't been told. In the first month of his basic training the instructors always claimed that you shouldn't trust anyone. Everyone lies. The lies may be harmless or irrelevant to what you were concerned with. But lies were lies and like a good many others of

14

his rank his distrust started at home. Right inside Century House.

Mallory took the notes back to his flat and sat in the kitchen with an apple-juice and sliced cheddar on wafer biscuits. He read it three times before he finally accepted that he was on a wild-goose chase. Almost all the scanty information covered events over forty years earlier. Anything later was supposition. Even the war crimes of which they were suspected were unspecific. He made notes of the facts for each name.

Stefan Wolff Born 17 Jan 1920. Osterode (Harz Mountains) Nieder-Sachsen. Joined NSDAP 1939. Joined Wehrmacht 1939. Transferred to Waffen SS 1940. Served Eastern Front then posted as 2 I/C of Einsatz Kommando based in Krakov. Responsible for rounding up Jews and subversives for despatch to Oswiecim (Auschwitz). Listed in CRASC document as war-criminal. Arrested by British Security in Bremen Sept 1945. Recruited as interpreter then used as informant in Hamburg area. Attended unit reunion in London in 1951 and was believed to be living in Birmingham working as security guard at Fisher and Ludlow (became part of Austin/Morris, now British Leyland).

Erich Keller Born 24 Oct 1919. Berlin. Father lawyer. Mother actress (musical comedy). Attended art-school in Berlin. Later worked as director of Staedtische Buehne (Local Theatre) in Brunswick and Hannover. Called up 1939 and because of language qualifications (English, French) was recruited by Sicherheitsdienst. Served first in Berlin and then in Amsterdam. Responsible for sending both Jews and non-Jews to camps. (Belsen-Bergen and Mauthausen). Arrested by 103 Field Security Section in Peine (near Hannover) in 1945 and taken to HQ in

Hildesheim. Was used in intelligence role by unit until 1950 when he was transferred to 21 Army Group at Bad Oeynhausen and believed used on line-crossing operations in area Helmstedt into Soviet Zone. No records extant. Last heard of as being given Canadian documents and possibly pension. Believed headed for Toronto with introductions to radio executives. Likely that Canadian documentation was genuine, not forged. A report was registered in late 50s that he was seen in London on two different sightings by former British intelligence officers.

Fritz Dettmer Born Jan 1914. Frankfurt. Nothing known until subject joined Gestapo in 1937. Mother Scots. Born Edinburgh. Née Maclean, Doris. Dettmer might have been earlier a member of Kriminalpolizei. Operated in Prague and then in Warsaw. Accused of torture of civilians and prisoners in Auschwitz where he was in charge of eight (8) blocks. Later was deputy head of Gestapo in Magdeburg. When 30 Corps pulled back to borders agreed at Yalta Dettmer was allowed passage to British Zone. Was recruited by Field Security to operate in line-crossing operation into Soviet Zone. Believed under control of Keller, Erich. In 1952 was allowed to go to UK. Destination believed to be Glasgow or Edinburgh. Nothing further known. Believe holds British passport.

Mallory decided that he would drive down to Birmingham and see what he could find out about Stefan Wolff. He went back to the flat and packed a bag and left a message on her answering phone for Debbie.

He turned off the M1 on to the M45 and wound his way past Coventry and eventually turned off the main road into Castle Bromwich. At a newspaper shop he got directions to the old Fisher and Ludlow factory next to the Dunlop works. It was now part of British Leyland.

At the factory's main entrance the guard stopped him and he asked for the chief security officer. The guard phoned through to security and then showed him on a map of the sprawling site where the main offices were. He was amazed at the size of the place, so large that it had its own internal bus service.

He pulled into the visitors' carpark and walked back to the main office. The receptionist phoned through to Security and a secretary came down and escorted him to a lift. On the second floor he was taken down a long corridor that led through a room with staff watching panels of surveillance monitors, to an office that was obviously used only as a meeting room. The man who shook his hand said, 'The boss is away but maybe I can help you. I gather from your ID at the gate that you're SIS.' He smiled. 'We're more used to spies from rival manufacturers.'

Mallory laughed. 'Do you get many of those?'

'My name's Jack Heyford. Do sit down.' When Mallory was settled Heyford said, 'We used to get quite a lot of industrial snooping but we put up a novel idea to management and to our surprise they accepted it. We invited our rivals to come and look us over. Engineers, designers, production people – the lot. And that was the end of the spying.'

'That was quite a risk, surely?'

'As a matter of fact it wasn't. Our philosophy is let 'em look. If they copy something we do it'll take them six months to put it into practice. And in six months from now we'll be doing it differently. Quicker, better, cheaper – you name it. Our production managers have to justify keeping equipment that's more than a year old. Our philosophy is: surely there's some better way of doing it, whatever it is.'

Mallory grinned. 'Maybe governments'll get round to thinking that way and we can close down SIS.'

'Nice thought. Now – what can we do for you?'

'I'm trying to trace a man named Wolff. Stefan Wolff.

We believe that he was at one time working here as a security guard.'

'When?'

'When the plant was still called Fisher and Ludlow.'

'That's way back. I'd think he would have retired by now. Can you wait while I have him checked out?'

'Yes.'

Heyford phoned through instructions to someone and then hung up.

'We put most of our records on computer some years back. If we're lucky it won't take too long.'

'What's your main work here as security people?'

'Physical security – against kooks who think autos pollute the atmosphere. Petty theft and organised theft. Mainly spare parts. And to some extent we liaise with Special Branch in the City regarding subversives. But strikes aren't the problem they used to be.'

A girl brought in a sheet of computer print-out and Heyford took it from her and read it carefully as she left. He looked up at Mallory.

'Your information was right, Mr Mallory. He did work here. Seems to have been a satisfactory employee. Retired on pension three years ago. He died a year ago this month and his widow is receiving a standard pension as of now. Seems he had two strokes one after the other and died a few hours after being received at the General Hospital.'

'There's proof of death?'

'Yes. We received the family doctor's report and we have a photostat of the death certificate. And a member of our staff attended his funeral at Witton Cemetery.'

'Have you got an address for the widow?'

'Yes, she's still at the old address. Two hundred and five Mere Road in Erdington – not far from here.'

Mallory noted the address. 'May I have a photocopy of the death certificate?'

'Of course.'

*

The house in Mere Road was just over the brow of the hill. Victorian red-brick with bay windows up and down and a substantial porch over the steps that led to a door with coloured-glass windows and a heavy brass knocker.

The woman who answered the door was wiping her hands on the flowered pinafore she was wearing. Her face was impassive as she said, 'What is it?'

'Are you Mrs Wolff?'

'Yes. Who are you?'

'I wondered if I could have a word with you about your late husband?'

'Are you from the Prudential about the insurance?'

'No. I just wanted to ask you about how you met him and what he was like?'

She sounded suspicious. 'What do you want to know that for?'

'Just a personal interest.'

'Did you know him?'

'I knew of him from others.' He smiled. 'I wouldn't take up much of your time.'

For a few moments she hesitated and then she said, 'You'd better be quick then, I've got my cleaning job to go to in an hour.'

She led him a few yards down a narrow corridor and opened the door to a room with dust-sheets over a three piece suite. She pulled the sheets from the two armchairs, folded them carefully and pointed to one of the chairs, as she took off her pinafore and sat facing Mallory.

'Where did you meet your husband?'

'At the social club on Slade Road. Up by Stockland Green. Bingo and old-time dancing.' She smiled. 'He was the best dancer there even if he was one of the older ones.'

'Did he work then at Fisher and Ludlow?'

'No, he worked as a collector for the Pru then. That's how we got the insurance. He went to the factory just before we got married. Said it was better pay and more interesting. But it was a long bike ride to Tyburn Road.'

'Was he born in Birmingham?'

19

'Oh no. He was born somewhere in Germany. I think he was a refugee. Came over just before the war. They interned 'em when the war started. Enemy aliens they called 'em. Worked down the mines and then when it was over he came here to Brum. Got the job at the Pru. Thought the world of him they did. He had a way with people. Took no nonsense about paying next week and all that stuff.'

'Have you got a photograph of him?'

She smiled and pointed to a framed photograph behind him on an upright piano. It was a strangely old-fashioned face. Black hair plastered back, dark eyes and heavy eyebrows and deep lines from the side of the nose to the lips. It was an arrogant face. And he'd obviously told her a pack of lies.

'A handsome man, Mrs Wolff.'

'He certainly was.' She smiled. 'Had an eye for the ladies too. They all fancied him.'

'A good husband?'

'Oh yes.'

'Any children?'

'No. He said they were too much responsibility with the world as it is.'

'Well thank you for your time, Mrs Wolff.'

'What was it all about, the questions?'

Mallory smiled as he stood up. 'Just curiosity about a man I'd heard about.'

She still seemed suspicious but she showed him politely to the front door.

It took him forty minutes roaming around the vast, sprawling cemetery before he found the grave. There was a polished granite headstone that just said – Stefan Wolff 1917–1984. The year of birth didn't correspond with his notes but that could be a mistake on what was, after all, an insignificant file in SIS records. Or it could have been part of the deception by Wolff himself. Short of having an exhumation he could cross him off his list.

4

The entrance to the Crossfire Club was down a narrow alley off Frith Street. It was at the rear of an employment agency for catering staff that fronted the building, and the club was on two floors and a basement. It was licensed by Westminster Council as a social club with a drinks licence that extended to 3 a.m. except on Sundays. The two men who owned the building had bought it when there was the big crackdown on vice by the local council and rentals and prices had been decimated inside a few weeks. One of the owners was a successful stockbroker and the other was part-owner of several other similar clubs that made money out of conning tourists and home-grown suckers with exorbitantly priced drinks and hostesses. After the crackdown there was a truce between the conflicting interests of club owners and council. Less flamboyance on one side and minimal harassment by the other. The partners estimated that they had made just over 1.4 million pounds in twelve weeks when rents eventually went back to their old levels and higher.

There was an untidy heap of black plastic garbage bags alongside the club entrance. The operators of the Crossfire Club had refused to pay the extortionate bribes of the council garbage collectors and Louis had written a rather rambling letter of complaint to the Cleansing Department. Louis and Tony Fratelli, who ran the club for a syndicate, were paid a percentage. Not off the top, but a percentage on profits. They toed the line because even a not very bright accountant could make it no profits at all if he wasn't kept happy. Fortunately Artful Arthur who looked after the accounts was not only bright but had a liking for pretty girls and that made him easy enough to satisfy.

The bouncer on the door was an ex-Marine and he did a casual salute as he opened the door for Mallory. 'Have a nice time, Cap'n.'

Mallory smiled. 'You too, Sandy. How's the old woman?'

'In good nick, Cap'n. Had her teeth fixed yesterday.'

The lighting inside was dim and pink. Pink bulbs over the bar and pink shades on the tables. As he stood at the bar with a whisky from the bottle under the counter, he looked around. Most of the tables were occupied and he could see Debbie, laughing and chatting with two men at one of the alcove tables. Then she saw him and stood up and walked over to him.

'Hi. What are you doing here?'

'I'm catching the night train to Glasgow so I just popped in to see that you were OK.'

'I won fifty quid on a horse at Lingfield today.'

'Who are the two guys at the table?'

'They're in town for a sales conference. They've got fast-food franchises.'

'Which reminds me. I've stocked the fridge up with food if you want to use my place.'

'How long will you be away?'

'A couple of days. Maybe three. You'd better get back to your table, honey.'

'Let them wait.' But she turned and waved and smiled at the two men, who waved back. She turned her head to look at his face. 'Is it OK if I sleep at your place?'

'Of course it is.'

He took out his key ring and eased off the Yale door key and handed it to her. 'If I'm back before Friday how about we go down to the country for the weekend.'

He saw the pleasure on her face. 'Yes. Could we go to that place we went to last time?'

'You mean the hotel in Bath?'

'Yes. That's the place.' She put her arms round his neck and kissed him on the mouth.

She walked with him to the street door and stood in the alley and watched him walk away. She was disappointed that he didn't look back.

At the station Mallory made his way to his first-class sleeper. First-class night sleeper to Glasgow was almost the last form of civilised travel left and he slept solidly until six the next morning when the guard brought him a cup of tea and a biscuit half an hour before they were due in at Glasgow Central.

He spent three fruitless days in Glasgow and Edinburgh. There was no trace of anyone named Dettmer. He checked directories, voters' lists, rate payers, a credit status data bank and the Social Services records but there was no Dettmer. It meant trying to find war-time records of any Field Security Sections that had been involved in line-crossing operations.

As they drove down the M4 towards Bath she pointed at a road-sign pointing to Chippenham.

'That's where my family live.'

'Do you want to turn off and see them?'

'Good God, no. They'd be horrified if I appeared without a week's notice.'

He laughed. 'You're kidding, why?'

'I'm not, Charlie. I'm the black sheep of the family. The example they give to my sisters of what'll happen to them if they don't toe the line.'

'I've booked us in at the Francis, the same hotel that we stayed at last time.'

'I liked that place. Everybody was so friendly and old-fashioned.'

She was watching something being flambéed at a nearby table and then she turned to him, smiling as she whispered, 'Why is it always such creeps who want things flambéed?'

'I hadn't noticed that it was.'

'It is. I've noticed it lots of times.'

'Tell me about your family.'

She laughed. 'Things that could be better phrased – talking of creeps tell me about your family.'

He smiled. 'I didn't mean that. Must have been a Freudian slip or something.'

She shrugged. 'My father's a financier. He used to be a merchant banker in the City and he made enough money to go into business on his own account.'

'What the hell does a financier do?'

'I only know what *he* does. He provides capital for small companies on the way up. Makes a lot of bread too.'

'How does he decide if they're likely winners?'

'His accountant goes through their books. Checks them out and then Daddy interviews the principals. If he approves of them then he takes a shareholding.'

'What makes him approve or not?'

'It's what he calls their "demeanour".' She laughed. 'Like not wearing brown shoes with blue suits. And certainly not wearing brothel-creepers like you wear.'

'They're desert boots, my love.'

She looked at his face for a moment and then said softly, 'I like it when you call me your love. Even if you don't mean it.'

'You must get called a lot more flattering things than "my love".'

'It's who says it that matters. And how it's said. If I've got my clothes on it counts double.'

'What's he like as a man – your father?'

'Big. Moustache. Pompous. Self-satisfied – made my own way in the world – none of the advantages you gels have.'

'I've never actually met anyone who says gels.'

'Anytime you want – just say the word.'

'What happened after the convent?'

'It's more what happened *at* the convent.'

'Tell me.'

'The usual thing – boys.'

'Then what?'

'They chucked me out and I had to work as a typist at an estate agent's who was a friend of the old man.'

'And?'

'And he made passes at me and I didn't like him.'

'Why not?'

She shrugged. 'He was a real ass-hole.'

'So you left.'

'So he sacked me and told Daddy I was making passes at clients.'

'Then what?'

'I pinched a hundred and fifty quid from the old man's petty-cash box and came to London.'

'How did you end up at the Crossfire?'

'It was what you could call a voyage of discovery.'

'What did you discover?'

'That the only qualifications I had were a pretty face, big boobs and a talent for amusing the kind of men who go to places like the Crossfire.'

'And what would you like to be if you had the qualifications?'

She frowned as she thought. 'Sometimes I'd like to be an actress, sometimes I'd like to be a nun.'

'What kind of actress?'

'In the theatre. A proper actress.'

'You're still young enough. Go to RADA or take a job as an assistant stage manager and work your way up.'

She smiled. 'Maybe one day I'll surprise everybody and do something sensible.'

The Ministry of Defence asked for a written request before they would provide any information on occupation-time intelligence units in Germany and Mallory drove down to the Corps depot at Ashford and spent a day in the Corps Museum.

He came away with six locations and details of Field Security Sections that had operated along the Zone borders. He had names, ranks and group photographs. And what he valued most was the present address of the officer who had commanded the FS unit that had covered the border crossing at Helmstedt. He checked the War Office list and found that the man who had then been Captain Carter had been promoted to major when he was posted to 30 Corps HQ at Bad Niendorf. Major Carter (retired) now lived in Chichester.

It was one of those beautiful houses in South Pallant, its door right on the street. Genuine Georgian with mason's touches in the keystones to the windows. Dignified but not overbearing. A window box of primroses on the outer window ledge, undisturbed and not doomed to blush unseen. In London they would have been vandalised within hours of being displayed.

As he let the brass lion's-head knocker fall he heard it echo inside the house despite the solid door, and then a woman's heels on tiles before the door was opened. She was in her fifties with one of those faces whose eyes, mouth and bone structure ensured that she would still be handsome even if she lived to be a hundred.

She smiled as she said, 'You're from the Cathedral Fund of course. So glad you came. We've got two collecting tins absolutely crammed full.'

Mallory smiled. 'I'm sorry to disappoint you. I actually came to ask if your husband could spare me a few minutes.'

She smiled the smile of a woman who was used to fending off intruders on her husband's time. 'What exactly did you want to see him about?'

'About his time in the army.'

'Are you army?'

He smiled. 'Kind of. I used to be and still am in a kind of a way.'

'How interesting,' she said. 'You'd better come in. I'll

take you out to him. He's out in the garden, planting out the sweet pea seedlings, hoping we'll have no frosts.'

The garden was small. A walled garden in local brick and as well designed and laid out as the house itself. The man on his knees with a trowel looked over his shoulder, saw his wife and Mallory and stood up slowly.

'This young man wanted a word with you, Eddie. Army stuff.' She smiled at Mallory. 'I'll leave you two to get on with it.' And she walked back into the house.

Carter said, 'I didn't get your name.'

'It's Mallory. Charles Mallory.' He reached inside his jacket and handed Carter his SIS ID card, his green membership folder of the Intelligence Corps Association and his membership card of the Special Forces Club.

Carter looked at each of them quite carefully and then handed them back.

'What can I do for you. There's chairs on the patio and some lemonade.' He smiled. 'Real lemonade. Trixie's special.'

When the major had poured them each a glass of lemonade he sat down and looked at Mallory with eyebrows raised in question.

'I wanted to talk to you about a man named Dettmer.'

'Who is he?'

'I thought you might remember him. I think he worked for you in Germany after the surrender.'

Carter smiled. 'I doubt if I could name more than two or three of my own section. It's a long time ago.' He paused. 'What's he look like?'

'I've no idea.'

'So why have you come to me?'

'Because the records indicate that he was used on line-crossing operations into the Soviet Zone. The record says that he was previously Gestapo in Magdeburg so it seems likely he worked for us into that area. Your FS Section was more or less opposite Magdeburg.'

Mallory saw a change on Carter's face. He was sure Carter knew now who he was talking about.

27

'Tell me more,' Carter said quietly.

'His mother was a Scot and before the war he was in the Kriminalpolizei. In the Gestapo he'd been in Prague and Warsaw.'

'Where did you get the name Dettmer from?'

'It was one of three names I was given, along with some notes on each man.'

'If he's who I think he is his name was never Dettmer. He might have used it as an alias at some time but it certainly wasn't his name. Why are you interested in him?'

'We believe he could be classified as having committed war crimes.'

Carter held up his hand. 'And you're all scared of that garbage in that rag the other day. British intelligence using ex-Nazis and all that crap.'

'Not scared.' He smiled. 'Just taking precautions and checking the facts.' He paused. 'Is your man still alive?'

'Very much so.'

'Can I talk to him?'

'I don't think so.'

'Why not?'

'Who were the others on your list?'

'A Stefan Wolff. He's dead. And a man named Keller. Erich Keller.'

'Who gave you the names and the notes?'

'My boss at Century House.'

'And they think that I'll sell men down the river who worked for me and for British interests just because the gutter press can't pin some sex story on a government minister at the moment.'

Carter's pale face was growing pink with his indignation.

'I don't see any reason why you should see me just talking to the man as selling him down the river.'

'You don't, eh? How long have you been in SIS?'

'Twelve years.'

'Then you ought to know better than try to bullshit an

old hand like me.' He leaned forward aggressively, 'What do you want to talk to them about?'

'To establish if they did actually commit war crimes and how and why we used them.'

'And then what?'

'That would be for others to decide.'

'For Christ's sake, Mallory, what do you think the so-called "others" would do?' He waited for a moment for Mallory to reply and when he stayed silent Carter shouted. 'He'd disappear. One more corpse dragged out of some canal because they daren't let him be alive.' He leaned back in his chair, suddenly calm again. 'You'd better work it out my boy. This works both ways.'

'What does that mean?'

'It means that you could disappear too.'

'Are you threatening me, Major?'

'You bet your boots I am. But it isn't me you should be scared about.'

'Are you ashamed of what you did?'

'No way.'

'So why can't we talk about it?'

'Because you wouldn't understand.'

'Why not?'

'It was over forty years ago. You probably weren't even born then. How could you understand?'

'You could tell me how it all happened.'

'It would take too long.'

'I'm in no hurry.'

Carter seemed to hesitate before he said, 'What were your orders?'

'To find out if the three men were still alive and see what had happened.'

'Why?'

'Because SIS will carry the can if any outsiders find out that something illegal, or whatever, happened, and SIS have enough problems without some old ghosts being raked up.' He paused and then said quietly, 'So what do we do about the man called Dettmer?'

29

'You forget him, because you'll never find him without me. Nor Keller either.'

'From the notes I was given it seems as if Keller ended up with 30 Corps. And you ended up there too. Did you move there because Keller was your man?'

'More or less.'

'Dettmer, or whatever his name was, was controlled by Keller, yes?'

'More or less.'

'Did you know that these people had committed war crimes?'

'Yes, in general terms.'

'And you didn't feel that mattered?'

'I told you. You wouldn't understand. They risked their lives week after week to get information that we desperately needed. For me it was much the same as the police using a criminal to inform to prevent crime or at least identify the people responsible.' He paused. 'You're doing the same yourself right now. You think I've done things that were illegal or at least undesirable but you still want to use me to get the information you want.'

Mallory smiled. '*Touché*.' He was silent for a moment then he said, 'Would it be possible for me to talk off the record with Dettmer and Keller?'

'To what purpose?'

'I'm not sure. But maybe I could get things into more realistic perspective.'

'What makes you think that?'

'You.'

'Tell me more.'

'Well. You were a British army officer and you believe that what you did was right. You seem a pretty straightforward person to me. If you think what happened was justified then maybe you're right. And if it can all be justified, we don't have to do anything against these men, and if the media do pursue it and it comes out, we have all the facts to show that what was done was justifiable.'

30

'Would your bosses take that attitude?'

'Right now they wouldn't, they're aware of public prejudice, but the public accepted that German scientists who had worked on the rockets that killed a lot of our people were recruited to work for us and the Americans.'

'Are you going back to London tonight?'

'No. I've booked in at The Ship.'

'Do you have to report daily?'

'No. Weekly.'

'You don't need to report on today's talk immediately?'

'No.'

Carter stood up slowly. 'Let me think about it overnight and we'll meet and talk again tomorrow. Agreed?' And before Mallory could reply Carter said, 'It would be valuable in many ways if we could find a solution to this problem.' He smiled briefly as he put out his hand. 'Let's see what we can do.'

Mallory walked back to the hotel, wondering if he'd been conned. That elderly man had been running line-crossing operations against the Soviets before he was born. Even now, despite the baby face and the freckles that came with the red hair and the pale blue eyes, that old boy was still an operator. Carter knew all too well how the wheels turned inside SIS and there would be others like him, colonels and brigadiers from 21 Army Group who had run clandestine operations behind the Iron Curtain before Winston Churchill had even coined the phrase. They would know how to protect themselves and those who had worked for them. Somebody high-up would have had to give the nod to use those Germans, or at least turn a blind eye to what was going on. He'd met men of that age-group on Corps days at the depot. Men who looked like overgrown schoolboys, laughing uproariously at schoolboy jokes, with nicknames like Jumbo and Tiny and Lofty. But they were men who had DSOs and MCs and a few had been knighted. They weren't fools and they never had been. They were patriots and single-minded, ready to do anything that was asked of them. Their least worry, the chance of losing their lives in some NKVD cell in the Soviet Zone.

At the hotel he called Debbie but there was no reply at the flat or at her place. He had dinner alone and then drove over to Birdham and looked at the photographs of boats for sale in the glassed-in display outside the broker's office next to the boatyard. There was an old 30-footer, and as if to make Carter's point the description said that it had been one of the boats used in the Dunkirk evacuation. The photograph showed a stolid almost ugly boat but the description said 'very reliable'. To someone like Carter its Dunkirk connection and those two words would be the main attraction. He had never thought about it that way before himself but for the men who had fought in the war it made it a kind of club. A closed circle. You didn't have to say anything. You had been in the war, so you belonged. Like Henry V's speech before Agincourt. St Crispin and – there are 'gentlemen in England now abed . . .'

As he drove back to Chichester and crossed the main Portsmouth road there was a sign to Tangmere, the airfield where the Spitfires had taken off to fight the Battle of Britain. It was over these lush green fields that that battle had been fought. Maybe it was a sign that he should take notice of what Carter had to say.

5

Carter phoned him at the hotel just after breakfast and suggested that he came to the house mid-morning. When he arrived Carter took him into the dining-room where there were what seemed to be two sheets of a large-scale Ordnance Survey map laid out on the table. The difference was that they were over-printed with various symbols and with their legends and notes in German instead of English.

As he bent over the maps Carter pointed with a pencil.

'You'll see that there is no double-lane road to Portsmouth and that the roads east–west and north–south go straight through the centre of Chichester whereas the whole area around the Market Cross is now closed off as a shopping precinct.

'That's because these maps are 1938 maps and the details are all in German because these are the maps produced by the German General Staff for operation "Sealion" – the invasion of Britain.

'Now I want you to look here. Fishbourne. A mile outside the city. A small village. But you'll see that there's a long narrow creek from the Channel right up to the village. That was to be a main landing point for an amphibious tank division.'

He moved his finger up the map.

'And here's Midhurst just north of us. That was to be established as forward HQ for all German forces on the evening of Day One. A farmhouse on the Military Canal near Appledore in Kent was to be HQ for the 2nd Group,

33

and the race-track at Goodwood is designated as a POW camp for British prisoners.' Carter straightened up and looked at Mallory. 'You'll be wondering why I'm showing you this stuff.'

'No. I think I know why.'

'Tell me.'

'You probably feel that the young people of today don't understand what sacrifices were made in the war and don't appreciate the courage and sacrifice of the people who were involved. And you see me as judging what happened in those days by today's different standards.'

'It angers me, Mallory. It wasn't just the service-men and women. It was the civilians too. Half-starved, working long hours in factories, and at night in air-raid shelters. And now we have bleeding hearts beating their breasts about dropping the bombs on Hiroshima and Nagasaki. Or the bombings of Hamburg and Dresden. They don't mention the bombing of Coventry and Birmingham. They don't mention what it would have been like if we had lost. Because, mark my words, those are the bastards who would have welcomed the Germans.'

'People don't take any notice of them, Major.'

'Don't you believe it, my boy. Why the hell do you think you're in my dining-room now?' He paused and faced Mallory. 'Because some creep on a gutter newspaper wants to make a quick buck with so-called revelations of how we tried to keep the Russians from coming over the border in 1946.'

'Were they planning to come over the border?'

For long moments Carter looked at Mallory's face and then he said quietly, 'You've got an awful lot to learn, young man.'

Mallory half-smiled. 'Maybe you can teach me.'

'That's exactly what I propose doing. If you're will-ing.'

'You said it would take a long time for me to understand. How long?'

'Hours. Maybe days.'

'Then I'd have to ask permission from my brass.'

'You don't need to ask them.'

'I'm afraid I do.'

'I've spoken to them and they agree. Not enthusiastically I'd admit. But they agree.'

'Who did you speak to?'

'To Toby Young and after that to Mike Daley.'

'Do you mind if I check with them?'

'It wouldn't be wise.'

'Why not?'

'Use your loaf. They've given you a job to do. The whole point was that you would be independent. Not just carrying out orders. They're trying to play it square. If you end up reporting that there was no justification for what was done then at least they know where they stand. But if you report that it was necessary and are convinced that it was fully justified, they've got an answer that most people will accept.'

'Not the Opposition.'

'Don't be too sure. They can't afford to look too unpatriotic.'

'And the media?'

'They'd have the choice of an anti-British story, or a story of courage and sacrifice. That will last a lot longer than a scandal that nobody really gives a damn about.'

Mallory smiled. 'And how are we going to do all this?'

Carter said, 'We'll make a kind of pilgrimage. Back to the past.'

'And what if in the end I don't see it your way?'

'Nothing. But you will see it my way.'

'How do you know?'

'Because you were in the army yourself. In a cold war rather than a hot one. But they're much the same.'

Carter walked across to the sideboard and picked up a leather-bound photograph album, bringing it back to the table. There were two slips of paper marking different pages. Carter looked at Mallory for several seconds in silence and then said, 'I want to show you three things before we start. To make sure that we don't start our journey with a mistaken impression on your part.'

He opened the album at the first marker. He pointed at a page of photographs. 'That is what was left of a German town called Hildesheim after it had been bombed by the US Air Force. It was eighty per cent destroyed in forty minutes blanket bombing. It was a medieval town, rather like Stratford-on-Avon. No troops, no factories.' He pointed to a picture of a large house in its own grounds, two jeeps and a Mercedes saloon in front of the house. 'That was my HQ, right after the surrender.' He pointed at the third photograph. It was of a young man in army battle-dress. Solemn faced as if he resented being photographed. 'That's me,' Carter said, 'I'd just come back from . . .' He turned the pages to the second marker. It was a picture of a group of British soldiers, they were staring at a pile of naked corpses. In the background was a group of men in striped uniforms. '. . . I'm the one on the far right of the group of soldiers. The place is Belsen-Bergen, the concentration camp. Two hours after it had been liberated.'

For a long while Mallory looked at the photograph. It was much like those he'd seen in magazines and books. Except that this showed a man he knew. The young ghost of the man standing beside him. He turned to Carter. 'You said three things.'

'So I did.'

He laid his hands palm up on the table. 'At the base of both thumbs you'll see similar scars. The white bits. They were done by the NKVD. I was caught during the line-crossing days. But I got away. The marks are where they nailed my hands to a table. And you'll see that there's something wrong with both my little fingers. They broke them both. They usually bend them backwards and break the main joint. Painful, but the quacks can put them right. In my case they bent them sideways at the first joint. They can't do anything with them.' He shrugged. 'It was all part of the game. But

36

at that time nobody'd got around to laying down any ground-rules.'

Mallory nodded, and said quietly, 'Thanks for showing me those things . . . I got the message.'

'You didn't, my boy. Not yet. Not by a long way. I just laid out a few markers for you. Signposts.'

'So when do we start?'

'Let's start talking this evening. Come and have dinner with me and Trixie and then we can talk in my small study.'

Trixie had laid out drinks, glasses, mugs and a Cona with a jug of milk and bowl of sugar. Carter poured himself a Glenlivet and Mallory had coffee.

Carter leaned back in his armchair. 'We'd better start at the beginning. The war against the Germans ended at midnight on April 8, 1945. I was an I Corps officer, a captain then, attached to HQ 30 Corps.'

6

It was getting dark and the ominous blue-black clouds were beginning to cover the setting sun. There was a long queue of vehicles waiting to be checked through by the MPs at a temporary road block.

The red-cap sergeant who spoke to Carter asked him where he was going and when he said he was on his way to 30 Corps HQ at Bad Niendorf the sergeant noticed his green flashes and looked at the thick wad of papers on his clipboard. After turning several pages he said, 'All 30 Corps Intelligence not on detachment have to report to Bad Salzuflen. That's been designated as Intelligence HQ for both 30 Corps and 21 AG. I'm sorry sir, you'll have to turn back.'

'For Christ's sake. Where in hell is Bad Salzuflen?'

'Go back down the road to Minden . . .'

'I've just bloody well come from Minden.'

'Go through Minden and you'll find there are diversions taking you round Bad Oeynhausen. You go straight on to Herford and you'll see signs pointing east to Bad Salzuflen. About ten miles from Herford. You'll be going against the traffic so it should be an easy run.'

'Can I do a U-turn here?'

'OK. If you make it snappy.'

It was pouring with rain for the last fifteen miles but he'd made it in a couple of hours and a Field Security sergeant had directed him to the Officers' Messes. There was one for field rank, and another for captains and below. And as the Intelligence Corps didn't have second lieutenants that made the differentiation even more ridiculous.

It was a big sprawling house and the Mess Corporal found him a room. There were two camp-beds and his companion was an old friend from the depot training course at Winchester, a Welshman named Lewis. Carter took the free bed and shoved his kit alongside the army issue blankets folded on the bed.

'What's going on, David? Why aren't we at 30 Corps HQ?'

'This is going to be the permanent HQ for all intelligence staff. They're sorting us out here and then we'll be sent out on detachment.'

'Do you know where you're going?'

'A dump called Celle. The postings are on the notice-board in the corridor.'

'Was my name on it?'

'I don't remember. Have a look.'

There were half a dozen officers looking at the notice-board and alongside on the wall was a large-scale map with the areas to be controlled by 2 Corps and 30 Corps. The names were in no particular order and it took him several minutes to find his own name.

Carter E. 10350556. Int. Corps. Lieut. To OC 103 Field Security Section. Hildesheim. Captain's appointment. Effect. Immediate. To report s.a.p. to Major Hargreaves. GSO II I(b), Haus Waldheim, Bad Salzuflen.

He moved over to the maps and found Hildesheim south-east of Hannover. Measuring it roughly with the joint of his thumb it seemed to be about fifty miles if the minor roads were passable.

The Mess was crowded with officers with food laid out on long tables. Spam, bread, butter and some sweaty-looking ham. There were no seats and only beer in bottles or apple-juice to drink. Despite the news of the surrender the day before, the chatter was mainly about the rumoured plans for demobilisation. Points for time served and extra points for overseas service. Rumour had it that Int. Corps officers with special experience or qualifications would be excluded from the demob plans.

Dai Lewis was already asleep when he got back to his room.

Haus Waldheim had been the home of a local businessman. Twelve bedrooms which had been made into temporary offices and a ground floor used as living quarters for the senior officers. Major Hargreaves interviewed Carter in one of the converted bedrooms, furnished with a plain wooden desk but two of the previous owner's comfortable armchairs.

Major Hargreaves stayed behind his desk and pointed at a wooden chair.

'Sit down, Carter.' He waited as Carter sat and then said, 'You've no doubt seen your posting. Hildesheim. Mostly rubble they tell me but you'll find something you can take over for your chaps. The Town Major will do that for you.

'You've got a full establishment. Sergeant-major, twelve acting sergeants and a driver.' He picked up a Roneoed sheet of paper. 'You've got the same briefing as all the other FS sections. De-Nazification is the word. There's a book publication you can get from the office called CRASC. Lists tens of thousands of wanted people. We want a daily report of arrests. No names, just general classification – Gestapo, Sicherheitsdienst, Abwehr, Waffen SS, Allgemeine SS, Senior Party members . . .' He smiled. 'Should keep you busy for a week or two.'

'Where do I put the prisoners?'

'You do a quick establishing interrogation. If it's still standing use the local jail but when you've got, say twenty, let us know and we'll send a vehicle down to collect them. We've taken over a few German camps. Yours will be going to a dump named Westertimke. You'll draw rations from here but you can purchase locally if there's fresh stuff available. Any questions?'

'No, sir.'

'One last thing. You've been put up to captain but don't let it go to your head. You're not dealing with clods. Your chaps are bright, intelligent people. We expect you to run a tight ship so far as the Jerries are concerned but even with them it's due process of law and all that crap. Big responsibility for a young chap like you so don't play silly buggers. OK?'

'Yes, sir. Thank you, sir.'

'If there's a Lieutenant Thomson hanging around downstairs send him up will you.'

Carter put his cap on, saluted, and the major nodded. Carter felt that parade-ground stuff wasn't called for so he didn't stamp his feet as he about-turned and walked out.

At the Admin Office the sergeant-quartermaster checked his name and appointment on a list. He looked up at Carter.

'Your chaps are just down the road, sir. The CSM's been here already and they've loaded your G1098 stores, and two weeks' rations. They've been allowed to hang on to their motor-bikes – ' he smiled ' – except the Harley Davidson they liberated in Venlo. You've got a pick-up and Service Corps driver.' He smiled. 'You need an extra pair of pips don't you?' He walked to a nest of drawers and came back with a pair of green cloth pips. 'Here you are, sir.' He pushed across a pad of printed forms. 'Would you sign for the stores please, sir. On the bottom line.'

When he'd signed Carter said, 'Where are my chaps?'

'The sergeant-major, name of Phillips, is waiting for you in the next office. I think they're all ready to push off.'

'Any chance of phoning the Town Major in Hildesheim?'

'Lines are down for all the area. The only lines available are Royal Signals and only for urgent operational use. Sorry.'

'Thanks.'

*

41

The Town Major had requisitioned a large house in its own grounds for them. A house that had no virtue except that there were enough rooms to house them all, provide office space, interrogation rooms and a large ground-floor room that could serve as a Mess. The house was solidly built but of a lowering, grim appearance, surrounded by tall conifers. Dark, flint-like bricks and heavy sash-windows. The furniture which the former occupants had had to leave behind was solid, and the curtains and carpets were still of good quality. It reminded Carter of a film he had once seen called *The Old Dark House* with Boris Karloff.

There were eight wide steps up to the front entrance which gave on to a spacious hall with curved stairways on each side, leading up to a minstrels' gallery.

The sergeant-major allocated rooms for sleeping and offices and by the evening it was beginning to look vaguely official and operational.

Carter's driver, Jacko, had laid out his kit in the good-sized bedroom that had been put aside for him. He washed his face and walked over to the triple windows as he dried his hands. It was still light outside and a heap of rubble as high as a house lay across the street, flowing like lava to the steps of what looked like a public building. There were women working, loading rubble into wheelbarrows, pushing the barrows to a plank that led up to the deck of a steep-sided lorry. As they had threaded their way through the town to the big house the smell of rotting corpses was everywhere. How the hell they would be able to root out the criminals in this shambles he had no idea. There were a few buildings still standing on the edge of the town but there were no longer any streets. Maybe he'd better move his HQ out to one of the villages. He turned when he heard a knock on the door and shouted, 'Come in.'

It was his driver and the CSM.

'What is it, Jacko?'

'Just came to tell you I got you a nice Merc, sir.'

'Where from?'

'Found it in a garage.'

'That's looting, Jacko.'

'No, sir. The Town Major's requisitioned it for us.' He grinned. 'All official and above-board.'

'I'll talk to you about it later.'

Jacko smiled and walked away but the sergeant-major stayed.

'I've done a recce around the town, sir. It's not quite as bad as it looks. The Engineers say they're bringing in mechanical shovels and they'll have most of it cleared away in ten days. It took most of the beating round here but the south side's only damaged, not destroyed.'

'That book I gave you. The list of wanted men. While we're waiting put the whole section on it and get it put on cards. Just the names for our area.'

'OK, sir. Can I ask you about Messing arrangements?'

'I thought you'd picked out the big room downstairs.'

'I'm thinking about you, sir. You'll need a separate Mess. I'd like to check if the room I've set aside is OK with you.'

'Sergeant-major, I'll be eating with the rest of you. I know it'll cramp their style, but they'll have to put up with it.'

'What about if you have visitors from 21 Army Group?'

Carter smiled. 'They won't be in a hurry to come down to this dump. Let's wait and see.'

7

Two months later and those early days were forgotten. The town was almost back to normal, and already houses that were structurally sound were being rebuilt. But what was more important was that the card-indexing of wanted men that had filled up the dead time of the first three weeks was paying off handsomely. They had done so well that 30 Corps had given him extra men and he now had detachments at Peine, Göttingen, Holzminden and Osterode in the Harz mountains.

The section were working long hours, but they were getting results and there were no complaints. There were no legal formalities for bringing in a suspect. When they tracked one down they just brought him in, interrogated him to check that he was the man on the list and he was put in the local jail until the vehicle came from 30 Corps or 21 Army Group to take the man to one of the camps for further interrogation.

Military Government were beginning to establish a skeleton German administration for the town so that people could be found jobs and services could be revived. This meant another burden on the section; the security clearance of potential German officials.

By the third month a new problem arose for all the Field Security Sections on the borders of the Soviet Zone of Occupation. The Yalta conference had laid down the boundaries of the Occupation Zones but the surrender had left Allied troops well inside the territory that had been allotted to the Soviets. In places the Americans had to pull back 150 miles abandoning Leipzig, Chemnitz and

Weimar. For the British it meant giving up small areas around Hamburg and a wider strip west of Magdeburg. The behaviour of the Soviet occupying troops was by now well known and despite the secrecy of the pull-back Germans panicked and headed for the Allied Zones, leaving houses and possessions behind in their fear. They were coming over the borders in tens of thousands, a burden that the fragile, new local administrations couldn't cope with.

21 Army Group issued instructions that these refugees had to be screened before they were accepted. And in a top-secret signal they warned that they suspected that the Russians were using the flood of refugees to cover the insertion of NKVD agents into the Western Zones. Carter had to put together a special team who spoke Russian as well as German to interrogate those who were classified as suspect by the screening team.

All of the interrogation rooms were small because of the space taken up by the sound-proofing.

There was a small, wooden table whose legs were fixed by angled clamps to bolts in the concrete floor. Sergeant Harper sat opposite the man who was to be interrogated and Carter sat at the end of the table nearest the door. He was listening as the sergeant asked the questions.

'Your name?'

'Lubke. Ernst Heinrich Lubke.'

'Date of birth?'

'First January 1912.'

'Where were you born?'

'Berlin.'

'When did you join the Party?'

'1933.'

The sergeant looked up from his note-taking. By 1937 you had to join to keep your job. But in 1933 it meant you were a pioneer Nazi.

'Other party connections?'

'I was a member of NSKK.'

The NSKK was the party section for men in heavy transport.

'Your job?'

'Long distance lorry driver.'

'War service?'

'Wehrmacht. Tank brigade.'

'Where did you serve?'

'Holland, Belgium, East Front.'

'Were you taken prisoner on the East Front?'

'Yes. I was part of von Paulus's Army Group.'

'Von Paulus and his men are still prisoners in Russia. How come you're here?'

'I got sent to Poland to help repair tanks for the Red Army.'

'Go on.'

'They took me with them when they attacked Berlin. I did a bolt and got away.'

'Where to?'

'I got a train to Hannover. I think it was the last one out of Berlin.'

'Then what?'

'I hitched a lift to Magdeburg.'

'Why Magdeburg?'

'I had relatives there.'

'What's their name?'

'Westphal. Arnold Westphal.'

'What's his address?'

'He's got a farm, on the edge of the city.'

'What's the name of the farm?'

'I don't remember.'

'So how did you find it?'

'I knew the general area and then I asked about.'

'What kind of farming does he do?'

The man hesitated. 'Cows and pigs.'

'How long were you there?'

'Three months.'

'Did you work on the farm?'

'Yes.'

'What kind of cows?'

'Cows for milk.'

'I mean what breed?'

'I don't know. I think he said they were Friesians.'

'What colour were they?'

'All sorts of colours, mainly brown.'

Carter avoided the sergeant's eyes. Even he knew that Friesians were black and white.

The sergeant unfolded a map and looked at the man.

'Show me the farm on the map.'

The man looked at the map and then shrugged. 'I don't understand maps.'

'You mean you were in a tank brigade but you can't read a map?'

The man shrugged again but didn't answer.

'What Red Army unit were you with?'

'I told you – a tank brigade.'

'Which one?'

'I don't know. I don't speak Russian.'

'So how did they tell you what to do?'

The man was shivering and Carter said quietly, 'What's scaring you?'

'They said you'd kill me if you found out.'

Carter took over. 'What did they tell you to do?'

'They wanted to know about the British troops near the border. The signs on their jackets and on the vehicles.'

'How would you contact them?'

'They've got people over here. They said I'd be contacted.'

'Did you have a password?'

'Yeah.'

'What was it?'

'Their man would say *"Wo sind die Blumen"* and I'd say *"Drei rote Rosen"*.'

'Drei rote Rosen' was a popular German song from a film.

Carter turned to the sergeant and said, 'Give him a meal and then send him to 21 AG. I'll let them know he's coming.'

Carter sat in his room after dinner that night and read through his mail. There was a letter from one of his girlfriends saying that she was going to marry a US army lieutenant, and another from a girl named Trixie who wanted to know when he would be home on leave and if there was anything he needed that she could send him. There was a snotty letter from Boots library in Winchester about an overdue book, and a demand for a shilling and the book's return. It was a P.G. Wodehouse but he didn't recognise the title.

There was a long letter from his mother detailing the latest family news, gossip about friends and a warning in his father's handwriting about licentious behaviour and its inevitable punishment. There was a slip from Coutts bank showing details of his last pay cheque and the total in his account – £197.10.6. It was more money than he'd ever had in his life before. He put the slip in his diary and tore up the letters. It was a world he could barely remember. It no longer had anything to do with the grim realities of his present life. To the people back home the Red Army were still heroes, but here they were the much-feared drunken rapists, the men who tore out toilets to send back home and whose arms were encircled by a dozen watches torn from frightened Germans. And here they no longer behaved as Allies but enemies, intent on causing disruption in the Western Zones, openly defiant of any war-time agreements. Openly hostile and uncooperative. According to them they had won the war alone, the Americans and the British had been on the side of the German invaders.

8

Carter was walking to his Merc when the BMW swept into the semi-circular drive in front of the house and he stood, shading his eyes from the sun, as he waited to see who it was. The man who got out was Tony Hughes, a major from 21 Army Group, who walked over, smiling, as he held out his hand.

'Did you get my message?'

'No.'

'Ah well, things are a bit shambolic at 21 AG at the moment. Where can we talk?'

'Let's go in the house. Would you like coffee or a sandwich or something?'

Hughes smiled. 'Both if it's possible.'

In Carter's office Hughes seemed in no hurry to say why he was there.

'How are things down here?'

'We're coping – just about.'

'What would help you most?'

'More bodies and perhaps some of the responsibilities placed elsewhere.'

'Which responsibilities?'

'At the moment we're responsible for the whole de-Nazification programme, screening the refugees, screening Milgov employees, screening Germans for local administration, reporting on civilian morale and attitudes. A lot of that should be a Milgov responsibility. One of our men at Milgov could guide them in screening of their own people and local government Germans.'

'That's an excellent idea. I'll suggest we do that. Now.

Back to your other duties. Which of them take most of your time?'

'Our brief originally was the de-Nazification programme. We have sent to 21 AG and 30 Corps over a thousand suspects. It filled our whole time with long hours of work.' He paused. 'Perhaps it's worth pointing out that many of our arrests take place in the middle of the night for obvious reasons. The cross-border screening takes almost half our time now. So the de-Nazification has slowed down. 21 AG have belly-ached about the slow-down. They've also belly-ached about the time spent on the border screening. And they also complain about the small number of suspected agents we uncover.'

Major Hughes smiled. '21 AG and 30 Corps are under the same pressures as you are. With politicians sticking their noses in as well.' He paused. 'We want to take you away. We need you for something more important.'

'Like what?'

'We want you to run a line-crossing operation into the Soviet Zone. There will be four teams. You'll cover the area into Magdeburg.'

'Why me?'

'Because you did well in Africa against the Italians penetrating their stay-behind organisations.'

'Good God, operating against the Eyeties was a piece of cake compared with working against the Russians.'

'Maybe, but we're desperate to know what they're up to. Things don't look too good to us at the moment. But we're working on rumours, and rumours from people who wouldn't know a tank from a weapons carrier.'

'When do you want me to start?'

'We've got a replacement in mind to take over here, so as soon as possible. It'll take you some time to put together a team and train them.'

'Where the hell do I find them?'

'We've got a pool of about twenty possibles for you to choose from. We suggest a network of not more than half a dozen. And see how it goes.' He paused. 'It's a volunteer job. No harm to future promotions if you turn it down.'

'Have you got the other networks organised yet?'

'No. We wanted to try it on you first.' He smiled. 'Do you want a couple of days to think it over?'

'No.' He shrugged. 'If I think it over I'll probably want to back off.'

'It'll mean holding back your demob for at least another six months, maybe a year.'

Carter shrugged. 'I've not got anything lined up in Civvy Street.'

'SIS would be pleased to take you over if you wanted.'

'Let's wait and see how this lot turns out.'

Major Hughes stayed for dinner and afterwards he asked to look around the town. Carter took him down to the river and as they walked along the bank Hughes said, 'What are the locals like?'

Carter smiled, 'They call us the British Gestapo. They're a sorry lot really. Wives denouncing husbands. Anonymous notes denouncing neighbours in the hopes of moving in on their two rooms. Still scrabbling for food. The usual black-market in cigarettes and coffee.'

'How are the local troops behaving?'

'A bit mixed.'

'How's non-fraternisation working?'

Carter laughed. 'It never did work. It was a stupid idea.'

'Why?'

'Well it was supposed to show that we despised the Krauts so much that we wouldn't even talk to them. They've got a hell of a lot more things to worry about than us not talking to them. So you've got some of our chaps getting their feet under local tables for a change of company and a chance to have their socks darned. And others screwing away like ferrets because you can do it all you want for a packet of issue cigarettes.

'Mind you, our lot are quick learners, and they didn't need the Army Education Corps to teach them that there ain't much difference between the locals and their own folk back in Liverpool and Birmingham.'

'Despite the concentration camps?'

'Too horrific for most of them to grasp. Like hearing about a terrible earthquake in South America. And psychologically they want to blot it out because they've survived a war and they want to get on with that survival.'

'Are Milgov doing anything to bring home the concentration camps to the population?'

Carter stopped walking, hands on hips as he stared at Major Hughes.

'Look. God forbid that I could ever be caught saying a good word for those creeps in Milgov.' He paused. 'D'you know what they're trying to do in this dump? Trying to make it so that the sewage doesn't spread typhoid. Trying to make it so that there's electricity for the locals for at least two hours a night. Trying to stop Polish refugees from killing innocent Krauts for a loaf of bread and raping their wives and daughters just for the hell of it. Trying to build sheds for homeless people to live in. Trying to find work for people living in holes in heaps of rubble.' He glanced at his senior. 'And all 21 AG is worried about is have they rubbed the locals' faces in the shit enough for all the things that were done by fucking psychopaths. You people should come down here for a few weeks and see what it's like. They're still pulling kids' bodies out from under the ruins of bombed buildings. Why not bring the bomber pilots down here and all over Germany so they can see what *they* did.'

'They did it on orders.'

'You know, we've pulled in dozens of SS men and women who were guards at Auschwitz, Belsen and Treblinka – and that's what *they* all say. *"Ich war gezwungen. Befehl ist befehl."* – "We had to, orders are orders." I'm tired of hearing people say such crap.'

'How long since you had UK leave?'

'Don't flannel me. I don't need it. It's just that you people at Bad Oeynhausen live civilised lives. You're dealing with top level problems. Democracy and all that. People running Field Security Sections are just trying to sort out all the shit that gets left behind after somebody loses a war.' He laughed briefly. 'I'm sorry. I didn't even know I had these thoughts until you took the cork out of the bottle. Tell me about Willaby. What happened to him?'

'They sent him back to the depot. Dishonourable discharge but a reasonable reference for getting a job.'

'What did he actually do?'

'What did you hear?'

'Something about him stealing a musical instrument from some Kraut.'

'The musical instrument was a Bechstein grand piano and he got an RAF transport pilot to fly it back to the UK. And the Kraut he lifted it from happened to be a relative of the Dutch royal family.'

Carter laughed softly. 'Ah well. Like they taught us at the depot, time spent in reconnaissance is seldom wasted.' He paused. 'We'd better go back or you'll be driving in the dark. They sometimes string wires between the trees around here. Just high enough to take a dispatch driver's head off. And they can smash a windscreen too.'

'Nice people.'

'It's Hitler Youth. All the top brass. Old fogeys in their sixties. Feel guilty about not being in the Wehrmacht or the Luftwaffe.'

'God Almighty. They must be really sick those guys.'

They walked back to the house and as they turned into the driveway Hughes nodded towards some flowers. 'Lovely rhododendrons you've got there.'

'Is that what they are? Never noticed them before. It's generally dark when we get back from a raid.'

'You still think it's more effective to pick them up in the middle of the night?'

Carter grinned. 'Too true. When you're half asleep and only wearing a shirt and you're facing a wide-awake guy in a uniform you're inclined to talk more readily. What we don't get in that first interrogation we probably don't get at all.'

When they got to the BMW Hughes said, 'You don't want to change your mind?'

'No. Do you?'

Hughes smiled and shook his head. 'No. I'm relieved to have you. You're just what I want.'

Carter had little time to think about his new assignment during the following two weeks as the stream of suspected war-criminals were traced, interrogated and passed on to 21 Army Group for processing. The problem was made worse when London decided that tens of thousands of German prisoners of war should be released in September after complaints from Milgov that there were not enough German men available to gather the harvest, and despite widespread hunger it would mean that grain rotted in the fields. 'Operation Barleycorn' meant more processing for all Field Security Sections.

When the coded signal came ordering him to 21 AG there was no party, no explanation, not even a handing over to his successor. He left in the early hours of the morning when they were interrogating that night's haul of suspects. He stopped off in Hamelin for ten minutes with his successor and it was still dark when he arrived at Bad Oeynhausen.

The duty officer had taken him to a comfortable room in one of the detached houses. He slept fitfully for a couple of hours and then the Mess corporal had seen him wandering around and had offered him an early breakfast.

Hughes came over for him just after 9 a.m. and drove him to a big house outside the town.

'Do you know Colonel Stafford?'

'Only by name.'

'He'll be with us all day. He's in charge of all four operations and he'll be briefing you. He knows his stuff and he's down to earth – no bullshit.'

'I'm glad to hear it.'

'He's very calm and quiet but don't underestimate him. He got a good DSO.'

9

Colonel Stafford wasn't in uniform. A Viyella shirt and grey gabardine trousers and a pair of scuffed tennis shoes made him look even younger than his thirty years.

As they settled down Stafford said, 'Pleased to meet you, Carter. From now on you wear civilian clothes. There's an allowance and clothing coupons more than enough for what you'll need. OK?'

'Yes, sir.'

Stafford looked at Major Hughes. 'I assume you've told him that this thing is for volunteers only.' He turned to look at Carter. 'No reflection on you if you decide it's not up your street.'

'Yes, I know, sir.'

'Right. Let's get down to business.

'Army Group have been suggesting to London for some time that the Soviets are establishing forces in their occupation zone that go far beyond the needs of controlling the local population. RAF reconnaissance has to be very limited for diplomatic reasons but such as they've got gives credence to our evaluation.

'London – the Cabinet – have agreed that it's time we found out what was really going on over there. They've left it to us to decide how to do it.' He smiled. 'They just want the facts. How we get them is our business. They don't want to know. Most politicians are still living in cloud-cuckoo-land – the Sword of Stalingrad and all that stuff.' He paused. 'What they mean is that if we make a cock-up of it they'll sell us down the river. Outrageous behaviour by an untypical and unauthorised group of men who would like to start another war.' He smiled. 'You know how it would go.' He raised his eyebrows. 'Any questions, so far?'

'Will I still be I Corps?'

'Ostensibly you'll have been demobbed and recruited by SIS.' He smiled. 'Tax free money from now on. That's the army's bit of safety first so that if the balloon goes up they can't be blamed. Carter – never heard of him. Ah yes, but he went back to Civvy Street months ago.' He shrugged. 'So. Let's get down to business. You'll have a larger area than the other networks because your terrain provides better cover. The Harz mountains make the zone border rather conveniently confused. We want you to concentrate on Magdeburg. South down to Quedlinburg and north as far as Haldensleben. There's a map marked up next door. We'll go over it later.'

'Where shall I be based?'

'In Bad Harzburg. A couple of miles back from the border. It's in your old FS Section's beat.'

'Will they know about the operation?'

'No. Only a handful of people will know anything about it.'

'How many?'

Stafford closed his eyes as he thought. 'Four here at 21 AG. Four people who will be servicing you, including radio and transport. Your own people and a couple in London. The others in London only know that an operation will be mounted – maybe.'

'Who's funding the operation?'

'Source you don't need to know, but rest assured you'd get all the funds and facilities you want.'

'And what do you want from my people?'

Stafford leaned forward, intent on his explanation. 'I want a complete Order of Battle of all Soviet forces in the area. Names of commanding officers down to captain and all the personal background you can get. Then a picture of the NKVD set-up in Magdeburg. Names, ranks and the names of Germans cooperating with them.' He paused. 'And a report on the morale of both troops and civilians.'

'How long have I got?'

'As long as it takes.'

'When do I start?'

'When you've chosen your team from the pool of possibles.'

'How did they become possibles?'

Stafford grinned. 'Well. They're a very mixed bunch. Some educated and intelligent. Some just cunning. But they've all got one thing in common. They've got things to hide and they'll do anything in return for our protection.' He stood up. 'We've put aside this house for you to use in the first place and we've got a place as your HQ when you're ready to start.'

'Where exactly is it?'

'It's an old hunting lodge in the forest outside Bad Harzburg. We're doing it up and there's plenty of room, and we can make it secure.'

Stafford held out his hand and when Carter took it Colonel Stafford said, 'Your promotion to major will be published in next week's Part Two Orders. Plus your demob.'

'Is this just part of the cover?'

'The majority's for real. The demob's for cover.'

It took Carter nine days to give preliminary interviews to the twenty possible recruits. He hadn't discussed with them what they would be doing if they were selected, but he made it clear that the work would involve risk and danger.

Out of the first interviews there were only two he was quite certain that he'd recruit and two others who looked possibles.

At the end of the nine days Stafford and Hughes joined him for an evening meal and a discussion. It was Stafford who started the discussion.

'Not much progress so far, Eddie.'

'I wouldn't say that, sir. Even a negative interview is

some kind of progress. I've got two certs and two possibles, that's a pretty good start for an operation where we have no criteria about what makes a man suitable.'

'Fair enough. Tell me the things that made you turn people down.'

'I tended to discard men who have had no armed services experience.'

'Why?'

'A lack of discipline. Unlikely to stick to orders.' He smiled. 'And I guess, prejudice. I know how to deal with soldiers or ex-soldiers.' He sighed. 'There were nine in that category but at least four were hardened criminals. I wouldn't be able to believe a word they told me and there won't be time for me to sort out information they bring back that is deliberately false.'

'You could get rid of them if they did that.'

'No. I can't. They'll know too much to let them go. I want to start with people I'm prepared to take risks for.'

Stafford nodded what looked like agreement. 'Tell us what your doubts are about the two possibles.'

Carter smiled. 'They both have basically the same problem but from opposite points of view. They're emotional problems. One is desperately unhappily married. His wife lives on our side of the border. He sees going over the border as a release from his problems. The other is unhappy in love. He loves a girl who used to live in Magdeburg. He doesn't know where she is now. He may have her too much in mind.'

'And how do you propose to work out the right solution?'

'Oh. I'll talk it over with them. Openly and frankly. I'll want their own views. And I want my two certs to give me their views. We're going to be a team. None of us are experienced in this work, and none of us is without his disadvantages. As long as we know what they are we can cope with them.'

Stafford said, 'What would you say are your own disadvantages?'

Carter thought for a moment. 'First, age. I'm a bit young to be bossing these men. In the army OK, there's a framework around one. But not on this job. And secondly I don't have enough knowledge of Soviet forces to evaluate what I'm getting.'

'Would you like me to give you a British officer who is an expert on these things?'

'Provided he doesn't interfere.'

'That would be up to you. You're the boss.'

'Have you got somebody in mind?'

'Yes. I'll arrange for you to meet him. Now tell us about your two certs as you call them.'

'Both intelligent. One of them intellectual, the other imaginative. Both strong characters. I actually discussed the operation with them. Separately and together. They are born leaders but with different styles. One a driver, the other a persuader.'

'Who are these two?'

'One's Becker and the other's Keller.'

Stafford smiled. 'I thought they might be. What about their Nazi backgrounds? They would both undoubtedly be classified as war-criminals.'

'Colonel, you've given me a job to do and I'm choosing men who I think can get me results. That's my only criterion. If a man was very marginal and I had other choices then his past behaviour might count. But I'm not looking for marginals. I'd rather go in under strength than take risks by eliminating people for what they did in the war. Quite frankly I don't want to know.'

'But you're obviously aware that what they did in the past is probably the main reason why they're willing to cooperate.'

'Yes.'

'Would you hold that over them if you needed to?'

'If I had to – yes.'

For a few moments Stafford was silent and then he said, 'Let's go in the next room and have a look at the layout of the hunting lodge and see if you agree with the alterations.'

10

Erich Keller, as always, was carelessly but elegantly dressed in a tweed jacket, pale-blue shirt and light brown slacks. Fritz Becker wore a black polo-necked sweater, black trousers and with his swarthy face he looked like some gangster out of an old black and white American film. Keller was leaning back, relaxed, and Becker was leaning forward, fists clenched as he made his point.

'In my opinion they're both OK. If we're going to spend this much time on deciding it'll be months before we get started.'

Keller smiled. 'Could be over before we've got started if they're not suitable, Fritz.'

'What have we got against Vorster?' Becker sounded angry. 'He wants out from a lousy marriage. He was at least honest and told us about it as one of his motives. We wouldn't even have known about it if he hadn't told us.' He paused. 'And the same with Heinz Schmidt. OK, he may spend some of his time looking for his girl. So what? We've all got some hang-up even if we don't recognise it.'

Keller laughed. 'What's yours, Fritz? I'd love to know.'

Becker shrugged. 'God knows . . .' He smiled. 'And if I did I wouldn't tell *you*.'

Carter stood up and walked over to the sideboard and brought back two cans of beer and the two Germans poured their drinks while Carter poured himself another cup of tea from a Thermos flask.

'OK. If they didn't have these problems. Or we didn't

know about them would either of you be against us taking them on?'

Becker shook his head. 'No. Not me.'

'Nor me,' said Keller.

'OK. I'll brief them tonight and we'll have a foursome tomorrow. Have you decided what jobs you're going to have as cover?'

Becker said, 'Something in admin. I'll take anything. But there's a shortage of skilled men so I shouldn't have a problem.'

Keller said, 'Did you get me the camera and the dark-room stuff?'

'Yes. A Leica 3c, is that OK?'

'That's fine. How much was it?'

'Four hundred Lucky Strikes.'

Keller smiled. 'Not bad. And the darkroom stuff?'

'It's in the bedroom upstairs.' He paused. 'You two had better move in with me tonight. And if the other two come on board we'll all move down to Bad Harzburg tomorrow. We can start your training on Red Army uniforms and weapons in a couple of days' time. And I'd like you both to give some thought to where you'll aim for over the other side.'

'I want Magdeburg. I won't make a living anywhere else.' Keller looked ready for disagreement but nobody said anything.

Becker said, 'Are we going to use cut-outs?'

Carter shook his head. 'No. We'll work as a team. But we won't discuss with each other our locations or our new identities. Just the military stuff. It's better we all know right from the start that we sink or swim together.'

Keller laughed. 'Sounds like a communist cell.' He looked at Carter, smiling. 'What can we call you?'

'My name's Eddie. Just call me that.'

'Any chance of some cigarettes for tonight?'

'Help yourself, there's plenty on the sideboard.' He paused. 'I thought you didn't smoke?'

61

Becker laughed. 'She's overcharging you, Erich. Is it the little girl who works next to our billet?'

'Never you mind, my friend. You're just jealous.'

As Carter went back to his room he was aware that the two of them were more worldly-wise than he was. Their country was a shambles. They'd lost the war. But already they knew the rules of the new game. And he was supposed to be telling them what to do. Maybe he'd better learn the new rules himself.

Carter saw Schmidt and Vorster together. They had similar problems so far as he was concerned, but otherwise they were entirely suitable.

When they had made themselves comfortable with a beer he asked them their own opinions of the chances of their emotional problems getting in the way of their work. It was Paul Vorster who spoke first.

'I don't see *any* disadvantages in my case. In fact in some ways the fact that I want to leave a lousy marriage behind me should be an advantage.'

Carter said, 'She might be so incensed at you leaving her that she wants some sort of revenge on you. Denounces you for being in the SS.'

Vorster smiled. 'She won't. She's got more guilt on her side than I have.'

Schmidt chipped in. 'Tell him, Pauli. He should know.'

Vorster shrugged and looked at Carter. 'It's nothing special. I married her when I got back from service in the SS in the *blitzkrieg* in the Low Countries. I was posted to Norway and then Poland. First time I had leave I discovered she was sleeping around. She didn't deny it, in fact she seemed rather proud of it. Next thing I heard was she'd sold the flat and the furniture and had moved to Hamburg with a black-market guy. When I came back after the surrender I got a room in Hannover and the bitch just walked in one day and said she was back. There's no courts so I can't divorce her so I walked out and went to Magdeburg. When I heard the Reds were moving in I came back over the border and got picked up because of my rank in the SS – Hauptsturmführer.' He shrugged. 'That's it.'

Carter looked at Schmidt. 'What do you think?'

'I don't know why you were bothered. There's always going to be some damn thing.'

'What about you then?'

'I had to come over the border in a hurry and my girlfriend was away visiting relatives in Dresden and I had no way to contact her. She didn't like Magdeburg so I've no idea where she is now. I want to find her but I'll do it only when I've got time to spare.'

'And if you find her?'

'I'll bring her over the border if you'll give her documentation.'

'And then?'

'I'll go back so long as I know she's safe.'

Carter said, 'OK. I'll take you both down to our new base tomorrow. We've got a lot to plan before you go over the border.'

It was snowing as Carter pulled off the road to the track that led into the woods and the hunting lodge. Although he had seen the photographs and layout plans he was surprised at the size of the lodge when they finally drew into a small courtyard.

Hughes had said that it had been the property of the Duke of Brunswick in the old days and had then been a rest-home for SS officers recuperating from war wounds. It had been empty since the Occupation but had been refurbished on Stafford's orders.

The main building was a long low structure of rough stone and heavy timbers on two floors and there were outbuildings of the same materials. The whole compound was surrounded by dense woods of conifers and oaks.

Inside, Hughes was waiting for them. He showed Carter around. There were seven large bedrooms and five smaller bedrooms that had originally been for the hunt staff and domestics. Hughes introduced him to a sergeant from the RASC who would be their resident cook, and an ATS corporal who would be in charge of all housekeeping. She spoke good German and had already checked sources of supply in Bad Harzburg. But most of their rations would be delivered direct from a local infantry brigade HQ. A painted sign outside said – NO. 3 SIGNALS UNIT.

On the ground floor was a dining-room, two general living-rooms and an operations room that was entered by a steel door.

Hughes had eaten with them that evening and had talked in guarded terms of the objectives of a line-crossing operation and the kind of information that was needed. Just as they were ending the meal a lieutenant arrived. Lieutenant Maclean, Scots Guards, was the expert on identification of Red Army insignia and equipment. Hughes left an hour later and Carter was on his own. It was up to him how long the training went on and when the operation would actually start.

The operations room had been laid out like a classroom with six individual desks. On each desk was a file containing descriptions and illustrations of Soviet uniforms and insignia. When the curtains had been drawn, slides were projected on to a silver screen showing actual uniforms and armoured vehicles.

When Lieutenant Maclean had finished Carter took over and explained some of the less obvious sources of information. Germans doing humble jobs in Soviet Army clubs and sports clubs. Signatories and titles on public notice-boards, permits and passes. Information from suppliers of goods and services to Soviet units. Information from black-market operators and prostitutes. There were many sources of information that would put one more piece in the jigsaw puzzle.

By the end of the first week Carter was surprised at how much the four Germans had absorbed and he turned to the actual passing back of information either by the use of dead-drops or coming back over the border. But how they would eventually do that would have to be decided once the four had settled down on the other side.

At the end of the second week they were given documentation, codes and cash so that they could go over on the Sunday when things were generally quiet.

There was no actual border but the line was marked with white-painted stones and in some places with a two-strand wire fence that was more a marker than a hindrance. There were patrols by soldiers with dogs on the main roads and lanes leading to the West. Nobody was expecting anyone to voluntarily move from the British to the Soviet Zone.

They left at half-hour intervals in the early hours of Sunday morning and Carter had gone with them to the chosen crossing point. Two of them had taken cycles with them and Carter had waited for the pick-up truck to collect him and the cycles the other two left behind.

Lieutenant Maclean went back to 21 AG later that day but was on permanent stand-by if Carter needed him. The hunting lodge seemed strange with the others gone. They had got to know one another well in the two weeks of training. Discovering each other's characteristics and foibles well enough to joke about them. There was no way of communicating with them until they had come back with the locations of suitable dead-drops so they were coming back over the border in two weeks' time to discuss the situation. Until then he just had to wait.

11

It took Erich Keller three days to get to Magdeburg, about seventy kilometres from the zone border. He made for the church near the main square. It had lost its stained-glass windows but otherwise it was still intact. There were half a dozen women sitting on benches near the altar. A priest was reciting a prayer and the women murmured responses. Keller stood at the back of the church and eventually the priest walked down the aisle with the women. When the women had left, Keller spoke to the priest and asked him if he knew where there was a room he could rent.

'Where have you come from?'

'From Berlin, Father.'

'Do you have papers?'

'No, Father.'

The priest glanced at Keller's Wehrmacht greatcoat that had been dyed black. 'What rank were you, my son?'

'A corporal.'

'That's an officer's coat you're wearing.'

'I took it off a dead man, Father. If I didn't take it the Russkis would have taken it.'

'Is it very bad in Berlin?'

'Berlin's finished. Just rubble and corpses.'

The priest sighed. 'There is a lady, Frau Hartman, who has an old house in Einbeckstrasse. Number 57. Tell her Father Simon sent you. I believe she has a room you could rent.'

'Thank you, Father.'

'God bless you.'

The priest turned away abruptly as if his blessings had become a ritual that he no longer believed in.

Frau Hartman was in her fifties with the big, shifting, brown eyes of someone permanently alert for where the next blow would come from. She looked at his face for a long time and then said, 'How can you pay for the room? Not Reichsmarks.'

'I could pay ten cigarettes a week.'

She closed her eyes, moving her lips and Keller guessed that she was trying to work out the black-market value of ten cigarettes. When she opened her eyes she said, 'For twelve I could do it. Weekly in advance. If you ever get coffee we could talk again.'

The room was quite large, with a single bed, a wardrobe, wash-basin and stand and a small bed-side table. It was on the top floor and was rather dark because the roof and the windows had been covered with a tarpaulin because only the roof-timbers were in place, the roof tiles long gone.

Frau Hartman had a relative on a farm just outside the town and had offered to get him eggs, butter and milk in exchange for cigarettes, and by the end of the first week she was well-disposed to her new lodger. She found him charming and polite, and in return for a share of the food she cooked for him and they ate together in her basement kitchen.

On the second evening after they had eaten he asked her if there was a photographer in the town. She made enquiries and came up with an address and a name. Herr Franke.

The address was the remains of what had once been a small warehouse and Herr Franke was an old man. Keller knocked on the outer door and when there was no answer he opened the door and walked inside. The main part of the room was obviously a studio. A swivel chair and a white sheet as a background and two tungsten lights with battered rear-dishes were obviously intended for portraits. A corner of the room was closed off from the rest and a hand-written notice claimed it as a darkroom.

When Keller knocked on the door the old man came out, his wire-rimmed glasses up on his forehead.

'I'm sorry, mister. Got no film until next week. Try me about Wednesday.'

'Are you Herr Franke, the owner of the studio?'

'Indeed I am, on both counts.'

'Herr Franke. I'm a photographer. I have a camera and film, printing paper and chemicals. Could we work together do you think?' He opened his hand so that the old man could see the two cassettes of 35 mm film.

They had talked for an hour and the old man had seemed relieved to find a partner with enterprise and seemingly with access to materials that could keep the business going. Most of the business was darkroom work, copying documents, birth and death certificates, wedding certificates, wills and certificates of training and education. He had plenty of work but had very little film and material left. And what he had was barely usable after he had dug it out from the ruins of his old studio in the centre of the town.

By the middle of the second week Keller was getting business from several local factories that were starting production again under Soviet control and needing photographs for identity cards for employees. And he was helping the old man with his copying work.

12

Keller was the first to appear at the hunting lodge, followed not much later by Becker and Vorster.

Keller had brought back photographs of a wide variety of passes and permits which Carter could pass up the line so that they could be reproduced at 21 AG. He had no information on Soviet Military but a couple of dozen names of Russian and German officials and their official posts.

Vorster had little to report except that he had got a room and a job at a garage but he was, with his training as a lawyer, advising a number of people with problems with either the Soviet or German authorities on how they should tackle those problems, drafting letters and explaining the new regulations laid down by the Soviet Occupying Power. He had even had an indirect approach from the Town Hall about setting up an advice centre for the general public.

Becker had notes of a number of Soviet military vehicles and their insignia. He had a room but no job. However, his landlady was using her influence on his behalf with a relative who worked at the Town Hall in the hope of him getting a job there.

When they had completed their reports Carter said, 'You've all done amazingly well. Let's talk about a few side issues. What's morale like with the Germans?'

Keller said, 'They're scared of the Russians. They hate them. In the first few weeks the military let the troops loot and rape, and although they've calmed down a bit now it's going to be a long time before the majority forget what went on.' He shrugged. 'Some people are cooperating with them. Mainly officials like the police and civil servants. And the local Communists, of course, they get extra rations from the Soviets.'

Vorster laughed bitterly. 'Even with ration cards you might not get any food. The Russians send out raiding parties on to the farms looking for food. They don't get much. The farmers learned how to keep it hidden away in Nazi times and the new boys don't even speak the language.'

'What about the morale of the Soviet troops?'

Nobody had enough knowledge to comment but Keller said, 'From what I've heard the Soviets have shifted most of their troops outside the city.'

Carter looked at his watch and then at the others. 'It's mid-day. What do you think's happened to Schmidt?'

Nobody had anything to offer and Carter went on, 'I've got cigarettes and cash for you. Anybody want anything else?'

Keller nodded. 'I need film and paper and chemicals. Agfa and Kodak sell cans of 200 metres of film that I can cut up and put in my Leica cassettes. I'd prefer Agfa because I might get asked how I got hold of Kodak film. If you could get me a Leica cassette loader it would help too.'

Carter made notes and then looked at Keller. 'Any time after ten days you can come for the film. Meantime I've got your paper and chemicals and four dozen cassettes.'

Keller smiled. 'How many cigarettes? They're better than cash.'

'Four packs each. Eight hundred cigarettes. Marlboro' or Luckies – your choice.'

Vorster said, 'When's the next meeting?'

'From now on you can come across any time you want. I'll be here.' He turned to Keller. 'Any chance of you photographing the dead-drops, Erich, and then I could come over and pick up your reports myself and save you taking risks coming over the border.'

Keller frowned and shrugged. 'I need time to do that, Eddie.' He laughed. 'It's crazy but I'm up to my ears in work. I'm building up my contacts and I've got to deliver.'

Carter smiled. 'OK. I leave it to you, but remember the locations of the drops.'

They all ate together and then Vorster left, cigarettes and a kilo of real coffee in a canvas holdall. Becker left shortly afterwards but Keller seemed in no hurry to leave. When Carter suggested a walk in the woods Keller seemed glad of the chance to talk to him alone.

'Are you worried about Schmidt not coming?'

Keller shook his head. 'No. You've probably seen the last of him.'

'Why do you say that?'

'Loving a pretty girl is one thing. Being obsessed about her is something else. Schmidt is a romantic and these aren't times for romantics. Just surviving, just staying alive is about all you can expect. If you do better than that – fine. A bonus. But it's not a time to depend on human beings.'

'I'm depending on you, Erich. And on the others.'

'No, you're not. *Relying* on us maybe to do our jobs. Relying on us not to renege. But there's a big difference between relying on us and depending on us.' He paused, standing still on the narrow path through the trees. 'If we all disappear, Eddie, well it will be a bloody nuisance. You've wasted some time. But you ain't gonna die of grief. And that's what friend Schmidt will do if he doesn't find the girl. Even if he finds her and they marry and have four kids it won't be enough for Schmidt. He wants a solution for all his problems. Losing the war, the shambles we live in, guilt for the past. He needs a priest, not a girl.'

'So why did you agree to him being part of the team?'

Keller shrugged. 'Because in the end it doesn't matter. He won't talk about this operation – I'm sure of that. If he does what you want that's fine. If you never hear from him again, what does it matter? Even if he talks what can he tell them? The Russians aren't going to find three men from vague descriptions in a population of millions. So they discover that we're putting people over the border to spy on them. You can be sure that they're already doing the same themselves.'

'I hope you're right, Erich.'

'I am, Eddie. Don't worry about Schmidt.' He laughed. 'Maybe he'll turn out to be the most successful of all of us.' He sighed. 'I'd better get on my way.'

Carter walked with him to the border and watched his figure disappear into the rising mist across the fields.

Keller was looking through some postcard sized prints of wedding groups when the man came through the door. He was wearing the khaki tunic and baggy blue britches of a Soviet officer and the shoulder-bands of a tank captain. He was young, in his late twenties with corn coloured hair and blue eyes.

Keller said, 'Can I help you?'

'I speak very bad German. I want wedding photograph two days at my place. You can take for me?'

'Where is your place?'

'Thirty-first Tank Regiment.'

Keller frowned. 'But where is it?'

'Is at farm – Gut Hohenburg – ten kilometres on Leipzig road. I send car for you.'

Keller smiled. 'Is it your wedding?'

The captain smiled back. 'Yes. Car here at eleven hours, yes.'

'I'll be here.'

The car that came for him was a battered Willys Knight jeep still with its US Army insignia stencilled in white. The driver was smartly dressed but spoke no German and Keller sat in silence for the ten-kilometre journey to the Russian unit's HQ at a farmhouse just off the Leipzig road. The groom came over to him and explained in his halting German that the photographs were to send home to his and the girl's family in Kiev. They were ready to start the ceremony.

The bride was a sergeant in one of the Guards units and was wearing a man's shirt with rank and arm of service badges on the shoulder straps. The only concession to femininity was that she was wearing a blue skirt and belt that was cinched tight to emphasise her waist. Over her right breast she wore the much coveted Guards badge and a single gilt star on her blue forage cap.

The ceremony took place in the open air and they stood together as a man in civilian clothes read from a printed sheet. Keller discovered later that the official was the unit's commissar.

There were tables laid out at the back of the farmhouse loaded with food and drink. Keller took photographs of the couple with the commanding officer, then with the commissar, and finally with a group of the groom's fellow officers.

Then the drinking began in earnest and a man with an accordion played a sad haunting melody before the music gave way to czardas, and wild energetic dances that the men could dance to.

Keller took the couple to the small orchard at the side of the farmhouse and photographed them holding hands in a cloud of apple-blossom. Then other officers came and with the groom interpreting they asked for their photographs to be taken. He took several of the commanding officer including a couple of portraits because he had a strong, handsome face.

Keller told them that he would work all night and get prints ready for the driver by mid-morning the next day, a Sunday.

On the Monday the delighted groom had come in especially to thank Keller for the photographs and to pay not only for his own but for his colleagues' photographs as well. Payment had been made in roubles and tobacco and Grigor Levchenko, the tank captain, had said that he would recommend Keller to the officers of other units. Everyone wanted a photograph to send back home.

It had been no idle comment and there was a constant flow of requests for his services. Sometimes to be taken at the studio, and sometimes at a military unit. But it was the personal invitation from Colonel General Katusov to take photographs of him and his staff at his villa just outside Magdeburg that was to change Keller's life in so many ways.

The photographs he was to take at the magnificent villa were not taken for simple soldiers to send home to the Ukraine or Georgia or Uzbekhistan. They were pictures of a powerful man who controlled the lives of not only hundreds of thousands of Soviet soldiers and airmen but millions of subjugated civilians. Colonel General Ivan Ivanovich Katusov was a czar, a ruler. A ruler who made up his own rules. The German legal code still applied. Just as the Criminal and Civil Codes of 1922 still applied to the Soviets at home and abroad. But legal codes could be brushed aside by a strong enough Caesar. And Colonel General Katusov was certainly strong enough. A brilliant war-record, a shrewd mind, and his distance from Moscow gave him all the power he needed. Ambition was the spur that made him bend his ear to Moscow's tune, even if he heard his own *leitmotif* threading its way through the official score.

The Colonel General had spoken good German long before the war. He had chosen German instead of Law as his subsidiary subject when he was at Frunze Military Academy. Like many other graduates of the Academy he had never believed that the Molotov-Ribbentrop Pact meant security for the Soviet Union. Colonel General Katusov was always described as 'a soldier's soldier', but he had mapped out his career with the shrewdness of any member of the Politburo.

All that first day Keller had photographed the General's staff officers and finally he had photographed the General himself.

As he worked that night in the darkroom Keller spent a long time on the enlargement of the portrait he had taken of the Russian General. It had been lit simply with the only available light from a side window, and the face that looked back from the developing dish was magnificent. It was the face of a Cossack, a proud eagle's face with penetrating eyes and a hooked nose. The deep shadows on one side only emphasised the man's awesome aggression. He did two further enlargements, burning in the eyes and holding back the shadows on the side of the face. He had used a lot of his scant supply of paper but his creative instinct knew that this was something special. It was a magnificent face but the photograph had added to the handsome features. It was hard to describe what had been added but Keller knew that his portrait told more of the man than perhaps the man would wish the world to know.

It was two days later when he heard from the General. He sent a car and driver to take him out to the villa. When he arrived a Red Army captain had shown him to the General's private quarters.

It was early evening and as he walked into the large living-room the General came in, drying his hair on a rough towel and wearing a bath-robe, his face still wet and glowing from a bath. He pointed at a leather armchair and when Keller was seated he sat down himself, his feet up on a glass coffee-table.

'How long have you been a photographer?'

'You mean a professional or just taking photographs?'

'Both.'

'Professionally just a few months but I've always had a camera since I was a kid.'

'How old are you?'

'Twenty-five next month.'

'And what did you do before the war?'

'I went to art school in Berlin and then I worked as an assistant director at the theatre.' He smiled. 'It sounds

75

important – assistant director – I was sweeping up and learning.'

'You seem a very perceptive and intelligent young man – are you?'

Keller shrugged. 'I don't know, General. That's for others to decide.'

'How much do you make a week?'

'Just enough to live on and pay rent and buy materials.'

'No money to put on one side?'

Keller smiled. 'I'm afraid not.'

'And you hate the Russians, of course. All Germans do.'

'There was a small concert at the Town Hall last week. Just amateurs. They played a Rachmaninov cello sonata, the Tchaikovsky violin concerto and the Glazunov violin concerto. They were all Germans in the orchestra.'

'What's the point that you're making?'

'That it all depends on what the Russians you know have done. You may hate a man who rapes defenceless women but you can still admire a great musician.'

'You should tell that to the Waffen SS who killed and raped our women. They weren't playing Brahms when they invaded our country. They were animals.' He shook his head dismissively. 'I'd like you to spend two or three weeks photographing the daily lives of my men. I want a record to show what our lives were like in this country. I don't want propaganda photographs, I can get a hundred men from Moscow to do that. I want photographs as perceptive of my men as the one you did of me.' He paused. 'We would provide all the materials and facilities you want. And we'd pay you well – anything you wanted – roubles, cigarettes – anything you want.'

'When would you want me to start?'

'As soon as you can.'

'I'd need five days to clear up my backlog of work.'

'That's OK. I'll send for you on Saturday.'

*

Eddie Carter was surprised when Keller walked in. He was eating his breakfast and looked up from his plate.

'Are you OK, Erich?'

Keller smiled. 'I don't know. We'd better talk.'

'Have some breakfast.'

'OK.'

Carter called the cook and Keller asked for fried eggs and bacon and settled himself down at the table with Carter.

'Tell me what's going on.'

Keller searched inside his jacket pocket and pushed over a bulging brown envelope. Carter reached over for it, opening it carefully. For long minutes he looked at the photographs. Keller said, 'The names and details are on the back. Some I didn't get.'

Carter looked at him. 'How the hell did you get this lot?'

Keller told him and Carter said quietly, 'My God. 21 AG will be amazed. So what's the problem?'

Keller told him about the Colonel General's new order.

'But it'll be invaluable, Erich. What's worrying you?'

'If they start looking into my background I don't stand a chance. They'd shoot me out of hand.'

'What have you told them so far?'

'Virtually nothing. They haven't asked anything about the war. But I'm scared that they will.'

'What about the papers we gave you?'

'Whenever they've been checked there's been no problem. But a casual check by a Russian who barely speaks German is one thing. A proper investigation by professionals is something else. They could check every damn thing.'

'How long can you stay now?'

'He's sending for me Saturday so it's three days at the most. But I'd rather be back at least a day earlier.'

'OK. Carry on eating and I'll talk to 21 AG.'

'What can they do?'

'I don't know but I want to check.'

*

Eddie Carter was away for twenty minutes but he looked pleased as he sat down at the table again.

'They're sending a specialist down this morning. He's a specialist in background stories and documentation. He'll ask you a lot about what you were doing during the war and then he'll devise a story that fits in, and the Document Unit will provide you with papers that will stand up to any checks the Russians care to make.'

Keller smiled. 'Thank God most of the German records have been destroyed.' He paused. 'Any chance of a sleep before the chap comes from 21 AG?'

'Of course. Your room's still there. I'll wake you when he arrives. You'll get a couple of hours.'

Colonel Stafford had come down from Bad Oeynhausen with a man in civilian clothes who was referred to only as George. George spoke with a faint trace of an accent that Carter couldn't identify.

It was Stafford who made clear what 21 AG wanted.

'Your man Keller could be our most valuable source of information from over the border. It's an opportunity we can't let slip. But I've got two worries about the situation.' He paused. 'The first is the man's safety. George here will give him a cast-iron story but we ought to warn him that if he were uncovered they'd have no mercy.'

'I think he recognises that. That's why he came back to talk about it. What's your other worry?'

Stafford said quietly, 'Are you quite sure that he's still ours?' He paused. 'They could have turned him. It works both ways, you know.'

'Perhaps you should talk to him yourself.'

'What do *you* think?'

'From what I know of the man I think it's highly unlikely that they could have turned him. And apart from that, the way he has got alongside the General is too accidental not to be believed. If he'd been turned they could have given him a better cover story and it wouldn't have included even a tenuous relationship with some Russian General.'

Stafford nodded. 'OK. I'll have a chat with him myself. Is he around?'

'He's asleep. I'll wake him up.'

'How long have we got?'

'A couple of days. He has to be back early on Friday.'

Stafford spent an hour chatting to Keller and then handed him over to George and left them alone.

Back with Carter, Stafford seemed satisfied. 'One can't be sure but I think we're OK there.' He looked at Carter. 'The fact that we've got his war-time history is a kind of insurance anyway.'

'If *we* ignore his past they could do the same.'

'True enough. Anyway, let's carry on as if the only problem is keeping him safe. George will do that.'

'How long does he need – George?'

'By tonight he'll have everything he needs. He'll get back to 21 AG, work out a cover story, provide documents and back-up material and he should be back here the day after tomorrow.' He paused. 'I told Keller that what he had provided so far was first-class. I told him too that we'll see him well rewarded when the operation's over.'

Stafford and George left at 1 a.m. and Keller seemed in no hurry to go to bed. He looked across at Carter. 'Seems a long time since we were all sitting around wondering if we'd survive over the other side but it's only a few months. Have you heard anything from friend Schmidt?'

'No. Not a word. I think we can write him off.'

'I think your pal, Stafford, wonders if you ought to write me off too.'

'No way, Erich, he's delighted with what you've been doing.'

'That man George. What nationality is he? He's real smart that one.'

'I don't know. I don't know anything about him.'

'He says he'll be back late tomorrow.'

'I'll be a lot happier when you've got better cover.'

'Me too.' He paused. 'What do you want from the Colonel General?'

'Everything you can get. Particularly about the Russian intentions in their zone.'

'I can't rush it you know, I'm just a photographer. I can't ask leading questions. I've just got to keep my ears open.'

'This job he's given you about making a record of the day-to-day lives of his troops. D'you think you can do that OK?'

'Yeah. No problem. It'll be good.'

'Not too good, I hope.'

'It'll be as good as I know how, Eddie. When you were instructing us you said we should never think of having a cover. Whatever we chose to be that's what we must be. I'm a photographer and I'm a good one.'

'Have you always been interested in photography?'

'Not really.'

'So what makes you good at it?'

'I worked in the theatre when I was a youngster before the war. When I got the chance to direct I spent hours analysing the characters in the play. Trying to understand them. Why they did what they did. It's looking at people that makes you a good photographer. A camera's just a camera. It's your heart and your mind that makes good pictures. Most people just look at the world around them. If you're creative you don't just look – you see.'

'Tell me about your family.'

'What do you know already?'

'You were born in Berlin. Your father was a lawyer and your mother was an actress. I think the record said you went to art school.'

'That's about it. The old man joined the Party right at the start. Mama was much younger that he was, but they got on well together. She hated politics of any kind.

Wouldn't join the Party. Not even to please the old man. Not even to secure her own position.'

'What happened to them?'

'I'm not sure. The last I heard was that the old man had been arrested by the French in Berlin. I don't have any news about my mother. She was in Berlin when it fell. Maybe she survived.' He shrugged. 'Who knows?'

'Why did you join the Sicherheitsdienst?'

Keller laughed. 'You don't *join* the Sicherheitsdienst. If you've got qualifications they want – you're in. And that's that.'

'What qualifications did you have?'

'Languages. English and French.' He smiled. 'They liked bright young men who knew which knife to use for spreading the butter. They were rivals of the Abwehr and Abwehr officers were gentlemen. So we had to have a few gentlemen too. They thought I was one.'

Carter knew it was unwise to probe further about Keller's war-time record. That was Stafford's worry, not his.

George had come back mid-afternoon on Thursday and had spent two hours going over the new cover-story for Keller. When he had finished Keller said, 'What if they check on the documents?'

'The doctor's certificate has the signature of a man who specialised in heart complaints. His name is correct, the signature is copied by a specialist too. The hospital is a real hospital and all its records have been destroyed.

'The theatre where you are supposed to have worked during the war has been destroyed too. The pay-slips are careful copies. Nobody can check on them. The birth certificate is genuine. The newspaper cutting of the play review is printed on the correct paper and has been processed for age.' He smiled. 'I don't think you have anything to worry you.'

Becker arrived late on the Thursday night and the three of them had eaten sandwiches and drunk coffee before going to bed. It was when Carter was pouring a last cup each that Becker said, 'I've got a problem. I need some advice.'

Carter said quickly, 'We don't talk about what we're doing – except to me.'

Keller stood up. 'I'm off to bed anyway.'

Becker looked up. 'I'd rather you stayed. At least you know what it's like out there.'

Keller hesitated and Carter signalled to him to stay. As Keller sat down Carter said, 'What's the problem, Fritz?'

Becker sighed. 'I'd better start at the beginning.' He sighed again. 'I told you I'd got myself a room and that my landlady was trying to get me a job at the Town Hall. I went for an interview and they gave me a job. Just a clerical job on food coupons. Then I was transferred to the Arbeitsamt, registering people who wanted jobs, and registering people who needed workers. First of all I just dealt with the two factories. The cement works and the optical instruments works. Then all municipal employees had to fill out a questionnaire. I filled mine in – there were four pages of questions – like an old Party *fragebogen*. That was two weeks ago.

'The day before yesterday I was told to go to the main police-station of the Kriminalpolizei. I thought I was going to be arrested. I was scared as hell. But it was about that bloody form. You had to give the languages you took at school and I'd put the truth – English and Italian.

'He gave me a document in English to translate and when I'd read it to the guy he called in another man who was obviously very senior. He asked me about my job and how much I earned and was I married. And then he said he was going to have me transferred because they had a lot of material in English and they wanted it translated. He said I'd got to start next week.'

Keller roared with laughter. 'It's crazy. I don't believe it. My best friend is a Red Army general and Fritz is going to work for the Kripo.' Still laughing he looked at Carter. 'What more could you want.' He turned to Becker. 'What's the problem, Fritz?'

Becker shrugged. 'I thought maybe I should pull out and come back.'

Carter nodded. 'Are you scared?'

'Yeah.'

'Of what?'

'Being right in there with the Kripo.'

'What was the document you translated?'

'It was a report by the British Military Government detachment in Magdeburg before the British pulled back.'

'What was it about?'

'How to deal with panic by the public when they found the British were leaving.'

'What were the other documents?'

'I don't know. They didn't say. But they looked official.'

'Were you given any chance to refuse the job?'

'No. You're told where to work. If you don't go there's no coupons for food and no residence permit.'

'What do you want to do yourself, Fritz.'

Becker shrugged. 'We made a deal. I'll do whatever you say. But I want to know that if I stay you'll get me out if I'm in trouble.'

'I'll talk to 21 AG and we'll discuss it tomorrow. OK?'

Becker nodded and looked across at Keller. 'Saw you the other day out front from the Town Hall. You were taking a photograph of a pretty girl by the statue of the man on the horse.'

Keller smiled. 'That's Otto the Great, my friend, and that statue's survived for seven hundred years.'

'And who's the pretty girl? She looks more like sixteen.'

'I don't remember. If you're a photographer you take pictures of lots of pretty girls.'

It was the first time that Carter had fully realised that already there were things in Keller's life and Becker's life that were nothing to do with their mission over the border.

He phoned Stafford, who didn't have any doubts. Becker should take the job. His point was that working at the Kripo Becker would hear about what the German officials thought the Russians were up to and he'd be in a perfect position to give a picture of what was going on in the whole of the area controlled from Magdeburg. Any inducement needed to make Becker stay should be offered. And again Stafford emphasised how valuable Keller's information had been. 21 AG wanted all he could get on identifying units and their locations.

It was obvious the next morning that Keller had been talking with Becker. Becker's doubts had gone. He'd take the job and accepted that the Kripo was far too busy to check up in great detail on the background of every low-level employee. As Keller said, 'They're Germans and well aware that everybody has some sort of skeleton in the cupboard. Including themselves.'

13

It took Keller six weeks to cover all the units under Katusov's command and two more weeks to process the results and decide what should be enlarged.

On the last day he laid out the 10×8 enlargements on a table in the outer section of the studio. He ended up with fifty enlargements that he liked and twenty-five sheets of contacts. A dozen times he moved them around and stood back from the table to look at them again.

There were groups of young soldiers, soldiers on motorcycles, at the wheel of jeeps and sitting on the turrets of tanks and on troop carriers. A gunner stood smiling and proud beside an anti-tank gun, and officers with artillery insignia posed beside heavy guns with their ammunition trucks.

But at least half were photographs of individuals. The stern, stoical faces of senior officers, the grinning faces of young men still proud of their victory, and sometimes the sad faces of men who were longing to go home. Young infantrymen who sat on ammunition boxes cradling their assault rifles in their arms like a mother holding a baby.

He was so intent on what he was doing that he barely noticed the old man standing beside him, looking at the photographs.

Finally the old man said, 'Why have you made those bastards look so good?'

Keller looked surprised. 'I just photographed them as I saw them, Papa.'

'They have murdered and raped from Poland down to here.'

'We had our turn, old man. But not everybody rapes and murders. They have been fighting for their lives and it's part of the price nations pay for waging war.'

'They have a sixth of the world's surface and they still want more.'

Very quietly Keller said, 'They didn't start it, Papa. We did.'

'It suits people now to say that. It's all propaganda. They are animals. Every one of them.'

'They're sons and husbands, brothers and fathers. They just want to go home.'

'Yes. To sell their loot in their God-forsaken country.' Keller laughed. 'What did you do in the war, Papa? Tell me.'

'I was too old to fight. I was an air-raid warden. I saved people's lives, not killed them.'

'You were lucky. Some of us had to do the killing.'

The old man looked at his face. 'Did *you* do killing?'

'That's my business, old man. You stick to your business.'

'They're good photos, Erich. You've got a talent for people.'

When Keller saw the photographs still in the envelopes on the General's desk his heart fell. The General was leaning back in his ornate chair just looking at him as he sat there in silence wondering how his photographs could have offended the Russian.

Eventually the General pointed to the envelope. 'I don't understand these photographs.'

'In what way, Colonel General? You said you wanted a record of your command. That's what I've tried to provide.'

'They're not military. No soldiers marching. No soldiers drilling. No soldiers firing their weapons.'

'I spoke to many officers and soldiers, sir. Most of them are not professional soldiers. They're civilian volunteers. I wanted to show what sort of men they are. The men who won the war.'

The General sucked his teeth noisily. 'I had visitors from Berlin. I showed them your photographs. What kind of reaction would you have expected?'

'It depends on what kind of men they are.'

'It doesn't matter. They were full of enthusiasm. In fact they suggested that they should be printed as a book with a text by one of our leading writers.'

Keller smiled with relief. 'I'm very pleased, General. I really am.'

'The writer is coming from Moscow. From the Film Institute. He'll be here in two weeks' time if his transport priority doesn't get over-ridden.' He paused. 'He'd like to spend time with you before he starts his writing.' He paused. 'You're a strange man, Keller. They said that you're a poet of the camera. Whatever that might mean.'

Keller smiled. 'I'm flattered, sir.'

'That place you work in, is that where you live?'

'Yes, sir.'

'They tell me it's no good.'

'I get by.'

'I've told my ADC to get you a decent place. I've also told him to find you a small car and see that you get all the petrol you need.'

'That's very generous, General.'

The General's ADC, a young artillery captain, had collected him, his photographic gear and his few possessions and driven him to his new place.

It was an old house near the centre of the town, its outer wall supported by large timbers with a crack down its length that had been roughly filled with cement. They had taken over the basement and the ground floor for his sole use and two army electricians were checking the wiring and putting up plasterboard panels for his darkroom. He had more than twice the working area than at the old

87

man's place. For his living quarters on the ground floor there was ample room. It had been requisitioned by the Russians and the owners had had to leave their furniture behind. It was almost too good to be true.

The car came two days later. A small DKW that had been requisitioned and checked by a Soviet transport corporal.

He spent two days setting up his darkroom and studio, and spent a few hours photographing in the old streets in the centre of the town.

It was three weeks before Sergei Rokowsky arrived and the General himself had introduced them. Rokowsky was to move in with Keller for a week's discussion and writing. Rokowsky was a little older than Keller but they took to one another immediately. The Russian spoke bad but fluent German.

When they got back to Keller's place he had shown the Russian what would be his room and they had sat together afterwards in the comfortable living-room.

'I loved your photographs, Erich. I can't wait to get on with the writing. And the General wants me to talk with you about doing a film.'

'What kind of film?'

'A film based on your book of photographs.'

'I don't have any experience with film and I don't have a cine-camera.'

Rokowsky smiled. 'I'll hold your hand on the filming and we'll soon get a cine-camera for you.' He paused. 'It's a big chance for you, Erich. It really is. It's got Moscow's approval.'

Keller's next visit across the border was brief but he had left contact sheets and duplicate negatives of a dozen rolls of 35 mm film. Over 400 different shots from his tour around Katusov's command area. And there were four pages of an index to the shots giving names, units and grid references of locations.

The analysis at 21 AG showed quite clearly that not only were the Red Army units across the border assault units not defensive units but that they were a force that would be overwhelming if they came over the border. The doves in London suggested that maybe there was no aggressive intent and that Moscow found it cheaper and more convenient to let its troops live off the land rather than burden Moscow with the responsibility. The hawks thought this was wishful thinking. But hawks are not popular when a country has just finished a long, gruelling war. The Americans had their minds on getting their rather undisciplined troops back to the States. They had done their bit for Europe and President Truman was well aware that the country wanted its boys back home. The French Zone did not touch the Russian Zone at any point and in Metropolitan France they were too busy taking revenge on one another to dwell on what the Russians might be doing. 21 AG recognised that a lot of people were intent on making sure that if the Red Army was massing troops just over the border then it was their hot potato. Not London's, not Washington's. If general advice was needed then it was – play it cool. Nobody wanted trouble. And the Russians were still our gallant allies. The bombs that had been dropped on Nagasaki and Hiroshima had sent message enough to Moscow. All the T-34 tanks in the world wouldn't balance that equation.

Stafford sat in with the evaluation team at 21 AG so that he could in turn keep Carter informed on what was most useful.

The discussion of Keller's photographs went on for several days and when they were finished a major from one of the tank regiments had gone over some of their finds.

'Most of these tanks are T-34s but a lot of them have been modified with fume extractors fitted mid-way along the gun barrel. There's a fair number of T-44s and only front-line units would get those. But what's most significant is this searchlight on the turrets. That's new. It's infra-red so it means the driver can drive in the dark and the gunner can shoot in the dark. We've never seen those fitted to any tanks before.

'When we look at individual soldiers they look fit and well-fed. But there's too many *polkovniks*, colonels, for my liking. All with plenty of campaign medals. Not the kind of troops you'd expect to be occupying a defeated civilian population.'

'What else can we get that would help you?'

'Petrol and diesel supplies. How much? What kind of storage and where?' He paused. 'And then personnel carriers. How many infantry support troops for follow-up?'

'What do you make of it?'

'That's for the top brass to say.'

Stafford persisted. 'But your own opinion.'

'It's hard to say. From the insignia there's at least twenty tank divisions opposite us at Brunswick and down towards Göttingen and the Americans at Kassel. They can't possibly need a force like this. But they're not hiding it. There's very little camouflage.' He shrugged. 'Maybe they just want to scare us. Or maybe Moscow's playing games. In Berlin all the crack troops have been taken back to the Soviet Union and there are only three tank brigades between Berlin and Warsaw. They're sending us some message, but God knows what it is.'

14

Vorster came over late on a Friday night. Discouraged by lack of opportunity to even see Soviet troops who were not allowed to go into the city. As he ate a good meal Carter talked about Vorster's new job.

'They set me up in an office near the Town Hall. People who want permits for building materials. Women looking for missing husbands and relatives. Anything that involves dealing with the Russian Commandant's office.'

'You must know a hell of a lot about what's going on in Magdeburg.'

'Yeah. But not about their troops.'

'OK. Forget troops. Just report on the German population. Their morale and their attitude to the Russians.'

'Most people hate them. Everybody's scared of them. But there's the usual rat-pack that suck up to the Russians. Denouncing people for being Nazis, or hoarding food, or for cursing the Reds in public. They call it "bringing the Occupying Power into disrepute". And there are the usual tarts who cycle out to the fields near where the troops are stationed.'

'What about jobs and food?'

'Most people, men and women, are put on six weeks' clearing rubble and then they might get a job in one of the factories. As far as food's concerned, it's the black-market or you starve. The soldiers sell food for jewellery and gold coins but if you're not careful they just take what they find. There are old Party members who get anything they want from the Kommissars and they've got more power than the German officials.'

'And what do you do?'

'I explain what the new laws are all about – when anybody knows what the law is. How to fill in the application forms and where to go.'

'OK, Pauli. Forget about the military stuff. Just concentrate on the local situation. The relationships between German officials and the Russians. Local morale and all the gossip.'

Rokowsky and Keller had gone through the photographs for the third time and Keller sat back in his chair.

'What do you think?'

Rokowsky smiled. 'I want to hear your ideas first. It's going to be your film, not mine.'

'Who's it for – the film?'

'You mean who's paying for it?'

'No. The audience. Who are we talking to?'

'The general public. All over the Soviet Union.'

'I'd like to make it a wider audience than that.'

'Tell me.'

'I'd like to make a film that's about men. Men who just happen to be soldiers. What they think and what they want for the future. Let them be average men whose attitudes can appeal to the soldiers of other countries. Even the Germans.'

For a few moments Rokowsky was silent and then he said quietly, 'That's brilliant, Erich.' He smiled. 'I can't wait to get started.' He stood up. 'While I'm writing the words for the book I'll make notes for the film.'

Becker's next visit brought bad news. Two lots of bad news. The Russians were to start up the Grenzpolizei again. The frontier guards. And there would be patrols along the Zone borders. That would make the crossings a real risk. It meant looking at their communications very carefully.

The second piece of news was in a copy of a top-secret report that Becker had been able to get hold of that had been sent to the Kriminalpolizei. Moscow was making plans for the Communist Party to become the sole official political party for the whole of the Soviet Zone. This would be a breach of Allied Potsdam agreements. The document was not yet a plan, merely a discussion paper but the German officials who had seen it were sure that it would go through in the next year. It also suggested that a Communist German government would be set up to govern the whole of East Germany. The events that would flow from that decision would be a direct challenge to the other occupying powers.

As he read through the twenty or so pages of the document Carter had no premonition of how the document was going to change the whole of his life. But he knew it was significant enough to phone Stafford immediately.

Stafford drove down early the next day and sat reading the document. He read it several times and then walked into Carter's office and sat down beside the desk.

'I'll take this with me, Eddie. This is for London rather than 21 AG.'

'What about the frontier patrols? I'll have to do something about that. It'll be too dangerous for them to keep crossing over just to deliver what they've got.'

'What do you have in mind?'

'The obvious thing is for me to go over and see them over there.'

Stafford shook his head. 'No way. That's far too risky. We need you here, in charge. I'll talk it over at HQ. Maybe we can find a courier.'

'From what Becker said it'll be some weeks before they've recruited people and trained them. They're going to be sharing their HQ at the Kriminalpolizei building where Becker works. He'll know when it's going to start. I told him we wanted to know well in advance.'

'Maybe Becker could apply for a job with the border police.'

'There'd be no point. He could be posted miles away from here.'

'But it would ensure that you'd still have a way across even if it meant a long diversion. Keller and Vorster would be safe anywhere so long as they were over the other side. They can both find excuses to travel.'

'Not without a movement permit they couldn't.'

'Think about it. I'll be back sometime in the next three or four days.'

It was a week before Stafford came back. There had been no visits from the other side in that time and Carter was beginning to get edgy.

Stafford got straight down to business. 'London want your people to concentrate on the political stuff. The order-of-battle material is still very valuable but right now it's their political intentions that London want most. Maybe the two things go hand in hand. The big military build-up and then setting up a separate German state. And that means trouble on an international scale. But at least we'll be fore-armed.'

'Anything else?'

Stafford smiled. 'Yes. A present from your old Field Security Section. It was 103 FS wasn't it?'

'Yes.'

'Before we pulled back to the Yalta Zone lines you had a two-man detachment at a small dump named Wernigerode – yes?'

'Yes.'

'Exactly eight miles over the new border. In the Soviet Zone.'

'I don't remember. I never visited the detachment. There wasn't time before the pull-back.'

'Well one of your chaps, a sergeant named Hollins had a girlfriend. A farmer's daughter. He got her in the family way. So she's a mother now. And he's a father. And the girl's father is angry as a rattle-snake. He liked Sergeant Hollins and the sergeant had promised to marry the girl as soon as 21 AG allowed marriages between troops and Germans. The old man would do anything to make an honest woman of his daughter.'

'How do you know this?'

'Sergeant Hollins made a marriage application way back but of course once we pulled back it was pointless. But some bright spark at Bad Salzuflen made a note of the circumstances for possible future use.' He smiled. 'So Sergeant Hollins was sent on a little mission over the border, with a proposition for the old man. We bring the girl and the child back over the border. She marries Sergeant Hollins. All proper and above-board. In England. The old man gets a copy of the marriage certificate and everybody's happy. And the old man is perfectly happy to let one of his rooms to someone with the right word who'd like a couple of days in the country away from the big city.'

'When?'

'What's today? Thursday? Yes. Sergeant Hollins should be on his honeymoon today and next time one of your boys comes over he gives the farmer this.' And Stafford reached into his pocket and gave Carter an unsealed foolscap envelope. Carter took out the folded paper. It was an official copy of the certificate recording the marriage between Francis Hollins and Helga Braumann, with the previous day's date.

Carter looked at Stafford. 'London must be pretty desperate to go this far in such a hurry.'

'Desperate – no. Anxious to please – yes.' He paused. 'And how about you?'

'I'm still staggered at the effort. Cutting all the red-tape and that.'

'You should be flattered, Eddie. It's done for you and your operation.'

Carter shrugged and smiled. 'I'm flattered all right. Overwhelmed too.'

In fact, although Carter was amazed at the speed and effectiveness with which Stafford and 21 AG had responded, he was also resentful that momentarily the control of his operation had been usurped by others, no matter how effective they may be. It had turned his cosy but effective operation into a hard-edged military operation. And he didn't like it. But there was obviously nothing he could complain about. They had solved a major problem for him, almost overnight. He wondered if it might be wiser from then on to keep Stafford at arm's length. He had no justification whatever for adopting that attitude but he knew that it would be at the back of his mind in future.

Stafford had given him full details of the location of the farm, a photograph of the farm and a faded photograph of the farmer and his daughter.

Keller and Rokowsky were walking slowly around the main square. It was almost midnight and they had been stopped and their documents checked by both a Russian patrol and by two German policemen. They both had curfew passes and Rokowsky laughed as the Russian patrol moved off. 'There's something especially pleasing, almost exciting, about doing something that others can't do. It must be like this to be a millionaire or a member of the Politburo. Doing what others can't do.'

Keller smiled. 'Most people would count themselves lucky to be in bed rather than walking around the centre of Magdeburg in the middle of the night.'

'Are you in love with the little blonde girl who comes to see you?'

'Good God, no.'

'You just sleep with her?'

'Yes.'

'How old is she?'

'I'm not sure. Sixteen – something like that.'

'Why so young? They've never got anything to talk about.'

Keller laughed. 'I don't pick them for their conversation.' He paused. 'By the way. Do I have to have a cameraman?'

Smiling, Rokowsky said, 'Well they come in handy when you're shooting a film.'

'I want to shoot it myself with a hand-held camera, so that although it's planned it's more like just a documentary.'

'It's your film, Erich. If that's how you want it that's OK by me.'

'I was thinking of starting in about a week's time.'

'It's up to you. Just let me know what you want in the way of crew.'

'Like what?'

'A film-loader, a sound-engineer, maybe a lighting guy.'

'You can get them here in a week OK?'

'Let's say five days and that'll give you time to explain to them what you're after.' He smiled. 'You might get landed with a kommissar to see that you're not advocating counter-revolution.'

'If there's to be a kommissar then there's no film. Not from me anyway.'

'Don't press too hard, my friend. You're getting more rope than one of our film people would get. But there are still rules and regulations – even for you.'

'They can just scrap the film if they don't like it.'

Rokowsky stopped walking and Keller turned to look at him. 'What's the matter?'

'I think you've forgotten something. Or maybe you just didn't remember it.'

'What's that?'

'The war's been over less than two years. We lost eight million fighting men and at least eight million civilians. Right now we have twenty-five million homeless people. You people in this town live better than most people in the Soviet Union. The Germans invaded the Soviet Union and we shall never forget it. And despite your talents, Erich Keller, you're a German. So take the privileges that we give you because of your talent, but remember – you're a German, and even for me I can't forget it. Don't tell us what we can do or can't do. OK?'

For a moment Keller was silent and then he nodded. 'OK. You've made the point. I thought that with you and me we were just men.'

'And so we are. But for other Russians you're a German. And you and your people behaved like animals. And you lost despite all that.'

'We all lost, Sergei. The whole world lost.' He paused. 'But I'll remember what you said.'

As they walked back to Keller's place he said, 'Can you get me some footage of the defence of Stalingrad?'

'Miles of it. All you want.'

'And I can use it?'

'I'll have to get clearance but there'll be no problem.'

15

Carter stood at the edge of the woods. There were long
shadows from the trees across the meadow and then the
slope down to the small stream. He had studied the map
countless times and had stood there daily but there had
been no sign of any patrols, either German or Soviet. He
bent down, reached for the handles of the canvas bag and
walked into the waning sunlight.

Using the roads it would have taken him no more than
an hour but he kept to the field paths away from the few
solitary houses and it was two hours before he saw the tall
grain-barn of the farm. It hid the farmhouse beyond and
the row of farm buildings that housed the milking parlour
and the piggery.

It was dawn as he walked across the pot-holed concrete
to the farmhouse itself. There was a light in one of the
downstairs windows at the far end. He guessed it was the
kitchen. As he stood at the door he checked that he had
the photograph of the girl ready in his hand.

He lifted his hand towards a lever beside the wooden
door and heard the sound of a cracked metal bell inside
the farmhouse. It seemed a long time before he heard
shuffling footsteps and the sounds of heavy bolts being
drawn back. The door opened and was held by a chain
inside. He recognised Braumann's face and he held up
the girl's photograph.

'I'd like to talk to you, Herr Braumann.'

The old man reached for the photograph turning it
towards the lamp he was holding up in his other hand.
For long moments he looked at it and then turned to

look at Carter, shining the lamp through the half-open door to light up Carter's face. Again he looked for long moments before his hand went to release the chain and open the door just wide enough for Carter to enter.

When the old man had put back the chain and bolted the door he turned and beckoned Carter to follow him. The way led down a corridor of uneven flagstones into a large old-fashioned kitchen with a black cast-iron oven and grate, heavy beams supported the ceiling and an old kitchen table with four spindle-backed chairs was in the centre of the room. He pulled out one of the chairs for Carter, pointing to it as he sat down himself. Carter took out the envelope, placed it on the table and slid it across to the old man, who opened it, took out the folded document and unfolded it carefully, holding it down at both ends. He looked at it carefully, his lips moving silently as he read it slowly. He read it several times before he looked up and across at Carter. He pointed to the marriage certificate.

'Is this genuine? Official?'

'Yes.'

'How was it done so quickly?'

'That was the bargain we made with you.'

'The sergeant said you are an officer. A major, yes?'

'Yes.'

'You give me your word of honour she is married to the sergeant?'

'I give you my word, Herr Braumann.'

'You want to stop the night?'

'No. I'll go back.' Carter took two packs of cigarettes from his canvas bag. 'Do you have a travel permit?'

'Only as far as Magdeburg.'

Carter pushed across the cigarettes. 'If I wanted you to take a message to a man in Magdeburg could you do that?'

The old man smiled. 'With cigarettes I can get petrol so, yes, I can do that.'

Carter stood up and the old man stood up too and

walked with him to the farmhouse door, pulling back the bolts and releasing the chain.

'When do I see you again?'

'I don't know. I shall not come very often. When my people come here they'll give you the password.'

Carter held out his hand and the old man took it in his.

'Tell her I hope she is happy.'

'I'll get your message to her.'

There was a mist across the fields as Carter started on his way back, watching for the clumps of trees that he had noted on his journey. Twice he had thought that he had lost his way and he was relieved when he came to the wooden bridge across the stream. He heard a vixen bark as he approached the woods and twenty minutes later he was back at the lodge.

Becker came over two days later with the news that the border patrols were due to start in two weeks' time.

'You'd better give me your address, Fritz.' When he had noted it down Carter said, 'Do you happen to know Keller's address?'

Becker hesitated. 'You told us not to keep in touch, any of us.'

'But you know where he lives don't you?'

'What makes you think that?'

Carter smiled. 'Instinct. Experience.'

'Yeah. I saw him at a street market with a Russian. I followed him. He's in a street just near the main square. Corner of Lindenstrasse and Bülowstrasse.'

'How did you know that man with him was a Russian?'

'I heard Erich call him Sergei.'

Carter told Becker of the farm as a place which he could use to leave messages or arrange a meeting, and Becker was obviously relieved that he need not cross the border unless his news was urgent. Carter showed him on the map the location of the farm and showed him the photograph of Herr Braumann.

'Do I have to pay him if I use the place?'

'No. I'll look after that.'

'How will he know I'm OK?'

'I've given him a password – Rainbow.'

'Does he know about the operation?'

'No. Absolutely nothing. He won't ask questions, and you shouldn't tell him anything.'

'Apart from the patrols starting there was one other piece of news I picked up. The police chiefs were discussing it and they seemed very worried about it. I'm not sure why.'

'Tell me.'

'Well it's two things really. First of all the Russian Administration are going to appoint Party members to report on people – like the old *blockleiter* system. And as soon as they are in place they are going to make the SPD join with the Communists in one single party.'

'Is this just Magdeburg?'

'No, for all the Russian Zone, including Berlin. A German named Ulbricht is going to be the Party leader.'

'Did the Kripo people say why they were worried?'

'First of all the *blockleiters* will be reporting to the Russians direct and not to the Kripo and they know that merging the two parties means conflict with the Allies. They seem to think the Russians are getting ready for some kind of show-down with the British and the Americans.'

'And with the French?'

Becker looked surprised, shrugging as he said, 'Nobody ever mentions the French. I don't think the Russians count them as worth bothering with.'

'I want to talk with you about some way to contact you to arrange meetings at the farmhouse so that you and Keller don't have to risk coming over the border to talk to me and for me to keep you briefed and stocked up with coffee and cigarettes. Any suggestions?'

'I don't want to contact Keller.'

'Why not?'

'He's in with the Russians too good.'

'You mean you don't trust him?'

'No. I'm just scared of the Russkis. Even the Kripo chiefs are scared of them. They have to work with them but they don't trust them.'

'OK. We've got the farmhouse for meetings. Where can I leave messages for you?'

'There's nowhere that would be safe. There's building and demolition going on everywhere.'

'We could arrange a code. A chalk mark on a certain place. Just a cross or a plus sign that would mean that I want to see you at the farmhouse the next day.'

'But what if I don't notice the sign?'

'We put it where you can see it. Maybe on the building where you live. You check it every day. Maybe twice a day.'

'But I have to be at the Kripo offices every day.'

'OK, we make our meeting day for a Sunday.' He smiled. 'Let's say that I arrange for a white chalk cross by the door of the house and the meeting is always the following Sunday.'

Becker nodded. 'That sounds better. Is that for when the patrols start?'

'No. We'll do it like this from now on and we'll see if there are any snags.'

'I'd better get back. You've got my address?'

'Yes. Don't worry. Even if anybody stopped you you just say you're going to the country to see if you can get food.'

'I still need cigarettes and coffee to get by.'

'That's OK. I'll bring them over for you and you can take plenty back with you now.'

Stafford came down from 21 AG the next day with the letter for the old farmer that Carter had asked for. As he handed it over he said, 'Says how happy she is and there's a photo of her and the sergeant and the kid. Should keep him cooperating.'

Carter nodded and said quietly, 'It all seems to be going too smoothly. I'm waiting for the first cock-up.'

'Are you worried about the patrols?'

'No. They won't be all that good in the early stages.'

'So what's bugging you?'

'It's gone too well. We've got Keller giving us more than we could have hoped for on the order-of-battle material and Becker sitting pretty right inside the Kripo giving us the inside dope on the political stuff.'

'And Schmidt down the drain chasing his crumpet. And Vorster isn't producing much as yet.'

'Is that what 21 AG feel about it?'

'No. It's not what I think about it either. You chose well, you briefed them well and with just a wee bit of luck you're getting far more than we hoped for. So stop worrying about it.'

'How are the other operations doing?'

'One network's collapsed already, the other two are doing a good job. But not as good as you're doing.'

'What's their evaluation of what we've got so far?'

Stafford smiled. 'You don't need to know, Eddie. But they're more than pleased.'

16

Carter saw the crudely painted sign by the newly erected wire fence. It said simply: ACHTUNG GRENZSCHUTZ MIT HUNDEN. But he knew that the guard took an hour to walk his section of the border. He bent low, lifting the centre strand of wire and easing his way through.

An hour later he stood in the shadow of the barn and looked towards the farmhouse. A slight wind was blowing the line of poplars that were silhouetted against the skyline, bending them slightly and setting something metal flapping on the barn. The light was on in the farmhouse kitchen. He looked up at the night sky. It was the full moon. The harvest moon, big and full and low on the horizon, gold and shining like a theatre moon.

He reached down for the canvas hold-all with the cigarettes and jars of Maxwell House coffee and then, for some reason he couldn't have explained, he straightened up, leaving the bag on the ground. When he got to the farmhouse he gave the knock on the door. The well-known V sign in Morse. He didn't hear the old man's usual footsteps on the flagstones inside and, as he bent his head nearer the door to listen, the door was flung open and a powerful torch was blinding him. At the same time a hand reached out and grabbed at his hair, jerking him inside the farmhouse as the lights went on in the hallway. He had a brief glimpse of a man in an NKVD uniform at the end of the passage and then he heard the swish of something that smelled of leather before it struck behind his ear. The ground tilted and came up towards him as he lost consciousness.

*

Carter came to as the bucketful of cold water flooded over his face and for a brief moment he was aware of being in a room with maps on the wall and metal filing cabinets but as a hand clutched roughly at the collar of his shirt he passed out again. He heard somebody groaning when he surfaced again and then realised that it was he who was groaning. Then a face leaned over him and a voice said, 'He's OK.' The voice spoke in German. Hands pulled him to a sitting position and held him there, his head lolling forward and a pain like fire in his neck and shoulder. A rough hand jerked his chin up.

'What's your name?'

'Kraus. Werner Kraus.'

'Where do you come from?'

The closed fist landed on his cheek and there was a gush of blood from his mouth.

Somebody standing behind him pulled him to his feet and pushed him back against a wall. The man holding him up and the man beside him were both wearing Kripo uniforms, the NKVD officer was sitting on a wooden chair alongside a heavy wooden table. Fear pumped the adrenalin through Carter's system and he remembered what they'd said on the training course at Beaulieu. If you're caught, hang on for two days if you can so that the others in your network can be dispersed. If they didn't break you down in forty-eight hours you'd done OK – you'd have saved the others' lives. But there was nobody to come in and save Keller and Vorster and Becker. Stafford wouldn't even know it had gone down the pan for three or four days. And even then they wouldn't know what to do or where everybody was. There couldn't be any rough stuff from 21 AG, there wasn't a war.

The hand came forward, the fingers stretched as it clutched at his throat, forcing his head back against the wall.

'Where did you come from?'

'Dresden,' he said and he remembered what the instructor had said. Name, rank and number and don't answer any questions. Don't try and outsmart them. But there was no name, rank and number in this situation. And he had no idea why he had said that he'd come from Dresden. Why Dresden for God's sake? He didn't even know a street in Dresden. And then instinct took over and as he felt the man's breath on his face he gathered all the strength he had left and rammed his knee into the man's groin. He screamed and fell away and for a moment Carter was just standing there aware of the room and the NKVD man quite still, just watching as the second Kripo man lashed at him. He felt a hard fist in his face and a red explosion behind his eyes and a boot in his chest as he sank unconscious to the floor.

Becker was clearing his desk for the night. All the papers had to go into the wall-safe. He was just locking up when Otto came in. Otto Meyer was his immediate boss and he looked excited.

'They think they've got an English spy.'

'Who have?'

'The NKVD. We did the pick-up for them.'

'How do they know he's English? Has he talked?'

'No. They're giving him the works. He said he was from Dresden.'

'Where did they pick him up?'

'At a farmhouse near the border. Just this side of the Harz.'

For a moment Becker thought he was going to pass out as the wave of cold fear that swept through him almost stopped him breathing. And then the flush of heat that left him wet with perspiration. He turned to finish locking the safe before he dared look back at Otto.

'Where've they got him?'

'Down in the basement.'

'Who's interrogating him?'

Otto grinned. 'He kicked friend Heller in the balls.

107

They gave him the treatment and he won't come round for an hour or two yet.'

'How did they get on to him?'

'No idea. But the border patrols probably saw him come over and followed him.'

'What was he doing at the farmhouse?'

'They didn't say.'

'Probably trying to buy food, poor bastard.' Becker shrugged. 'What makes them think he's English anyway?'

'I think they put the heat on the old boy who runs the farm. Maybe he said that. They've got him too, in one of our cells.' Otto rubbed his hands. 'Anyway makes a change from drunks.' As he headed for the door. 'Time you were on your way. The bastards don't pay us for overtime.'

Becker stood there, still shaken, wondering what to do but knowing that he wouldn't have a moment's peace until he'd found out if they'd got Eddie. It was far too dangerous to go up to the NKVD section but he could bluff his way to the basement cells where Otto had said they'd got the farmer. For a moment he closed his eyes and then he took a deep breath and walked to the end of the corridor to where the cast-iron spiral staircase led down to the basement.

The first cell held a drunk, shouting obscenities and covered with vomit. Three cells further on he saw a Kripo man standing guard.

'You're not allowed down here, Becker.'

'I'm looking for Sergeant Otto. You seen him?'

'He'll be gone by now.'

'No he isn't. He was talking to me in my office only a couple of minutes ago.' He glanced towards the cell. 'Is this the chap he was talking about? The farmer.'

'None of your business, my friend. Nor Otto's neither.'

But Becker had seen enough. The bundle of rags on the slab of concrete was the farmer all right. His eyes closed and his face bruised.

'Don't look the kind to make much trouble anyway.'

'That's for others to say.'

Becker nodded. 'If you see Otto tell him I'm off home.'

'I told you. He's gone. He don't hang around once his shift's over.' He grinned, 'Don't blame him neither.'

It was raining when Becker walked out into the street and hesitated about which way to turn. Turning left he could be home in ten minutes. If he travelled all night he could be over the border before daylight. But then what? There would be no Eddie to put things right. By the time the others could do something it would be too late. Eddie would almost certainly be dead and so would he and Keller if Eddie was tortured and talked.

Almost without thinking he turned right and headed for Keller's place. He stumbled once as he closed his eyes for a moment trying to wipe out what was happening from his thoughts. There were no lights on at Keller's flat but there were lights from the ground-floor studio. He couldn't find a bell or a door-knocker so he banged on the door with his fist and stood waiting. The rain was heavier now and a stream of water ran down from a cracked cast-iron pipe. It seemed a long time before the door was opened.

Keller stared at him for a moment and then let him in.

'What the hell's going on? Why are you here?'

'They've got Eddie.'

'Who's got Eddie?'

'The Russians and the Kripo. They've got the old farmer too.'

'What happened?'

'I don't know.'

Keller, who had been working in the darkroom, was peeling off a pair of thin rubber gloves as he collected his thoughts.

'Tell me what you know. Everything.'

Becker told him what he had seen and heard, and Keller listened, head leaning forward as if he might miss some vital word. When Becker had finished Keller said. 'And why have you come here? Why aren't you on your way to the border?'

'I thought I'd better warn you first. See what you think we should do.'

'And what do you think we should do, my friend?'

'We ought to get over the border as soon as we can.'

'And our old friend, Eddie?'

'There's nothing we can do for him. He's down the drain.'

'Not the kind of thinking I'd expect from an ex-SS major, my friend. A distinct lack of comradeship.'

'What's that all about?'

'Are you scared?'

'You bet I am.'

'Too scared to help friend Eddie?'

'How can I help him? I can't even get to him, he's in the NKVD section.'

'But he's guarded by Kripo, yes?'

'Yes.'

'D'you want to go back over the border?'

'Yes. But with Eddie gone they won't want me – us – any longer.'

'But you want to go back?'

'Yes.'

'So we'd better get back Eddie with you.'

'That's impossible.'

'Have you eaten?'

'No.'

'Let's have a coffee and a sandwich upstairs in my place.'

'There's nobody else up there is there?'

Keller smiled. 'No. Well, just one of my girlfriends but I'll send her round to her mother's.'

They were still sitting at the kitchen table, Keller smoking a Russian cigarette and Becker all too conscious that his time for escaping was slipping by.

Keller said, 'Tell me more about this Otto chap, the sergeant.'

'What do you want to know?'

'Anything. Does he like the Russkis? Does he like his job? His family?'

'Nobody likes the Russians. I don't know about his job. He's been Kripo all his life. He hasn't got any family that I know of.'

'How long has he been a sergeant?'

'About ten years.'

'Does that mean he's not very bright?'

'He's got no education but I think he had some trouble way back towards the end of the war. He would have got the push but there was a shortage of men so he hung on.'

'What did he do?'

'I've heard he was greedy for money. Took bribes from prisoners, and back-handers from wealthy men who were being investigated.'

Keller just sat there, smoking for several minutes. Then he said, 'Where does he live, this Otto?'

'He's got a room in Kantstrasse.'

'Let's go and see him.'

'What for?'

'He'll help us get Eddie across the border.'

'You're crazy. Why should he help us?'

'A lot of reasons. Say fifty thousand marks, a good job over in the British Zone. A new start, and no Russians. And very grateful English.'

'And what if he refuses? He'd shop us to the NKVD.'

Keller half-smiled. 'He won't refuse.' He stood up. 'You can stay here if you want.'

Becker was obviously tempted and for a few moments he hesitated. Then he shrugged. 'No. I'll come with you. It might help that he knows me.'

As soon as he saw Otto Meyer and his room Keller knew that there'd be no problem. The Kripo sergeant was a big

111

raw-boned peasant, greedy for money and openly resentful of his lack of success in life.

Keller had done all the talking but he hadn't said anything about his and Becker's role with the British. There was an opportunity to make a new life and a lot of money with a minimum of risk. But Otto Meyer had got to decide right then and there. There was no time for bargaining or discussion or things would have gone too far with the NKVD's prisoner. He left the impression that the motives were the same for all three of them.

Meyer hadn't even haggled about the money. He was ready to cooperate. He had no ties, no roots, in Magdeburg. The sooner the better so far as he was concerned. They would do it the following night and would use Keller's car.

When the guard stopped them as they got to the dimly lit corridor where Carter was held Keller had used his pass from the General that said he was entitled to be anywhere in the Soviet Zone. It was in Russian and German and the guard had shrugged and unlocked the cell door.

What they had not expected was that Carter would be unconscious, but when they saw the state of Carter's face and hands they realised that it was going to be more complicated than they had expected. They were not removing a prisoner, they were removing a man who looked very near death.

The guard said, 'Where are you taking him?'

'To the military hospital.'

The guard looked at Meyer. 'What are you doing here? You're Kripo not NKVD.'

Meyer shrugged. 'Just carrying out orders.'

'You'll have to sign the release form before you go.'

Keller said sharply, 'Let's get him down to the car first.'

Keller turned to Becker and pointed to Carter's legs. 'You can take his legs. Lift him carefully.'

Carter showed no sign of consciousness as they carried

him up the stairs and through to the rear of the building where they had parked Keller's car in the official car-park for police vans and NKVD cars.

As Keller got into the driving seat Becker and Meyer got Carter into a sitting position on the back seat. Becker sat with him, one arm round Carter's shoulders. Keller drove out of the yard and down the main street and on to the outskirts of the city.

The rain had stopped but there was a mist hanging over the open fields. It was almost midnight when Keller pulled up a few kilometres past the last huddle of houses just before the last few kilometres before the border.

Keller turned in his seat to look at Carter. 'Are you sure he's alive?'

'Yes. He's breathing.'

'What have they done to him apart from his face?'

Becker held up one of Carter's hands. There was a jagged hole at the base of the thumb that went right through the hand. He could see the raw, bloody flesh and the white, shining glint of a bone. And the little finger hung loose and at a strange angle.

'They must have put a bullet through his hand,' Keller said.

'No. That's too rough for a bullet hole. Looks more like a wound from a knife of some kind.'

'We'll have to carry him over. Thank God he doesn't weigh much. When do they change guard details?'

Becker looked at his watch. 'About an hour from now.'

'How many on duty?'

'Only one at a time.'

'And he has a dog?'

'Not always. Most times at night, but there aren't enough dogs for every patrol.'

'Are they efficient or slack?'

'Depends on the man. Some are, some aren't.'

'What are they armed with?'

'AK47s and Schmeisser pistols.'

'Loaded?'

'Yeah.'

'Safety on or off?'

'Off when they think that they might have reason to need to use the gun.'

'Have they had weapons training?'

'Just a few firing sessions on the Kripo range. But no formal instruction.'

Keller looked again at Carter's bloody face and sighed. 'Let's go. We'll just have to take our chances.'

They drove on another three kilometres and then lifted Carter out of the car on to the damp grass at the side of the ditch. Keller looked up at the hazy moon, then pointed across the field. 'That's the way we should go.'

Slowly and carefully they carried Carter, stumbling over the tussocky grass of fields that had been abandoned to become part of the border. It took nearly an hour to do two kilometres but by then they could see the faint outlines of the wooden posts that marked the border itself. Keller took off his jacket and made a pillow for Carter's head. Then he turned to Becker. 'We'll wait until the guard goes by and then we'll go straight over. Once we're safely on the other side you wait with him and Meyer in the woods and I'll go to the house and get help.'

It seemed a long wait but it was barely half an hour. They heard the rattle of the loose magazine of the Kalashnikov before they saw the man. He walked slowly along the fence, smoking a cigarette as he went, and disturbed pigeons in the woods marked his progress. They waited until he was out of sight then lifted Carter, stumbling and half-running to the border. Becker forced up the loose bottom wire and they slid Carter across under the wire. They carried him a couple of hundred yards into the woods and then Keller went off alone.

He only had the vaguest idea of where they had crossed the border and where the house lay but he kept heading due west until he came to what he was sure was the track that led to the lodge. He followed it for about a mile and then he saw the long building. There were lights everywhere and two cars parked in the courtyard. They both had military number plates.

He was panting as he got to the door, perspiration running down his face, his shirt soaking wet. And for a moment he leaned against the wall before he pressed the bell. As it echoed inside he heard footsteps hurrying to the door and when it opened he recognised the man from 21 AG who had first interviewed him.

'I'm Keller. I need help.'

Stafford opened the door wide. 'Come in.'

He was led to a couch in the hall and as he sank down the man said, 'My name's Stafford. I interviewed you some time ago. What can I do for you? Is it about Eddie?'

'They caught him. The NKVD. We've brought him back over the border, Becker's with him in the woods. He's in a bad way. They beat him up.'

'Where are they?'

'Just this side of the zone border.' He closed his eyes. 'I don't feel too good. It's . . .' And Stafford caught him before he fell forward.

It took nearly two hours for them to find Carter and the two Germans. Stafford had stayed at the house and contacted 21 AG for a doctor.

Stafford stood watching as the doctor carefully checked Carter over. When he had finished he straightened up and looked at Stafford. 'What the hell was done to this man?'

'He was beaten up.'

The doctor shook his head. 'You don't end up like that just from being beaten up.'

'You do if the Russians think you're a spy.'

'Have you seen his hands?'

'Yes.'

'What did they do to them? Those aren't bullet holes. Nor knife wounds. Those holes are a quarter of an inch diameter and they go right through. The flesh is frayed.

115

It'll take fancy surgery and weeks of physiotherapy before he can even close his hand.'

'What's his general state?'

'He'll survive. Just about. But he's in shock. Some kind of trauma. It's a good job he's fit and young. I'll get him to hospital when I've done the basics.'

'He'll have to stay here. Tell me what you need.'

The doctor turned, angry and indignant. 'He needs surgery and specialist nursing. He needs to be in a hospital.'

Stafford pointed to the telephone. 'Phone 21 AG, ask for Colonel Shapiro. Tell him what is needed.'

'I want to put on record, Colonel, that I do this under protest.'

'OK. It's on the record, Major. Now get on the phone. There's a direct line. Just pick up the hand-set.'

An hour later an ambulance and a medical team arrived at the lodge and Stafford took them up to where Carter was being watched over by the major. He left them to get on with their work and went downstairs to where Becker and Meyer were eating.

Stafford asked Becker to bring his food with him to the room Stafford was using as an office.

When they were seated Stafford said, 'Where's Keller?'

'He's gone to bed.'

Stafford noticed the trembling hand that reached for another sandwich.

'Who's the other man?'

'His name's Meyer. Keller promised him money and that he could stay over here in the British Zone if we got Eddie back.'

'What part did he play?'

'He was guarding Eddie's cell in the NKVD section.'

'Tell me what happened.'

Stafford listened as Becker gave him a disjointed account of what he knew, and as he absorbed what was said Stafford realised, even from that garbled report, that Keller had not only taken great risks in taking charge and organising the

116

escape, but had done it when he could have stood aside and avoided taking any action. Or he could have left Carter and come back over the border to safety himself.

'You'd better get some sleep, Fritz.'

'Is it OK what we've done?'

'It was first-class. We'll look after you all. Don't worry.'

It was four days before Carter came to. The wounds in his hands were responding to the treatment and the bruises on his body had lost their livid rawness and were fading to the final stages of smooth yellow patches on his chest and shoulders. Stafford chatted to him several times on the following two days but never asked what had happened or how Carter had been caught. There were times when they chatted when it seemed as if Carter was not sure where he was or whom he was talking to. And Stafford had Keller to be concerned about too. His courage and initiative had been much admired by 21 AG and Stafford had been told that anything that Keller wanted he should have. And unbelievably Keller was intending to go back to Magdeburg.

When they discussed it for the third time Stafford said, 'Are you even sure that you'll be safe?'

Keller smiled. 'Sure enough.'

'That guard could recognise you or remember the name on the General's *laissez-passer*.'

'I kept my thumb over my name on the pass and he was too drunk to be of any use. They'll blame it all on friend Meyer.'

'What makes you want to go back?'

Keller shrugged and smiled. 'The filming. They're giving me almost a free hand. And they want me to move to Berlin.'

'What can we do for you?'

'There is something. A kind of insurance.'

'What?'

'A British passport. And British nationality. Genuine, not forged.'

'I'll speak to 21 AG. They'll have to talk to London.'

117

'I can only hang around another couple of days or they'll be wondering where I've been.'

'What will you tell them?'

Keller laughed softly. 'Nothing. Just hint that I was with one of my girlfriends. They'll believe that.'

To Stafford's surprise London had not only agreed immediately to Keller's request but the passport had arrived by special despatch rider the following mid-day. When he handed it over Keller said, 'How about Eddie? How is he?'

'Not too bad. I haven't talked to him yet about what happened.'

'He obviously didn't give anything away.'

'What makes you think that?'

'They wouldn't have gone as far as they did if he'd talked. And if he had then Becker and I would be in that jail ourselves.' He paused. 'You look doubtful.'

'No. Not doubtful. Just not sure. We'll have to wait and see what he says.'

'I saw those holes in his hands. That would be enough evidence for me.' He shrugged. 'Anyway. I'd better get on my way back tonight.'

'You know that if there's ever anything we can do for you you've only got to ask.' Stafford smiled. 'And I really do mean that.'

'You haven't asked me to keep you informed.'

Stafford looked surprised. 'I thought you'd say you'd had enough.'

'I'll let you know anything of real importance.'

'How?'

'I don't know. But if it's important and I think you would want it I'll get it to you somehow.'

'It seems too much to ask.'

'They mean mischief, Colonel. I want to stop them.'

'Well all I can say is that we'd be very grateful. Like you, we think that they are out for trouble. They're no longer our Allies.'

118

Keller smiled. 'They never were. No more than they were ours, despite our pact with Stalin.'

'But I heard that you'd made a film for them extolling the virtues of the Red Army.'

Keller shook his head. 'I did a film to show that soldiers are just men. Men who get homesick. Men who are encouraged to behave like savages because some group of powerful men make them so. The men in my film could have been Germans, or British, or American. Men from Glasgow. Men from Kansas, men from Essen – or men from Kiev. It doesn't make much difference to their lives whether they were winners or losers. They'll go back to their homes and they'll be exploited and then forgotten.'

Stafford smiled and shrugged. 'That's a very pessimistic picture you paint.'

'It's not pessimistic, Colonel, it's how it is. And you're right. Those boys are going to give you and the Americans a very rough time.'

'In what way?'

'I've heard senior officers on the General's staff talking of cutting off all land communications with Berlin. Any Allied troops wanting to go to Berlin would be checked and searched by Soviet troops.'

'We'd never agree to that and what's the point of it?'

Keller shrugged. 'To show who's top dog. They're sure you won't fight your way up the road to Berlin.'

'And then what?'

'The Soviet Zone of Germany comes to an end and they create another Germany. A Communist Germany.'

'But that would be a total breach of the Four Power Pact. We'd never let them get away with it.'

'You'd go to war for it?'

'I don't know.'

'When Berlin is closed how will you provision your troops? Yours and the Americans. And who'll feed the population of your three zones in Berlin?'

'You really think they'll do this?'

119

'I don't know. I'm only telling you what they're talking about. Maybe it's just wishful thinking but no doubt you've noticed that while you and the Americans are sending your troops home the Red Army is sending more and more men into their zone.'

'That's just a cheap way to feed their men at the expense of the Germans.'

Keller stood up. 'We'll see. We'll see. Give my regards to Eddie when he can understand. Yes?'

'Of course. And thanks for your courage and your loyalty.'

'He's a nice man your Eddie. I must go.' He held out his hand and Stafford took it in both of his. 'We shan't forget, my friend. I promise you that.'

17

It was beginning to get light when Carter finished talking. Mallory had listened and from time to time had scribbled notes on his pad. He realised that he had been listening to a small piece of history. Carter had put the clock back so well that Mallory felt as if he had been there himself when it was happening.

Carter said, 'You must be bored stiff with all that old stuff. You'd better get some sleep. So had I. How about we meet again this evening?'

Mallory smiled. 'I certainly wasn't bored, Major. Just eager to hear more.'

'More about what?'

'How it all ended.'

Carter shrugged. 'It hasn't ended, my boy. That's why you're here.'

'Can I ask you some questions tonight?'

'You can ask me anything you like but I probably won't tell you what you want to know.'

Mallory smiled. 'Thanks for telling me the story so far.'

Carter stood up shakily. 'Let's say seven this evening. We'll go down to my boat.'

Back in his room at the Ship, Mallory put the 'Do not disturb' label on the doorknob, undressed and lay back on the bed. He was asleep in minutes but it was a troubled sleep that left him tossing and turning from the random disjointed images that surged through his brain. Black and white newsreel images of the war, but none of them in any way connected with anything that Carter had told him. A grainy film of Chamberlain getting off a plane and holding up a piece of paper that fluttered in the wind. Spitfires taking off from a grassy airstrip. Hundreds of bombers flying in formation against a night sky and Montgomery signing the surrender document in a tent.

Almost without waking he got up and ran a basin of cold water and washed his face, his eyes half closed as he stumbled back to the bed. It was his room phone ringing that woke him.

'Hello.'

'We did say seven didn't we?'

Mallory looked at his watch. It was 8.30 p.m.

'I'm terribly sorry. I must have overslept. Do you want to leave it over until tomorrow?'

'Do you?'

'No, but I don't want to inconvenience you.'

'I'll expect you in about an hour. OK?'

'Sure. Thanks.'

They drove straight down to Birdham where Carter's boat was berthed and with the covers off they settled down in the comfortable saloon.

There were drinks on the table and a thermos of tea and Carter held up his glass of whisky to the light as he said, 'You must have been bored stiff, my lad, at all that guff I gave you last night.'

Mallory smiled. 'Can I ask you some questions?'

'I said you could.'

'What happened to the line-crossing operation when they got you back?'

'They called it a day. Left a couple of I Corps lieutenants at the lodge in case anybody contacted the place.'

'What happened to you?'

'It took nearly two weeks before I could talk and the medical team worked very hard.' Carter smiled. 'They had a new drug they kept on about called an antibiotic. They used it on my hands and other places. I was getting around in about six weeks.

'They sent over a team from London. Said they were there to de-brief me.' He shook his head. 'They wanted to check if I'd talked.'

'But Keller would have been arrested if you'd talked and Becker too.'

'They could have been in it with me. I get caught. Get beaten up. Tell them what they want. They do a deal. The rest of our lives in jail or we cooperate.' He paused. 'London didn't like it that Keller went back. How did he know that they wouldn't be waiting for him when he got back if he really had helped me escape?'

'That's a reasonable thought in some ways.'

'Indicates a very limited vision.'

'Why?'

'We were a team. Keller was a big man. A big mind. All he cared about was his photography, his films. He would have filmed for us but it wasn't on. Our people weren't interested. He would have filmed for any government that would have supported him. And he'd been a soldier. He was loyal. For him I was a comrade. His passion for filming overrode everything else.'

'Why did the London team think that the NKVD would have gone along with the escape?'

Carter shrugged. 'My freedom in return for working for them.'

'You mean they believed you could have been turned?'

'No. They do their thinking the other way around. They want to know why I should not have been turned.'

'How could you prove that for God's sake?'

'I couldn't. They knew that. But they thought that if they kept on and on. The same old questions again and again. They might wear me down. I might make some slip and then they could be sure.'

'You must have hated them.'

'No. Not really. They were doing their job. It angered me at first that they should even think I might have betrayed my people. But in the end I consoled myself.'

'How?'

'They weren't soldiers. They were civilians. They were SIS.' He smiled.

'And what did they decide in the end?'

'Who knows. They didn't tell me.'

'What happened to you after they'd finished?'

'Those people never finish. The file is left open.' He laughed drily. 'They offered me a job in SIS.'

'What did you do?'

'I said no thanks.'

'And?'

'I had no qualifications. My demob was long overdue. They gave me an excellent reference. Resourceful, leader of men, honest and loyal.' He sighed. 'But the post-war jobs had already been taken over by the men who'd already been demobilised and anyway employers weren't looking for leaders of men. They wanted men who had some sort of qualifications. I had none. I wrote dozens of applications, had several promising interviews. At least four companies virtually offered me jobs – the offers were withdrawn a couple of days later. Regrets but finally decided I wasn't quite what they had in mind. Hoped I would be successful elsewhere.' He looked at Mallory. 'And then, out of the blue Stafford rang me up. There was a chap he knew who was looking for somebody like me to sell cars. Rolls-Royces and Bentleys. New and second-hand. Was I interested? I met the chap and he hired me on the spot. I was still living with my parents and the job meant that Trixie and I could get married. After a couple of months training at the works my new boss sent me to his concession in Stockholm. That was where the money was after the war.'

Mallory smiled. 'And you lived happily ever after.'

'Not quite.'

'Why not?'

'I discovered that it wasn't fortuitous that it was Stafford who had contacted me.' He paused and looked at Mallory as he said, 'I found that many operators of overseas Rolls-Royce concessions in strategic cities were ex-SIS officers. My boss was no exception. I also realised why I hadn't got those other jobs. When people applied for references SIS put the boot in. All part of the game.'

'How did you find out?'

'My boss asked me if I'd like to be full-time SIS. I asked him if I'd lose my job if I refused and he said no. He'd give me a long-term contract if it would put my mind at rest. He also told me that his concession and four others in Europe were all actually owned by SIS.'

'And you carried on?'

'Yes. About four years after I left Germany they paid me a quite generous tax-free compensation and I get a decent pension too.'

Carter smiled as he saw the look on Mallory's face. 'If you ask me if I think they paid me to keep me quiet I just don't know. I never made my mind up.'

'What happened to the Germans?'

'What did Century House tell you about the Germans?'

Mallory bent and opened the brief-case on the seat beside him and took out the two sheets of paper that Daley had given him. He glanced at them briefly and then handed them to Carter.

Carter read the sheets slowly and then read them again before he handed them back to Mallory.

'Are you telling me that that stuff was all they gave you? That was your briefing?'

'Yes.'

Carter looked away slowly towards the cabin windows to where the sun was going down behind the trees on the far side of the bay. It was a long time before he looked back at Mallory.

'What were you doing before they gave you this assignment?'

'I was on a small arms refresher course at Hythe.'

'No. I mean your previous assignment.'

'I was in Berlin.'

'Doing what?'

'I'm afraid I couldn't discuss it.'

Carter smiled. 'Was it against the KGB?'

Mallory smiled back and shrugged. 'Maybe.'

'Was it a success, the operation?'

'It's still on-going.'

'But there was no cock-up on your part?'

Mallory laughed. 'No. Why should there be?'

'Did they say why they had given you this job?'

'They said it was because I was too young to be involved and that would make me impartial.'

Carter nodded. 'So why did they give you that rubbish as your briefing?'

'Is it rubbish?'

'I didn't find more than two correct facts in the whole lot. Somebody concocted that crap.'

'Are you sure?'

'Quite, quite sure. They were my men for God's sake.'

'Maybe this is what's on the record. It must be pretty old stuff.'

'If you'll believe that, my boy, you'll believe anything.'

'But why would they deliberately give me rubbish?'

'That's for you to work out. Maybe I'm too cynical.' He shrugged. 'You asked about the Germans.'

'Yeah.'

'Meyer was no problem. We let him join the Kripo in Essen to keep him well away from the Russian Zone. Oddly enough Heinz Schmidt eventually came back about two weeks before we closed down the base in the woods.'

'Had he found his girl?'

'Yeah. She was living with a black-market baron in Leipzig.'

'Did he bring back any intelligence?'

'Not a thing.'

'What did you do with him?'

'We got him a job as a truck-driver for a firm in Bremen. That's the last I heard of him.'

'The chap Wolff on my list. The one who died. Was he one of your people?'

'No. I think he was part of a line-crossing operation run

from Hamburg. I heard his name mentioned a few times as an efficient operator.'

'And what about Keller and Becker?'

'You still want to pursue them?'

Mallory smiled. 'Pursue isn't the word I would have chosen. I still want to find them.'

'Well . . .' Carter paused. 'Well, this is where you and I part company.'

'Am I right in thinking that you know where they both are?'

Carter shook his head. 'I've done my bit, Mallory, I've given you the background. That's all I intended to do.'

'But they are both alive?'

For a moment Carter hesitated and then he nodded. 'Yes,' he said quietly. 'They're both still alive.'

The following morning Mallory bought a small painting of Chichester harbour for Carter, and a Hermes scarf for his wife and arranged for them to be delivered. He checked out of the hotel and drove back to London, stopping in Midhurst for lunch and a chance to collect his thoughts.

18

At the flat Mallory unpacked his bag and put his shirts and underwear in the washer. When he had stripped there were enough items to warrant switching on the machine. As he walked into the bathroom he saw the array of cosmetics jars and tubes and bottles arranged on the glass shelf over the wash-basin, his shaving kit shoved to one end. He walked into the bedroom and stood there smiling as he looked at the girl on the bed. Lying there naked except for her panties, her head resting on one arm, her face turned towards the bedside lamp still alight on the table beside the bed. A paperback lay open on the floor beside the bed – '*Your Zodiac Sign and You*'. He walked round and slid aside one curtain so that there was sunshine in the room. On his way back to the bathroom he switched off the bedside lamp.

In the bath he lay thinking about what he had heard from Carter. And he thought about Carter himself. Carter must have been in his early twenties at the most when those things were happening and looking at him now it was hard to imagine him having been involved in such things. Seen in the street or meeting him at a party he would seem to be an uncomplicated, straightforward Englishman. Stolid and reliable and at the end of a successful business career living happily with his wife and pottering in a much-loved garden. And he was all those things – stolid and reliable, uncomplicated and straightforward. But if you pressed that button the clock went back and those pale blue eyes were cold and angry. No longer was he all for King and Country, no longer was he the good citizen. There were different rules and different loyalties and different criteria for judging a man, that you'd never suspect just from looking at him. And Keller and Becker would be the same. They too would look mild and ordinary and whatever war-crimes they had committed they would be all wrapped up and tucked away in some closet marked 'Do not disturb'. But if you pressed their button who could guess what their reactions would be? They were both probably ex-SS officers and they had been pressured to work for us rather than stand trial as war-criminals. If they hadn't done something serious they wouldn't have been vulnerable to any such pressure. They were risking their lives working for us in the Russian Zone. Was this, in fact, absolution enough for those past misdeeds?

With a bath towel draped around him he walked back into the bedroom. She was still asleep. Breathing gently and evenly like a child, a wisp of hair across her face, the long dark lashes following the curve of her cheek.

He dressed slowly and used the extension phone in the living-room to phone Mike Daley. Daley wasn't around but his secretary fixed a meeting the next morning for him.

Ten minutes later he heard her stirring and walked back into the bedroom. She smiled. 'I heard you talking on the phone.' She paused. 'Are you OK?'

'Yes. How about you?'

'I guess I overslept.' She grinned. 'D'you want a cuddle?'

An hour later they got dressed and he took her to dinner at Leoni's before she went to the club.

Daley kept him waiting for half an hour and then seemed more interested in some papers on his desk as Mallory reported on his time with Carter. When he had finished Daley said, 'What's your next move?'

'To try and find Keller or Becker.'

'How're you gonna do that?'

'I'm not sure. I'll just ferret around for a bit.'

'What did you think of friend Carter?'

'True-blue Brit. One of the old school.'

'Sounds like he gave you a lot of his time.'

'That was only to convince me that the Krauts should be left in peace. Let sleeping dogs lie and all that.'

Daley half-smiled. 'He didn't convince you?'

'He convinced me that they'd done a good job but that's only half the story.'

'What's the other half?'

'The other half's what they had done, that made them potential war-criminals.'

'The notes I gave you give you a rough indication.'

'Carter said the notes were phony.'

'You showed them to him?'

'Yes.'

'He was never told what they had done so he's just stirring you up.'

'You think the notes are accurate?'

Daley hesitated for a moment. 'Maybe not accurate. But a good guide.'

'Do you know what they did?'

'Roughly.'

'Like what?'

'Let's say enough to make it difficult with hindsight to justify using them. Could be made to look pretty bad today.' Daley smiled. 'The general public isn't going to get the benefit of hearing Carter's story as you did.'

'So we tell them.'

'And admit that we were spying on our allies?'

'Why not. They were spying on us and have been ever since. How about Philby and the other two. And Fuchs and Lonsdale.'

'You said Philby and the other two. What were the names of the other two?'

'I can't remember. They were Foreign Office weren't they.'

'Exactly. Like you, the public don't even remember their names let alone what they did. But Philby was SIS.

And they still use that against us. People are tired of the war. It was over forty years ago.' He shrugged. 'What's the date today?'

Mallory looked at his watch. 'July twenty.'

'It's an anniversary of something. What?' Daley was smiling as he waited for an answer.

Mallory shook his head slowly, and Daley said, 'It seemed fantastic at the time.'

'I've no idea. What was it.'

'It was the date of the attempted assassination of Adolf Hitler. He had the ring-leaders hung with piano-wire from meat-hooks.'

'Are you telling me something?'

Daley looked surprised. Genuinely surprised. 'No way. I'm just warning you that there's no easy solution. That's why you were chosen to look into it. You weren't even born when those things went on. But you still need to know how things were in those days.'

Mallory got Records to check the issue of a passport some time in late September '47 in the name of Keller but there was no record of such a passport being issued in that name in that six month period. Then Mallory remembered that other name. Stafford. Lieutenant Colonel Stafford. Maybe there was some record of him at the I Corps depot at Ashford.

He spent a day in the Corps Museum. He found only two references to Stafford. The first was a copy of Part II Orders notifying the appointment of Colonel Stafford DSO as Brigadier General with effect from January 1, 1949. And his posting to the War Office. The second item was a photograph in the Corps magazine of the wedding of the Brigadier's eldest daughter, Patricia, to Wing Commander F.W. Wright of the RAF. The wedding was at St Mary's church in Bath, Somerset. There was no date but it must have been before Bath was incorporated in the new county of Avon.

*

There had been few marriages at St Mary's church in the small village outside Bath and he found the entry in the register quite easily. Her father's entry merely said 'Brig. Gen. Stafford DSO' and his address was given as 'Camelot House, Brook Street, Bath'.

Mallory spent the afternoon in the back-issues library of the local paper. But it was the elderly registry clerk who was most use. He asked Mallory if he needed any help.

'I'm looking for background details on Brigadier Stafford.'

'Ah, yes. The Brigadier. A very brave man. Good war record and now he's retired, a great boon to the community.'

'In what way?'

'Serves as a magistrate. Town councillor and chairman of two committees. President of the town British Legion. He's a good citizen.'

'What did he get his DSO for?'

'Near as I can remember it the citation said he risked his life while saving the lives of a group of British agents in a prison somewhere in France.'

'What kind of man is he?'

'Very much the officer. And very much the gentleman.' He shrugged. 'What more can I say?'

Camelot House was a narrow-gutted three-storey house built of the local Bath stone and in the traditional style. Two wide, stone steps gave directly on to the street and a wrought-iron carriage light hung beside the oak door. A worn brass plate with the house name engraved on it was in place above the brass letter-box. A bold lion's-head knocker looked as if it was the original it was so smooth, and so heavy. Mallory knocked twice and was taken aback by the noise he made.

He knew as soon as he saw him that the man who opened the door was Stafford. He wore a tweed jacket, khaki drill trousers and a checked Viyella open-necked shirt.

'Brigadier Stafford?'

'Yes.'

'I wonder if you could spare me a few moments?'

'What about?'

Mallory showed him his SIS identity card with its red diagonal stripe. Stafford looked at it carefully but didn't touch it. He looked back at Mallory.

'You'd better come in, Mallory. But I can't give you much time.'

He led the way to a small study off the tiled hall and waved Mallory to the leather armchair.

'Sit you down.'

When they were both seated Stafford said, 'What's it all about?'

'Major Carter mentioned your name, sir – I thought maybe you could help me.'

'Carter, eh. How is he these days? Still in – where is it now – Winchester?'

'Chichester.'

'Ah yes. The Royal Sussex depot. I heard it was the Redcaps depot now.' He laughed and slapped his thighs. 'Bit of a come-down if you ask me. That was the first of the modern barracks built when Hore Belisha was Minister. A useless bugger but at least he got us better housed.' He lifted his chin. 'So what are you and Eddie up to?'

'He was telling me about the line-crossing operations into the Russian Zone.'

'He should have got a gong at least for that. Poor old Eddie. First the Reds beat him up – I'm sure you saw his hands – and then we do him over. Standard routine they said. But all those queers like Philby and Co. They didn't treat *them* like that. We're a funny lot in this country. First-class chap. No doubt about it.'

'What happened to Keller and Becker?'

Stafford frowned. 'Who?'

'Keller and Becker. The two Germans.'

'Was that what they called themselves?'

'That's what Eddie called them.'

'Well he'd know. They were his chaps. Which one was the film chap?'

'That was Keller.'

'Bright fellow but obsessed by his bloody filming.' He frowned. 'Let's see. We gave him a UK passport and he went back over the border again. Sent us back warning of the Berlin blockade and later on he warned us about the bloody Wall going up. No flies on that fella.'

'And Becker?'

'That was the other one who helped get Eddie back?'

'Yes.'

'I thought his real name was Hartmann, but anyway I can remember him turning up in the middle of the night at that place we had in the woods. Absolutely shattered he was. He stayed on our side. We gave him a few thousand dollars and a pension. Went up to Hamburg. Opened a bookshop I believe. That's the last I heard of him.'

'And Keller stayed in Magdeburg?'

'Oh no. The Russkis took him to Berlin.' Stafford chuckled like a mischievous boy. 'We worked a bit of a flanker for him in Berlin. The Russkis had to get a de-Nazification clearance from us for him. We put on a bit of an act. Pretended we didn't approve of him. Hung it out a bit. Gave him a cover if ever they were suspicious of him.' Stafford put his hand to his forehead, thinking. Then he looked at Mallory. 'They transferred him to Moscow. Seem to remember he did a big film for them. Forgotten what it was about. But the Moscow film lot were jealous. Foreigner making Russian films and that sort of crap. They shipped him off somewhere. South America if I remember rightly. Good chap. Pity he was a Nazi.'

'What sort of war-crimes had the two Germans got up to, sir?'

'God knows. I don't remember. I'm not sure I ever knew. They'd all been processed by a special team at 21 AG. All of 'em. Not just Eddie's lot.' He paused. 'It's odd you know, you popping in to chat. Eddie left a message

134

for me to call him on the answering machine. But I didn't get back from London until late last night. Sounded in a bit of a tizzy. Is he all right? No problems?'

'He seemed all right to me, sir.' Mallory paused. 'You don't have any photographs of Eddie's people by any chance?'

'I don't think so.' He laughed. 'If you can come back tomorrow I'll look through my cardboard boxes for you. I doubt we took any pictures. Security you know. I'll have a look.'

'Thank you, sir. And thanks for your help.'

Stafford stood up slowly. 'Why all the interest in those days all of a sudden? They writing a book about it or what?'

'Just getting the record straight, sir.'

Stafford grinned. 'First time they've ever got the record straight if they do. Let me show you out.'

Mallory called the flat but there was no answer and the answering machine was off. He tried the club but they said she hadn't come in yet. He looked at his watch. It was nearly midnight.

He ate in the hotel restaurant and the pianist played 'Smoke gets in your eyes', and it reminded him of the girl. It was her favourite tune. He'd always been slightly surprised that she should even know the ballad, Stevie Wonder was more her style of music. She was a strange creature. So open and yet so shrewd. So innocent and yet so street-wise. He had never been able to work out which was the real Debbie. She obviously had a vague idea of his work but she never probed. Just as he had never probed about what she did when he wasn't around. He had more than a vague idea of what she got up to. In the early days he had been jealous but slowly he had realised that he was wasting his time. If she had ever loved anybody it was him and the life at the club was another separate world. It wasn't just a way of earning a living, it was a way of life itself. Gossip, chatter, being chatted up by every man who saw her and behind it all that strange juvenile defiance of her parents and family.

He phoned Stafford the next morning to see if he had had any luck with the photographs, and Stafford was very frosty. Apparently Carter had spoken to him and told him that Mallory was out to make trouble. Stafford said that Mallory was obviously no gentleman and he had no intention of helping him further. And then he hung up.

He paid his bill at the Francis and headed back to London.

19

Mallory sat on his bed reading through the notes that he had made. Although Carter probably hadn't told him the whole truth he was sure that what he *had* said was the truth as he saw it. He at least had a lead to pursue. Becker/Hartmann and a bookshop in Hamburg. And as he read through his notes he realised that there was one other possible lead. Carter had said that the lodge in the Harz mountains had been given the cover-name Number 3 Signals Unit. When it was closed down some sort of record must have been kept. There might be a clue in those records.

He sent a request through Archives for a copy of the de-commissioning report on 3 Signals Unit and was surprised to receive it the following day. It was obviously done to give no clues to the unit's function. It recorded that the contents of the lodge had been taken over by the Town Major (Brunswick) and all members of the staff returned to their previous units for re-posting.

He walked down to the next floor to Facilities and drew travellers-cheques, sterling and Deutschmarks along with an open return ticket to Hamburg. He asked them to book him into the Baseler Hospitz for a week.

Mallory had had several stints in Hamburg when operations based in Berlin spilled over into Hamburg and Hannover. He knew his way around the city and had amicable contacts with both the police and the local office of the BND, West Germany's intelligence service. His contact in Hamburg was Leutnant Werner but he didn't want to contact him on this job if it could be avoided.

He borrowed the local telephone directory from the reception desk. There were forty Beckers listed, not counting those in the outer suburbs and there were over a hundred Hartmanns and about the same number with only one 'n' at the end of their names. There were two Hartmanns listed as booksellers. One was quite near, in a small arcade off the Goose Market. It was within walking distance of the hotel and ten minutes later he found the shop. The window was full of secondhand copies of specialist books on history and philosophy. Most of them published well before World War II. From the handwritten sales tickets they seemed to be expensive books. Some of them were priced in the hundreds of D-marks.

An old-fashioned bell over the door jangled as he opened the door and a woman in her fifties came towards him.

'Can I help you?'

'I'd like to talk to Mr Hartmann.'

The woman frowned. 'What Mister Hartmann do you mean?'

'The owner of the bookshop.'

'There hasn't been a Hartmann connected with this shop since 1931. My father bought the shop in 1936. His name was Freund. He was killed in the war and he left the shop to me.'

'D'you know a bookseller named Hartmann in Hamburg?'

She thought for a moment. 'No. And I'm quite sure I should have heard of a Hartmann running a bookshop. Our name is very important to us. We do business with collectors all over the world. Somebody would have told me if there was another Hartmann.'

'What about Becker? Do you know a bookseller named Becker?'

She shrugged. 'Not off-hand. But the name would have no significance for me. There could be a half a dozen Beckers without me being aware of it.' She paused. 'Are you a collector? Is that why you're interested?'

'I'm just trying to contact a man who I was told was a bookseller in Hamburg and his name was either Becker or Hartmann.'

She smiled. 'I can only wish you good luck.'

The second Hartman was the other spelling and the shop was in Gross-Borstel, not far from the airport. It was empty and there was a typewritten card inside the glass panel of the door that said that Mr Mencken, the proprietor, had retired.

Mallory realised that he could spend years trying to track down every bookshop in the city of Hamburg, and when he got back to the hotel he phoned the number he had in his book for Leutnant Werner.

'Werner speaking.'

'Hi. This is Mallory.'

'Who?'

'Charlie Mallory. I came to see you a couple of times about a joint enterprise in Berlin.'

'Charlie. My apologies. Is this the Berlin thing again?'

'No. Could I come and see you?'

'Where are you staying?'

'At the Baseler Hospitz.'

'How about I come round to you?'

'Fine. When?'

'In half an hour, OK?'

'I'll be waiting for you downstairs.'

Heinz Werner looked much the same as last time he had seen him. *Typisch Deutsch*. Blond hair, blue eyes and a lively smile.

When the girl had brought them coffee Werner said, 'What's it this time, Charlie?'

'I'm looking for a guy and all I know about him is that his name is either Becker or Hartmann or it could be Hartman with one 'n'. And he probably has a bookshop.'

Werner grinned. 'Or he could have some other name and maybe it isn't a bookshop. You're joking. Even our

IBM370 doesn't keep records as vague as that. What else do you know?'

'Nothing.'

'So why are you looking for him?'

Mallory hesitated and then shrugged. 'It's confidential, Heinz.'

Werner smiled. 'So's ninety-nine per cent of everything I deal with. The same applies to you I guess.'

'It's got complications. Goes back to the end of the war.'

Werner sighed. 'Let's not play games, Charlie. I can't help you if you don't give me what you know. I probably can't help you even if you do.'

'Can I ask that it's confidential between just you and me?'

'No way. But if it doesn't have any significance for us then it won't need to go beyond my boss.'

'This chap, whatever his name is, worked for us, the Brits, on a line-crossing network into the Soviet Zone for a couple of years after the war. The network was stood down and there's no record of what happened afterwards to any of the Germans. I've been told to trace them. There were three who mattered. One's dead. Another probably in Moscow and then there's this guy.'

'I can tell you the rest. There was a piece in *Der Spiegel* some months back about so-called war-criminals who worked for the British and the Americans. There was a suggestion that they might be prosecuted.'

'That's it.'

'It's too late to try people for war-crimes. That legislation ran out some years back. But you could do them for so-called "crimes against humanity".' He paused. 'Or you could be real shits and, if they're in the UK, extradite them to wherever they committed the alleged crimes and let them deal with them. If it was behind the Iron Curtain you might just as well knock them off and save the fare.' He sighed. 'Where was the network based?'

'In the woods near the border. In the Harz.'

'They were working Magdeburg I suppose.'

'Yes.'

'And if they didn't work for you guys they ended up in Nürnberg, yes?'

'I guess so.'

'What had they done?'

'I don't know.'

'Have you checked with the War Crimes Tribunal records?'

'No. Where are they?'

'In Berlin. They've been put on computer.'

'Would they be on if they hadn't been tried?'

'It's an international register. If this guy had done anything serious a complaint will have been made by someone. An individual or a group of people.'

'How do I get into these records?'

'It'll take time. There are formalities. You'd have to apply from London. And without a computer input it would take a long time when you've got so many unknowns.'

Mallory looked at the German. 'Any chance of you cooperating?'

'Let me think about it. I'll phone you here this afternoon. OK?'

'Thanks.'

Leutnant Werner didn't phone. He went to the hotel himself and when reception called Mallory he asked them to send Werner up to his room.

Mallory poured a whisky for the BND man and a tomato juice for himself.

Werner grinned. 'You still on the wagon, Charlie?'

Mallory shrugged. 'I've never been off it, Heinz. I just don't like the taste.'

Werner nodded. 'Tell me what you call a bookshop.'

'A shop that sells books.'

'What would you call a shop that sells magazines?'

'A newsagents.' He smiled. 'You're going to tell me that Becker or whatever he calls himself now is a newsagent.'

'No not exactly.'

'But you traced him?'

'Yeah, I traced him all right. Quite a naughty boy. And you were right. He's one of our locals.'

'And he's got a newsagents shop?'

Werner laughed. 'He's got shops. Ten of them. But they're not newsagents. They're sex shops in the Reeperbahn and Grosse Freiheit. Got lots and lots of money. A nice house in Blankanese. Three-metre chain-link fences all round, electronic surveillance in every bush, a couple of live-in heavies and a posse of Rottweilers.'

'What were his war-crimes?'

'That I can't tell you.'

'You said the records gave details of the accusations.'

'I know. And they do. I didn't say I don't know. I said I can't tell you. That was ruled out by my boss.'

'Does that mean you're covering up for him because he's German?'

'No way. It just means that we're playing it formal. The records are there in Berlin. If your people make an official application for details they'll get them in a couple of hours. But at local level we cooperate with you by telling you that the details are there in Berlin.' He shrugged. 'It's protocol, Charlie. If he's done the things that are alleged he deserves all he gets. But somebody, somewhere has got to provide enough evidence to warrant him being extradited. And I don't see London being able to do that. He didn't commit the alleged offences in the UK and he wasn't a British national at the time.'

'What do you mean – at the time?'

'He's got a Brit passport that was issued in Bonn in 1947. It's up-to-date and still valid. He's got a West German passport too.'

'What country would be interested in extraditing him?'

For a few moments Werner hesitated and then he said, 'Israel.'

'Is there any mention on the records of him working for us or a reason why he got the UK passport?'

'No. Anyway it wouldn't be considered relevant. The

records are for war-crimes.' He paused. 'But we've got some details of what went on.'

'Like what?'

'The line-crossing operation. There are some rough notes about it at our HQ at Pullach.'

'Tell me.'

'Off the record? Strictly off the record?'

'Of course.'

'The guy's real name is Becker. There was another one called Meyer. He's deputy head of the Kriminalpolizei in Kassel now. Due to retire in about a couple of months time.' Werner looked at Mallory quizzically. 'Do you know of any others?'

'There was one named Schmidt. He used the network to try and find his girlfriend. She was living with some black-market baron and he came back but he hadn't done any intelligence work for us.'

'And you got him a job as a lorry driver?'

'I believe we did.'

'Yeah. He hanged himself a couple of years later. So you can cross him off your list.'

'Did you have any details on Keller?'

'Keller? Tell me about him.'

'Got well in with the Russians. Did a good job for us. Almost certainly saved the life of our chap who was running the network. He went back to Magdeburg.'

'What was his cover?'

'It wasn't a cover. It was for real. He was filming for the Russians. I think they moved him to Berlin and then to Moscow. There was some talk that he'd gone to South America.'

'But you don't know the name he uses now?'

'No. Do you?'

'Yes. But you'll have to trace him yourself, if you really want to pursue it.'

'Why is he the exception that I can't be told about?'

'You'll know why when you catch up with him. If you do.'

'Well thanks for the dope. Can I have Becker's address?'

'D'you remember my boss? Fischer?'

'Vaguely. In his fifties. With a beard. Tall and thin.'

'That's the one. He thinks your people in London want to do a white-wash job on these people. Is he right?'

'I was just told to try and trace them. Check what they'd done and give an opinion on what action to take. Then if the media have got these people in mind we can justify what was done way back. The newspaper stories could have been about people like von Braun or other scientists, not necessarily people used for intelligence work.'

Werner smiled. 'If you want to interview Becker then I'll need to go with you. That's how Fischer wants it played.'

'That's OK with me. When shall we see him?'

'I'll contact him. Tomorrow afternoon OK for you?'

'Sure.'

Mallory was having dinner in the hotel restaurant when Werner joined him at the table.

'Have you eaten, Heinz?'

'No, but I can't stay. We've got a crisis at the office.'

'What's the news with Becker?'

'It's bad I'm afraid. I went to see him myself and he was very aggressive. I told him that if he wouldn't talk to me I'd bring a senior Kripo officer along with me if he wouldn't cooperate and he said that he'd give no interviews to either you or me or the Kriminalpolizei without his lawyers being there. And it was lawyers – plural. My boss, Fischer, wants me to back out – he said do it diplomatically.'

Mallory shrugged. 'So I'll call Becker myself.'

'You'd be crazy to do that, Charlie. You'd end up face-down in the Aussen-Alster inside twenty-four hours.'

'So we'll go through the hoops and get the details from the Commission in Berlin.'

'First of all there isn't enough information there to act

against him and secondly you'd have to apply to a German court for his extradition. And you wouldn't have a cat in hell's chance. He didn't commit his alleged war-crimes in either the UK or Germany. And he wasn't a British subject or his crimes committed on British soil.'

'We'll still have a go. We'll expose him, and what he did.'

'Charlie. You're not thinking. He sells hard porn. He's got millions stashed away. You won't shame him. He's a crook and a very tough one.' Werner paused. 'If you want to pursue him there's a better way. Establish what he actually did and let London submit it to Bonn. If it's the right stuff they couldn't ignore it. They wouldn't want to anyway.'

'That would take me months, maybe years.'

'I can give you a short cut, Charlie.'

'How?'

'I'll give you a name. A man who can tell you what both your two Germans were up to during the war. I don't think that your people realised that Becker and the other guy – the film guy – operated in the same area.'

'Where was that?'

'The Netherlands. The Hague and Amsterdam.'

'That wasn't where they were in the brief I was given.'

'Who compiled the brief?'

'I've no idea.'

'Fischer is sure that your people are up to something.'

'Why?'

'Well there's very little chance of the media being able to pin-point your Germans. Not even their names, let alone where they are now and what they did in the war.' He smiled. 'It's been tough enough for you, Charlie. So why do your people want you to track those guys down? It'll only embarrass your people. If the media got hold of it they'd run it for months and SIS would have the choice of looking like suckers or hypocrites. So why not let sleeping dogs lie?'

'Because from what I've already found out those Germans did a first-class job for us. Some might say that wipes out the past.'

'Do *you* think it squares things off?'

'I don't know until I've found out what they did.'

Werner hesitated for a moment and then he reached inside his jacket and brought out an envelope, placing it at the side of Mallory's plate.

'The name and address of the man you should contact is in the envelope, Charlie. He can tell you what those two guys did. All of it. Or most of it. And it'll be up to you to sort out what it all adds up to.' He stood up and held out his hand. 'Best of luck, Charlie.'

20

It always seemed to be summer and sunshine at Schipol. An airport that was laid out to suit passengers rather than bureaucrats. Mallory went through immigration and then customs and finally a security check where his bag was searched, not for cigarettes or whisky but Semtex, detonators and heroin.

He bought a Falk street plan at the airport bookstall and took a taxi to the Damrak where he had booked a single room by telephone from Heathrow.

The typed name and address on the plain sheet of white paper just gave the name Paul van Kempen, and an address near Rembrandts Plein. He checked for the entry in the telephone directory but there was no entry under that name.

After dinner he walked down to Rembrandts Plein. The address was a house in a small street leading down to the Amstel river. It was one of those beautiful traditional Dutch houses with tall elegant windows on the ground floor, and two further floors and a window above in what must be an attic. It looked calm and peaceful in the last of the day's sunshine and he decided to leave his call until the next day. He had no idea who the man was or why he could shed any light on what Becker and Keller had done during the war.

The man who opened the door the next day was in his sixties. Tall and good-looking with white hair and light blue eyes. He wore a black roll-necked sweater, a loose suede leather jacket and light-weight slacks and sneakers.

He smiled. 'I think you must be Mr Mallory.'

'How did you know?'

'My old friend Bernd Fischer phoned me. Told me what you looked like and that you'd probably call on me.' He smiled. 'You'd better come in.'

Van Kempen led Mallory down a wide corridor through a large room and into a smaller room lined with books on three walls. The furniture was all antique, mainly Flemish oak and Georgian, except for three comfortable soft, leather, button-backed chairs. When they were seated Mallory said, 'Did Herr Fischer tell you why I wanted to talk to you?'

Van Kempen smiled and nodded. 'Yes. He told me you wanted to talk about two Germans.' He paused. 'Tell me why you're interested in them.'

Mallory explained what he was doing and then said, 'I hope it doesn't seem rude to ask, but could you tell me how you come into this?'

Van Kempen sighed. 'You might well ask. I suppose the simplest explanation I can give you is that I was in the Dutch resistance and your two Germans were our enemies. One in the Gestapo – Becker. And one in the Sicherheitsdienst – the man you called Keller when you spoke to young Werner.'

'Were you part of SOE?'

Van Kempen smiled and shook his head. 'Only for a short time. Thank God.'

'Why "thank God"?'

'Special Operations Executive in Holland was a total disaster. It was only luck that allowed me not to be entangled with those people.'

'What did they do wrong?'

'Some said they were just fools. For me they were traitors.' Van Kempen looked at Mallory. 'Nearly one hundred brave Dutchmen and maybe half a dozen Englanders died because of the top people in Norgeby House.'

'How do you know this?'

'After I escaped my contact was only with British

Intelligence. Not SOE. They were rivals and between them they sacrificed my countrymen.'

'What did they do about it when the war was over?'

Van Kempen laughed. 'They covered it up.'

'Why didn't the Dutch resistance stop it from happening?'

'You have to remember – we were not like the French resistance. We were not soldiers, we were civilians. We had very few contacts in Britain. We listened to the BBC broadcasts of course. We found having the Germans as our enemies very strange. They were our neighbours. We knew them well until Adolf Hitler bewitched them. To us they were Brahms and Beethoven, Schubert and Schumann. And suddenly it was all Wagner. A nightmare – but without the beautiful music.'

'You can remember Becker and Keller?'

Van Kempen smiled wryly. 'Oh yes. I remember them very well.'

'Would you mind telling me about them?'

Van Kempen rubbed the back of his neck as he looked towards the window and the pots of geraniums on the patio. When he looked back at Mallory he said, 'What does the 10th of May mean to you?'

Mallory frowned, and shook his head. 'Nothing that I can recall.'

'Fair enough.' He paused. 'That was the day in 1940 when the Germans attacked Holland. Without warning and without mercy. Thousands of innocent Dutch people died that day from the indiscriminate bombing. Nobody outside Holland remembers that date. Or what happened. Just one more small country went down to the Nazis.' He shrugged. 'We were only the beginning.' He smiled at Mallory. 'Do you really want to know about things that happened all that long time ago? Surely it must be boring to a young man.'

'If it doesn't disturb you to talk about it I'd like to hear what the two Germans did.'

'It won't disturb me. Not a day goes by without me

thinking about it. About brave men who died. And girls too. We had a lot of brave girls in the resistance.' He sighed. 'And what are you going to do about the Germans after I've told you what they did?'

'If they committed war-crimes I shall report to my chiefs and recommend that they are tried.'

'You know, of course, that it's too late for the courts to hear war-crime prosecutions.'

'Depending on what they did they could be tried for crimes against humanity.'

Van Kempen nodded and smiled. 'Crimes against humanity. It's a remarkable phrase. Almost poetry, and vaguely romantic. Rather like a flag waving in the breeze. Yes, you *could* do that. But do you think anyone would take action against them?'

'Do you think they did commit such crimes?'

Van Kempen pursed his lips. 'Well let's see what we've got. Say twenty thousand Dutch Jews to the gas-chambers. About a hundred Dutch resistance people killed. Some of them tortured before they died. The whole population deliberately brought to starvation point as a punishment for not loving the occupying power. Do you think that might be enough?'

'I'm sure it would be. Particularly if we could have witnesses.'

'Most of the witnesses are dead. And some who witnessed what went on and did nothing to save the victims would prefer to forget. It won't be easy for you. It was a very tangled web we all wove in those days.' He smiled ruefully. 'We weren't all brave all the time. Not even our heroes.'

'Can you spare the time to tell me about it?'

'Why not. Maybe it would do me good to say it out loud for once. Not to have it bottled up inside me for the sake of diplomacy and not causing distress to the families of those who betrayed us and our country.'

'Can you tell me about your life now?'

'Of course.' He paused to collect his thoughts and then

went on. 'I'm a widower. I have a housekeeper. I read a lot. I paint in oils, but not very well. I have a quite generous state pension and a good income from the family firm which deals in textiles. I'm a licensed radio ham and I play chess two or three days a week.' He smiled and spread his arms like a Frenchman. 'I'm sixty-eight. That's about it. There's nothing more.'

'Do you have children?'

'No.' He shook his head. 'We had seen what can happen to children and their parents in war-time. We neither of us had the courage to have children ourselves.' He paused and then said softly, 'I saw one day a line of Jews being put on a train to be sent to one of the camps. They were crying and shouting prayers in Hebrew. There was a woman standing there holding the hand of a small boy. I suppose he was seven or eight years old. He was wearing a cap that was too big for him and a man's jacket as a coat and he just stood there passively in all that clamour. Pale face, big dark eyes with no hope in them. He wasn't a child any more. The thought of that boy still haunts me. I saw many worse sights but that stays in my mind. The utter surrender of one small soul. The grief and fear of people who knew they were going to die. To die without blessing and to die without dignity.' He sighed deeply. 'If there is such a thing as a crime against humanity – that was such a thing.'

The old man stood up awkwardly, but smiling as he held out his hand. 'Where are you staying?'

'At the Damrak.'

'Very nice too. How about you come round tomorrow and we'll talk again.'

'I'd be very grateful.'

Van Kempen said, 'Don't be too sure of that, my boy.'

21

Van Kempen was looking through the window to the garden, shifting in his chair so that he could see three or four blue tits swinging upside-down as they pecked some peanuts in a string sack on a branch of an apple tree. Reluctantly he looked back at Mallory as if he regretted having to talk.

'There were about a dozen of us, girls and boys. Many of us had known each other since we were kids. But the reason we were together that night was because we were all students at Leyden University.

'We'd finished the Spring exam that day and we'd got six weeks to go before we got the results. So we decided we'd have one last party that night. An all-night party. We went to a small restaurant in Rotterdam that we knew well and their other customers left just after midnight. Somebody, I think it was a boy named Maas, Jan Maas. Anyway he gave the *patron* fifty guilders to let us carry on as long as we wanted.

'It was already beginning to get light when we finally ended up in a bunch on the street. Singing and shouting and making the usual nuisance of ourselves. And then – it was unbelievable. Wave after wave of planes. They seemed to be going terribly slowly, and flying so low that the noise of their engines was deafening. And the ground seemed to shake and we realised that they were dropping bombs. You could see buildings collapsing, not exploding but just sort of folding up. We could see fires burning all over the centre of the city and the air was full of stone dust and brick dust and the smell of burning wood and hot metal.

'We stood there paralysed for what seemed like ages but was probably no more than five minutes. When we started to talk and move off a policeman on a motor-cycle told us not to go into the town centre because it was impossible to move around as the streets were full of rubble.

'We had two cars between us and we drove out on the road to Utrecht and stopped in a village where we could all phone our homes. By then everyone was panicking a bit including our parents. We stayed in a village inn and one by one we were picked up by our parents. And by the end of a couple of weeks it all seemed to settle down. We were occupied by the Germans but they were promising that all would be as usual.'

'What did you do yourself?'

'I hung around for a couple of months rather aimlessly and then a few of us got together to produce an underground newspaper. I wrote pieces for it, so did others, including former politicians. It was quite good. Amateurish but well-informed. It was printed surreptitiously and then we all had to distribute it personally and collect money to keep it going. We formed what we called an underground resistance group. It was rather pathetic really. All talk and no action. Which wasn't surprising because none of us knew anything about resistance. And not everybody was convinced that resistance was a good thing. The Germans were being '*korrekt*', so why cause trouble?

'But I knew that in the end we would have to fight them and the only way I could start was by going to England and joining the Free Dutch forces.'

'What did your parents think?'

'I didn't tell them. I didn't tell anyone. Not even my girlfriend.'

'Who was she?'

'A girl named Anna. Anna van Steen. I only saw her once since I left Holland. Not to talk to. I went to where she was working and watched her go home. She was killed during the liberation. She had become a nurse and was nursing in a hospital in Arnhem.'

'How did you escape?'

'We used to go for weekends and holidays to Walcheren. We had a boat there. Just a pleasure boat. A glorified rowing boat with an outboard engine.

'I moved down there to a chalet we had and I planned it all very carefully. I traded things for charts and petrol and food for the voyage. The way I planned it it was going to take me somewhere between eight and ten hours. I talked to fishermen about tides and currents and winds and I even found an old man who had helped others to escape by boat.

'But the most important thing was that he knew about the German security. Their boats and the Wehrmacht patrols on the beaches.

'I wanted as many hours as possible in the dark so that I could row without the engine.' He smiled. 'I was strong and tough in those days but I didn't realise how foolhardy my plans were.

'Guards changed at midnight and I pushed off and clambered into the boat.' He smiled. 'Two pairs of thick socks over my shoes to deaden the sound. I rowed for two hours, getting slower and slower until I was barely making any headway. I switched on the engine and it sounded terribly loud.

'I won't go into details of the journey. It was bad but it was bad for everybody who escaped that way. When light came it was just sea all around and I'd already been going six hours. But the engine kept puttering away. Twice I saw ships, but fortunately they didn't see me. Finally the engine died. No petrol left. I started rowing again and it was like a nightmare. I was talking aloud, shouting to God. But no sight of land. Finally I passed out and I didn't come to until a Royal Navy seaman was hauling me up a rope-ladder on to his ship. They were very kind. Fed me biscuits and milk and made me sip some brandy.

'I had been aiming to land on the Essex coast but I'd

ended up just off the Kent coast. They took me to a town called Margate and handed me over to the local police. I was in their cells for four days and then an army sergeant and a private took me to a small truck and I was told I was going to the Patriotic School. I had no idea what that was but I really didn't care. I'd done it. I was going to fight the Germans.' He laughed. 'When we got to the place it looked like a prison from a Dickens book. Very grim. And then it started. The questioning. Day after day. The same questions over and over again. No clues as to what they were thinking. Very formal, no smiles, no jokes. No hero's welcome. You've no idea what it was like.'

'So tell me.'

'It'll take some time.'

Mallory smiled. 'So go ahead. Tell me about it.'

22

'Tell me your name again.'

'I've told you and the others my name a dozen times already.'

The captain sitting on the other side of the table said, 'I thought you had understood what I explained to you. Everybody who comes to this country from Europe is suspect. The Germans have tried infiltrating people to act as spies. If you want to fight the Germans you should be glad that we take such precautions.'

'If I were a spy would my name matter – if it was true or false you wouldn't know.'

'The problem for us about you is that you can give us no address to check on in Holland.'

'I told you. I lived with my parents until about nine months ago. Since then I've been in the resistance and moved from place to place.'

'So give us your parents' address.'

'They are not involved in the resistance. I don't want them to be put in danger.'

'Give us the name of one of your colleagues in the resistance then.'

'I told you. One of my jobs was organising the distribution of an underground newspaper – *Het Parool* – any Dutchman in this country can tell you who the editor is and you can contact him about me.'

'Tell me again about your journey.'

'I started from Walcheren Island as soon as it was dark. I rowed for two hours and then used the motor. The Royal Navy patrol boat saw me just off the coast at Margate.

I was drifting and I'd run out of petrol. And I was too exhausted to row any more. They picked me up and took me ashore and handed me over to the police.' He paused and shrugged. 'And now I'm here.'

'Why did you aim for Margate?'

'I didn't. I was heading for somewhere on the Essex coast.'

'Where?'

'Anywhere. I just looked at a map and that looked a suitable area. I suppose I must have read the compass wrong or I didn't allow for the wind and the current.'

'Where did you learn your English?'

'At school and university.'

'Which school and which university?'

'School in the Hague and Leyden University.'

The officer opened the buff file and took out a photograph and pushed it across the table.

'Do you know that man?'

It was Jan Maas, a friend of his at the university. But van Kempen's face showed no recognition as he looked back at the captain.

'No. I don't know him.'

'He knows you, van Kempen.'

'Who says so?'

'He does. I've arranged for him to be here. He's in the next room. He tells me his name is Jan Maas.'

Van Kempen had been too depressed by his reception by the British not to be overjoyed at the thought of seeing Maas again. Big, awkward Maas who was taking a general degree because he wanted to be a teacher in a primary school.

The captain pressed the button on the far side of the desk and a few moments later the door opened and Maas walked in, smiling that rather stupid lop-sided smile of his. As he went to walk round the table to van Kempen the captain stopped him with an outstretched arm.

157

'Is this Paul van Kempen?'

Maas grinned. 'It certainly is.'

They were walking in a kind of garden, if you could call a dark square of almost brown grass and a few trees a garden.

'How long have you been in England, Paul?'

'I make it a week exactly. I didn't expect a hero's welcome but my God I've been treated like I was a German spy. What is this place anyway?'

'It's called the Royal Victoria Patriotic School. The Patriotic School for short. They screen everybody here who comes from anywhere. Even the British have to go through the hoop.' He shrugged. 'It's best they do.'

'I came over to fight the Germans not argue with bloody Englishmen who don't believe a word I say.'

Maas laughed. 'Stop moaning. They'll be interviewing you about joining one of the services as soon as you leave here.'

'How long have you been over here?'

'Just over six months.'

'How did you get here?'

'We're not allowed to talk about that.'

'What did they ask about me?'

'About your background. Your family and so on.'

'So the bastards knew already. They must have been amused by me refusing to talk about my parents.'

'No. They'd give you good marks for that. Most of the questions they ask you here they already know the answers.' He paused and then said, 'How are Ockersen and van Laan?'

'The Gestapo got Ockersen. And van Laan was in a group in Amsterdam.'

'And your Anna?'

'She's in a group that finds hiding places for Jews on the run.' He looked at Jan Maas. 'It seems a long, long time since that day in Rotterdam. Standing there watching the Dorniers coming over in waves and buildings collapsing

158

all round us. And then all the parachutes. Sometimes I don't believe it really happened.'

'May 10, 1940. Over two years ago now.' He turned his head to look at van Kempen. 'I shouldn't really tell you but Bogaard is over here now. You'll be meeting him soon.' Pausing for a moment he said, 'How are things back home now?'

'They're bad. Getting worse every day. The Germans are showing their real face. Hunting down Jews like they were animals. Train loads being sent off to the camps. You can't practise any profession or trade without registration and approval. Hostages taken at any sign of civil disobedience or protest.'

'What about the resistance?'

'Who knows? There are groups all over the country. But what can they do? There's almost no contact with London and there are always collaborators and traitors who work for the Germans.'

'And what do you want to do about it?'

'I want to go back and set up regular communication with London and organise real resistance.'

'You'd have to be trained first.'

'So much the better. I'll do anything they want.'

The small Georgian house in Mayfair was in a mews off Berkeley Square and the civilian who had escorted him there handed him over to a Military Police sergeant at the reception desk. He handed over the card he had been given, the sergeant checked it against details on a clip-board on the desk before picking up the phone and dialling two numbers.

He looked at van Kempen as he hung up. 'Somebody's coming down for you if you'd like to take a seat.' He pointed to a row of straight-backed chairs along one wall. But van Kempen was too tense to sit down and walked with his hands in his pockets to look at various notices and posters on a board on the far wall. There was a type-written page of instructions on what to do

159

in case of fire. A poster warning about careless talk. A notice about drawing cigarette and chocolate rations. An official document that confirmed that the building had been requisitioned by the Custodian of Enemy Property from its owner Baron Freiherr von Teller.

Then a girl's voice said, 'They're waiting for you, sir.'

She was an ATS sergeant in uniform, and very pretty. When he asked her her name she just smiled and pointed to an open door at the end of a short corridor. 'In there, sir.' She stood and watched until he was in the office.

There were two officers in uniform. Both captains and both with the red and white flashes of the Royal Sussex on their sleeves. They were both quite young but one of them was almost completely bald.

It was the other one who held out his hand. 'My name's Parker and my colleague is Captain Watson. Glad to see you. Sit down. Make yourself comfortable.' He smiled. 'Please relax. You're not at the Patriotic School now. That's all over and done with.'

When van Kempen didn't respond Parker went on, smiling amiably. 'There's just one formality we have to go through.' He looked intently at van Kempen's face. 'You will be trained thoroughly for the work you've volunteered for but I want to point out that it's dangerous work. Particularly in Holland. If you have any doubts we can arrange for you to join the Free Dutch forces. The army or the navy. They'd be delighted to have you.'

'I don't have any doubts.'

'Are you quite sure? Maybe you'd like time to think again?' He paused. 'The problem is that once you've started your training you know a lot that the Germans would like to know. And once we've started we can't rub it out. You understand?'

'Yes. I understand. And I don't have any doubts. It's why I came to England.'

'This is your first time in England isn't it?'

'Yes.'

'Well I'm going to hand you over to Captain Watson and he'll be looking after you from now on.'

Captain Watson stopped the taxi in St James's Street and van Kempen watched as the taxi-driver was paid. Then Watson took his arm, smiling as he led him towards the offices that had a large sign saying – Metro Goldwyn Mayer.

Watson pushed open the glass-panelled door and led him through an office with desks and up a flight of stairs, then another two flights before he stopped and took out a bunch of keys. As he unlocked the door and flung it open he said, 'This is going to be home sweet home for a week or so.' He smiled. 'It's not bad.'

There was a living-room, a large bedroom with two single beds, a further single-bedded room, a small kitchen and a bathroom. Van Kempen's few belongings were still in the small canvas bag that he had taken on to the boat. A razor, an almost used-up stick of shaving soap, a shaving-brush and a comb. The narrow gold ring that Anna had given him, a Swan fountain-pen and a thick leather purse holding ten 100-guilder notes. His passport and all his documents had been kept by the people at the Patriotic School.

Watson made them a pot of tea and as he poured them each a cup he said, 'This afternoon we'll go out and buy you some clothes and a few odds and sods of toiletries and things. I've got clothing coupons and ration cards.' He smiled. 'The idea is you have a couple of days relaxing. We'll have a look around the town. Then a few days when I can go over the training programme with you.'

'How long will the training take?'

'About six months.'

'Six months! That's a long time. I'd hoped to be doing something useful long before then.'

Watson smiled. 'We want you to survive once you're back in Holland. There's a lot to be done.'

161

'What kind of training?'

'Operating a radio, Morse, codes, surveillance, avoiding surveillance, unarmed combat, explosives, weapons, map-reading, escape methods, gathering intelligence, organising groups, supervising drops and reception committees and a parachute course.'

Van Kempen smiled. 'You're right. That's quite a programme.'

'And that's the first time I've seen you smile. A good sign. Smiles mean self-confidence and confidence means success.'

'And when all the training is through?'

'Then you'll be dropped back in Holland.'

'To do what?'

Watson smiled. 'I don't know. And if I did I wouldn't tell you. When the time comes you'll be properly briefed.' He shrugged. 'As you well know – things change in occupied countries.'

It was in the evening when they were having a coffee before going to bed that Watson said, 'Tell me about Anna van Steen.'

'How do you know about Anna?'

'Jan Maas told us.'

'She's my fiancée. Or she was.'

'What do you mean – or she was?'

'She'll have been shocked and probably angry that I left without telling her I was leaving. She won't know that I've come to England.'

'Is she in the resistance?'

'She and her mother have been placing Jewish children with safe families.'

'What about her father?'

'I think you must know about him or you wouldn't have asked.'

'So tell me.'

'He's a senior officer in the Dutch police in Amsterdam.'

'And he collaborates with the Germans.'

'Some people say that. But it's not true. He's as patriotic

162

a man as you could find. If he had resigned he would have been sent to Germany. As it is he uses his authority to smooth things for the general public. He loathes the Germans and what they are doing but he puts up a front of cooperation.'

'You normally live in Rotterdam, yes?'

'Yes.'

'How likely that you'd be recognised in Amsterdam?'

'Not likely. It would have to be very bad luck. Most of my resistance work was in the Hague and then I moved down to Utrecht where I was unknown.'

'Would the van Steens help you?'

'I wouldn't ask them to help me.'

'Why not?'

'Because I'm emotionally involved and if I was caught that could affect me.'

Watson seemed pleased with his reply but said nothing. They listened to the news on the radio and then went to bed.

23

Despite the sunshine there was a nip in the air that showed that the summer was turning to autumn. The long shadows of the chestnut trees touched the gravel driveway that surrounded the manor house. Van Kempen sat on the trunk of a felled tree and looked at the house. There was a jeep and two pick-up trucks at the front of the house and there was a group of five or six men standing around a sergeant instructor who was demonstrating with one of the group how to use a garotte. And as he watched, six low-flying Spitfires flew across in formation and he noticed that despite the roar of their engines none of the group looked up. It happened too often to arouse more than a brief glance. When the air was quiet again his mind went back to that terrible morning in Rotterdam. They had stood there, the six of them, four boys and two girls, coming home from a very late party, not really believing what they saw. And then the fear that quickly turned to anger. Two days later the news that the Queen and the Royal Family were safely in London. The Germans promising the country that life would go on as usual. It had taken only six months before all the promises had been broken and it was made clear that Holland was a vassal state. A minor appendage to the Thousand Year Reich.

And now, sitting there, looking at the house in the evening sunlight this all seemed just as unreal. In Holland it had seemed the only thing to do. Go to England and fight the Germans. But now it seemed ridiculous. He was twenty-one next week and he'd spent ten days learning how to kill men without making a noise and without a weapon. What the hell difference would he make to the Germans who occupied all of Europe and were now smashing the Russians on their way to Moscow and Leningrad? It was futile. Pathetic. A joke.

He stood up and slowly and disconsolately went back to the house.

Despite its beautiful exterior the manor house inside had been converted in a hurry and the single bedrooms were sparsely furnished cubicles and as he washed and made himself ready for the communal evening meal he was slightly ashamed of his pessimism. There were a lot of people who were spending time and effort to train him. He wasn't alone. He was part of a team. A team that knew what it was doing.

The meal with his fellow trainees revived his spirit. If they had doubts they didn't show it. They didn't know each other's real names but over the first few weeks they had grown to recognise each other's personalities and there was much joking about the instructors and their foibles. The instructors were all British at this stage. A mixture of NCOs and officers. Some very military and barely hiding their doubts about the value of the band of foreigners in their charge. The others, mainly those concerned with action training, treated them like children who had to be got through their exams before they faced the tough real world outside.

They were told that night that they would be going to Scotland the next day for two weeks' survival training. They assumed from the knowing smile on the instructor's face that it was going to be tough. There were mutterings about sorting sheep from goats. Not a phrase familiar to the foreigners around the table, and there was some discussion about which of the two animals the British thought was the more desirable.

The mud-spattered army 3-tonner truck pulled up alongside the stone hut on the crest of the hill and the seven men climbed out, stretching their cramped limbs from the long journey to the Scottish highlands. The sergeant-instructor told them to start unloading their kit and take it into the rugged building.

Inside there were no rooms, just an open space with rough stone walls and a cement floor covered with straw. When a couple of the men sat down with their backs to the wall the instructor yelled at them to stand up and listen to what he was going to say. The instructor was a sergeant in the Gordon Highlanders, born and raised in the tough back-streets of Glasgow and despite the attention the seven men paid to what he said they could barely understand a word.

As they pieced together what had been said it seemed that they were going to be taken out into the night and off-loaded one by one in different places. They would have an Ordnance Survey map covering the area and the grid-reference of the stone hut. Each would have a compass, a box of matches, six hard army emergency ration biscuits and a half pint of water. They had two days to find their way back to the hut. They would be dropped separately, roughly forty miles from the base, and the terrain was rough. They would be leaving in an hour and there would be a plate of hot porridge for each of them before they left.

By midnight on the second day only three of the squad, including van Kempen, had made it back to the stone hut. Two arrived late on the third day, one of them in a state of complete exhaustion. One had been arrested as a suspect spy in a village nearly sixty miles away, and one had been found unconscious by a forest ranger. Back at the Surrey manor house they were given two days to rest and recuperate before they went up to Ringway just outside Manchester where they would have their parachute training.

Only five of them went up to Ringway but despite the fact that two of them were in their early fifties they all completed the course successfully.

Back at the manor house they were told that they

were going to spend the next two months at Beaulieu, a stately home and estate in the New Forest, not far from Southampton. They were told that from then on they would solely be concerned with instruction on being an agent in occupied territory. They were now lieutenants in the British Army so that if they were captured they would be able to claim the protection of the International Red Cross. A protection they would never receive as they would be in civilian clothes, with false documents and identities, and that meant that the Germans could claim that they were spies and treat them accordingly.

Their instructors now were very different men, ranging from ex-police detectives to historians and psychologists.

They spent four days on a lock-picking course with the police at Portsmouth and two weeks on surveillance and avoiding it, in Southampton. A week at the army School of Small Arms at Hythe in Kent and then three weeks on Morse and codes and signals security. Van Kempen and another man were to be radio operators for resistance groups already in Holland who had had no training in England.

There were several lectures by intelligence officers from the Free Dutch Army on the German forces occupying Holland, and a long talk by a minister of the Dutch government in exile about the relationship between the Germans and the civil government in Holland. Another Dutchman lectured on the various documents and permits that were needed for residence, work and travel.

Finally there were two weeks with a specialist on cover stories and new identities. This was done on a one-to-one basis so that nobody but the instruction staff and the agent concerned knew anything of the new identity or what the agent would be doing.

They gave him a small cottage on the estate and the day after he moved in his instructor came over from the main house to introduce himself.

'My name's Wyeth. Tony Wyeth. I'll be with you every

day now for the next two weeks. You're Paul van Kempen but that's the last time you'll answer to that name.' He smiled. 'We've got a name for you – it's Piet de Kruif. We all think it suits you well. How does it sound to you?'

Van Kempen laughed. 'Not bad.'

Wyeth nodded. 'Let's make ourselves comfortable shall we?'

When they were both seated in the comfortable armchairs Wyeth said, 'We have spent a lot of time going over your background.' He smiled. 'Part of the pay-off from all those boring questions at the Patriotic School. And we've tried to put together a cover that fits in reasonably well with the true facts. I'd like you to read it carefully over the weekend and note any comments you have on it and we'll discuss it on Monday.'

'Am I going as a radio operator?'

For a moment Wyeth hesitated. 'We'd like you to do that for the first few months until we've got other wireless operators in place. We've got a continuous wireless operators programme already in train. When we've got more in place we want to use you to organise and train the rather amateur existing resistance groups.' He smiled. 'You already know how uncoordinated they are.'

'When am I going to be dropped?'

Wyeth shook his head, smiling. 'All in good time. Can I ask you a personal question?'

'Yes.'

'Why do you want to go back?'

'To fight the Germans. To throw them out.'

'Don't you think it might be better for the civilian population in Holland just to knuckle-under and wait for the Allies to deal with the Germans in due course? I ask that seriously because we sometimes have people say that whose views we respect.'

'There will be tens of thousands of Hollanders killed by the Germans for one reason or another even if there were no resistance. Jews, the gypsies, so-called undesirables –' van Kempen shrugged ' – they don't need to pretend any more. They can do what they want. The resistance can teach them that it costs them to play those games with innocent people. Teach them too that the rest of the world is aware of what they're doing, and that sooner or later there'll be a day of reckoning and they'll be on the receiving end.'

'Does the whole country think that way?'

'Of course not. We're not a nation of warriors. No more than here. There were plenty of British who wanted peace at any price.' He shrugged. 'Including the Tory government.'

'Fair enough.' Wyeth paused, eyebrows raised. 'And what if they get you?'

For a moment van Kempen looked shocked and then he said quietly, 'What made you say that?'

'Because it happens, my friend. It happens.'

'I'd do what I was told to do.'

'Tell me.'

'I'd stick to my cover story.'

'Think about it.' Wyeth stood up smiling. 'See you on Monday. You can have use of one of the pool cars if you want over the weekend.'

Van Kempen spent most of the weekend studying the cover story that Wyeth had handed to him but on the Saturday he borrowed a car from the pool and drove over to Southampton and saw *Mrs Miniver*.

On the Monday Wyeth came early and they talked about the cover.

'Why have you made my birthplace as the Dutch East Indies?'

'Because they can't check up on the records there.'

'And why make my father an official out there?'

'The same reason. They can't check on someone in Surinam.'

'They could check the diplomatic records in the Hague.'

'Good thinking. But they won't bother. They may not even know they're available.'

'But if they do.'

Wyeth smiled. 'Then if they do they'll find that a Christiaan de Kruif is the acting consul in Surinam.'

Van Kempen was impressed and his face showed it. 'That's very thorough.'

'Of course. What else?'

'Why have you made me have book salesman as my trade?'

'Because we have somebody with a bookshop who will cooperate with the story.'

'If you know the bookshop then you know where I'm going to be dropped.'

'Maybe. But things frequently get modified at the last moment. So wait until you're told properly.' He smiled amiably. 'Any other points?'

'Yes. The security check in my radio traffic.'

'What about it?'

'We originally agreed that I'd put in the error in every message on the sixth word or multiples of six, and in your briefing it's been changed to multiples of nine.'

'Does that make it more difficult for you?'

'Not really but when you've spent weeks fixing something in your mind it's not easy to wipe it out and change it.'

'I agree. I'm not a radio or code expert but I'll take it up with the signals people and come back to you.'

'Apart from those points the cover fits in nicely.'

'I must emphasise that from now on you don't think of this as a cover. You are Piet de Kruif and you were born in Surinam. Your parents are still there and you're very worried about them. You've got photographs and background on Surinam and any other places you have been concerned with. Absorb it. All of it. And anything else you want to know about – ask me. In a couple of days we're going to put you through a tough interrogation. There will be two more interrogations before you are cleared. You'll be wearing genuine local clothes as from tomorrow and I'd like to recommend that you don't listen to the BBC in English. Listen to their Dutch bulletins and listen to Hilversum. Limit what you know about the war to what any Dutchman in Holland could know.'

Van Kempen smiled. 'I think you'd be surprised at how many listen to the BBC. Not just the Dutch programmes but the Home and the Light programmes. Especially the Sunday night news when they play our national anthem along with all the others.'

'That's interesting, I'll pass your comments on to the BBC.' He stood up. 'I'll see you again tomorrow.'

Van Kempen thought that the first interrogation had gone well. Four hours of question after question from two men. In the evening Wyeth had come over with a report on the interrogation.

'How did you think it went yourself?' Wyeth asked.

'Not too bad. I didn't give anything away that I can remember. What did they say?'

Wyeth looked at his clipboard and then at van Kempen. 'They failed you outright.'

Van Kempen looked shocked. 'On what grounds?'

'Right. First of all you responded twice when they called you Paul, not your code name – Piet. Second you responded too quickly to their questions. A normal person who has been arrested is confused and scared. When he's asked questions he doesn't respond eagerly. He's too confused. Thirdly they said you just talked too much. Far too sure of yourself. You showed that you knew why they were asking you the questions, even the oblique ones. An experienced interrogator would know that you'd been trained on being interrogated. You made it a battle of wits between you and them. All a normal person would want would be to be released.'

Van Kempen looked both resentful and disappointed. He shrugged. 'I wanted to show them that I was innocent and I wasn't scared.'

'Innocent of what? They didn't accuse you of anything. They just asked you questions about your background.

They've not seen your cover story so it was just a straight questioning. In their opinion you yourself turned it into an interrogation.'

Van Kempen sighed disconsolately. 'Well. They're the experts. I suppose they're right.'

'They are, my friend. Now take the next two days and don't spend your time mugging up your background facts. Just be it. You – are – Piet de Kruif – and you've lived a pretty quiet life. You sell books in a bookshop and all of a sudden you're in a prison cell being questioned. How would you be? How would you react?'

'OK. I'll do that.'

'It's for your own good. Remember that. In the end it doesn't matter what our two interrogators think. What matters is what a Gestapo man or an SD man would think.'

The second interrogation was by two different interrogators and their report was much less critical. Suggesting only that van Kempen seemed to be anticipating questions. Wyeth told him that the final interrogation would be some time in the next three days.

A dozen or so back copies of the Dutch underground paper *Het Parool* had been passed from London to Beaulieu and van Kempen sat reading them until nearly midnight. He had been one of the original distributors of the paper and had written several articles for it on how the Germans were breaking international law. A lot seemed to have changed in the last six months. What had once been derision at the German empire builders had become hatred and a call for revenge. It was obvious too that a lot of the hatred was levelled not only at Germans but at the Dutch who collaborated with them.

As he pulled the blanket up and switched out the bedside lamp he wondered what it would be like going back. He was asleep ten minutes later.

They came for him at 2 a.m. At first he thought it was a nightmare. The crash of the outer door, the splintering of wood, the light of the torch on his face and the black uniforms of the two Gestapo officers. The curses as they seized him, dragging him naked from the bed. The handcuffs searing the flesh of his wrists and his head wrenched back by his hair as they heaved him on to the wooden chair where he had placed his clothes.

And then the questions, the shouting, fists thudding against his face and belly.

It lasted for two hours and he was aware of the vomit on his body as they left. Nobody came for over an hour and then it was Wyeth and the army doctor, who assured him that there was nothing worse than bruises and what he described as minor shock. He had expected Wyeth to apologise or at least try to justify what had happened. But Wyeth merely told him that the team had praised his behaviour under stress. He would come back in the evening when van Kempen had had time to sleep and recover.

It was 4 p.m. before he woke and walked to the bathroom to run a warm bath and look at his face in the mirror. And slowly, despite the hurt he was pleased. They had done what they were told to do and so had he. He'd survived. He'd made it. He knew now what it would be like if he was caught. And he knew how to survive. There would never be that sudden shock of disbelief and fear again.

He was still soaking in the bath when Wyeth walked in, lowered the toilet seat and sat down.

'How are you feeling?'

'Not as bad as I expected.'

'If it's any consolation it's not likely to be as bad as that if they get you. There'll be the shock of course. The surprise. But even the Gestapo know that the more they beat a man up, the more angry and determined they make him. They want what you know.' He smiled. 'We'll have dinner together you and me. And your instructors on the course will be there too. Just to wish you well.'

'Does that mean I'll be leaving soon?'
'Next moon. Almost ten days.'
'Where are they dropping me?'
'You'll be told that tomorrow.'
'You still haven't told me about my security check.'
'They agree you can go back to the original. The sixth word or some multiple of six.'

24

Wyeth drove with him to the airfield at Tempsford and in one of the wooden huts he had stood naked as they checked over his clothes. Examining his own possessions. His wristwatch, a fountain pen and a worn leather purse with a few ten-guilder notes inside. A sergeant of the Royal Corps of Signals carried out one final check on his radio and checked the spares. A Dutch officer who had not seen them before sat at a small table and checked his documents. The passport, the faded birth certificate, the work permit, the identity card, the restricted travel permit and a doctor's certificate and a confirming note dated August 1939 to say that he was unfit for his military service due to the results of an attack of glandular fever as a child. The doctor who signed it had been killed in the attack on Rotterdam.

Finally everything was ready and they had sat waiting for twenty minutes before an RAF squadron leader told them the crew were ready. Before they left the hut Wyeth went over one last time the recognition signals that the reception committee would use.

There was an almost full moon and as they walked across the tarmac he could see the reflections on the fuselage of the Hudson. At the wooden steps Wyeth shook his hand and then walked away. The noise of the engines was too loud to make talking possible.

There were no seats for passengers inside the Hudson and van Kempen held on to a metal pipe with one hand as he sat on a wooden box as the aircraft gathered speed down the runway before lifting in a sharp climb, banking and turning as it headed down towards the south coast.

Although he was to operate in and around Amsterdam he was to be dropped in the south right on the Dutch-Belgian border. A few kilometres north-east of a small village named Slujs on the canal from Bruges.

About forty minutes later the turbulence indicated that they must be going over the coast. He felt his ears pop as the plane lost altitude as it headed low across the Channel. Twenty minutes later the navigator came back and told him that they would be over the dropping zone in ten minutes' time. He would open the circular flange that covered the parachute exit and stay with van Kempen until he jumped. They would have to check that the light signals from the ground were correct before he could jump.

The navigator removed the bolt, slid back the clasp and swung the circular cover to one side. He beckoned van Kempen over and pointed at the lights on the side of the fuselage.

'When the red light comes on it means we're over the drop. When the orange light is on it means the ground response is OK and then when the light's green you jump. OK?'

'OK.'

Van Kempen swung his legs into the exit hole and shook his head from the force of the draught coming in from outside. The red light came on and stayed on for over a minute. Then the orange light and almost immediately the green light came on, the tap on his shoulder and the command to jump.

He went out clumsily and then the weight of the pack strapped to his leg righted him, and gasping for breath he released the catch and he heard the whip-crack of the canopy opening and the feeling that he was being pulled upwards as the canopy filled. For a brief moment he saw the triangle of lights of the reception party and then the ground was rushing up towards him. He remembered to keep his feet together and his legs slightly bent and then the shock of landing, falling forward but forgetting all the drill about deflating his parachute as he was dragged forward until the canopy collapsed, his feet stumbling in tussocky grass.

He heard footsteps running towards him and saw the figure of a man reaching down to help him to his feet as he freed himself of the parachute harness.

The man held out his hand, smiling as he said, 'Welcome, Piet. Are you OK?'

'A bit breathless. I'll have to bury the parachute.'

'Don't worry. The others will do that.' He grinned. 'There's many a pretty Dutch girl wearing silk undies thanks to the RAF. We've got a van in the lane over there. Are you OK to walk? It's not far.'

'Yeah. I'm OK.' But he was panting as they walked together across the field.

There were two men waiting by the dark blue van in the lane. The first man said, 'It's OK. This is Piet. He's only shaken up. He'll be OK.' He turned to van Kempen. 'We've got a farmhouse to take you to. About ten kilometres away. There's a curfew here and it's dangerous to drive far at night. They can see us too easily.' He opened the rear doors. 'Jump in. There's some straw you can lie on.'

As they drove through the night van Kempen was relieved that all had gone to plan despite his clumsy landing. He wondered if they'd be able to let him sleep.

He heard a dog bark as the van slowed down and bumped along what felt like a rough track. Then the engine was switched off and the rear door was opened.

'You OK, Piet?'

'I'm fine.'

'Come in the house. There's nobody there but us.'

Inside it looked comfortable and they showed him a single room where he could sleep until they left to see their chief in the morning.

There was a small wash-basin with a jug of cold water and he washed his face which was still burning from the wind when he'd jumped. Like his training had taught him he lay down on the old-fashioned wooden bed with his clothes on. It was a long time before he slept. His last thought before he slept was realising that he'd forgotten to use the recognition password. But they'd called him Piet so they obviously knew who he was. He'd done everything else according to the book.

When he woke up the light was on in the room. He was sure that he'd switched it off before he got into bed. And then, as he turned, he saw the man sitting on the chair by the bed. It was the man from the reception group but he had a Luger in his hand. He was smiling.

'What's going on?'

'It's all over, my friend, you should have stayed safely in London, not coming back here to cause trouble for the population.'

'Where did you learn to speak such good Dutch?'

'I am Dutch. As much a Nederlander as you are.'

'And a collaborator?'

The man shrugged. 'Better that than being like you people who stir up trouble and get people killed.'

'Killed by Germans and traitors like you.'

'We're taking you to Utrecht. Let's see how tough you are when it's Germans you're talking to.'

'It won't be long, my friend. Remember that.'

'What won't be long?'

'Before you're facing a firing squad. Your turn will come.' Van Kempen saw that for a moment the threat had its effect. The man stood up and banged on the wall with his fist.

One of the other men came in, smiling as he dangled the handcuffs in front of van Kempen. They held him face down and shackled his hands behind his back.

He closed his eyes as he waited for the blows to fall but they rolled him over and told him to stand up. Ten minutes later they were on their way in a pre-war black Mercedes, his radio and kit-bag in the boot of the car.

The road signs had been removed but he knew as

they drove through Breda that they weren't taking him to Utrecht. They were turning on to the main road to Rotterdam. Van Kempen sat manacled uncomfortably in the back seat with the man who said his name was Bootsen. They had taken all his papers before they left the farmhouse and Bootsen looked through them as they headed towards Rotterdam.

The car stopped at a large house in its own grounds on the outskirts of Rotterdam. The gates were guarded by a Wehrmacht sergeant and two privates. The sergeant bent down to look inside the car, nodded to Bootsen and waved to one of the soldiers to open one of the tall wrought-iron gates.

There was a semi-circular gravel drive with a lawn and a display of plants that would have done well at a Haarlem flower-show, and there was an SS corporal at the entrance to the house.

Inside van Kempen was taken down to a cold, damp basement that had been converted into cells. Three on each side of the short corridor, with metal doors fitted with small circular inspection holes.

They pushed him into the first cell and the door clanged to behind him, the key grinding in the heavy lock as he looked around. There was a slab of concrete covered by a single worn blanket and a light behind a heavy grille in the ceiling. Otherwise the cell was empty.

An hour later he was taken from the cell up to the ground floor and then up the wide stairway to an office on the first floor. The guard knocked on the door and a voice shouted 'Come in'.

The office had obviously been the house-owner's library. Books on shelves from floor to ceiling on two walls, tall elegant windows and an antique desk with a trolley on casters to one side, holding two telephones and a wooden panel with half a dozen buttons.

The man behind the desk was only a very few years older than van Kempen. Maybe twenty-seven or twenty-eight. Well-dressed, tall and good-looking.

'Do sit down,' he said pointing to the single chair by the desk. As van Kempen sat down, his hands still manacled, the man stood looking out of the window, his hands in his trouser pockets. Van Kempen pressed his knees together to stop them from trembling. Then the man turned and looked at him, his hands on the desk top as he sat down.

'Herr de Kruif, my name is Keller and I'm a major in the SD. The Sicherheitsdienst. And of course your name is not de Kruif, is it. May I ask what is your real name?'

Van Kempen didn't reply and the German smiled. 'I speak some Dutch but I wondered if we might talk in English or German. I would find that easier. Which would you prefer?'

'Not German.'

Keller smiled. 'Let's not be childish, Mr de Kruif. I don't believe in the usual ritual that's called interrogation. So far as you are concerned the war is over. And despite what they told you in the talks at Beaulieu you are not a prisoner of war. And you have no rights of protection under international law. You have been dropped in Holland in civilian clothes with an English radio set and false documents.' He paused. 'In other words you are a spy and we are entitled to treat you as such.

'Some of our people who have been captured under similar circumstances in Britain have been executed. But some have been persuaded to change sides. Particularly radio operators. They send back messages concocted by MI6 in the hope that we shall believe that they are not working under duress.' Keller smiled at van Kempen. 'We should like to give you that choice. What do you say?'

Van Kempen shook his head but said nothing.

'Now before you make up your mind I think that you ought to know a little more about the situation here.' The German looked at a sheet of paper in front of him on the desk. 'I see that Captain Wyeth was your case officer.' He leaned back, smiling. 'A charming chap but I always felt that he was rather naïve. A bit too military. Too straightforward, to be involved in SOE's little games.

I expect you know about his wife. That little episode hasn't helped him. Left him insecure, with a tendency to want to believe what Baker Street tell him.' He paused. 'And there's something very wrong at Baker Street isn't there? Or you wouldn't be sitting on that chair right now. Did you sense that when you were at Norgeby House? A bunch of amateurs? A bit of a shambles?' Keller looked briefly at his watch then towards the window before he turned back to look at van Kempen. 'One of the problems we have with these situations is time. When a chap is willing to cooperate we have to get him back on air fairly soon. So bear that in mind. By the way I'll tell them to remove those wretched handcuffs.' He smiled conspiratorially. 'You Nederlanders are rather like us Germans, you like to keep to the rule-book.' He stood up, leaned forward and pushed one of the buttons on the panel on the trolley. 'Think about what I've said and we'll talk again tomorrow.'

When he was back in the cells the guard unlocked the handcuffs and slipped them in his pocket.

'The major said you were to have a meal. Which do you want: cheese omelette or toasted cheese?'

'I'll have the omelette.'

When he'd eaten, the guard came back for the plate and van Kempen asked if he could have something to read and he had been surprised when the guard came back with a paperback collection of the poems of Hendrik Walsman. Walsman had been drowned trying to get to England in 1940.

He lay back on the cement slab, the paperback unopened on his chest. He was shocked at what they knew about SOE. But he recognised that it was done to lower his morale. The SD major seemed civilised. Or was that just a ploy too, to be dropped when he didn't respond and they'd call up the thugs to make him talk.

Van Kempen was surprised the next morning when there was a young Dutch girl taking notes of the meeting with Keller.

'Have you made a decision, Mr de Kruif?'

'I'm not prepared to cooperate.'

'Why not?'

'It could cause other people to be caught.'

'Mr de Kruif, I have over twenty of your SOE colleagues in custody.' He pushed across a sheet of paper. There was a typewritten list of names. Van Kempen read them slowly and recognised five names. Three had been on part of his training programme, one was Jan Maas and the other was a man he had met at SOE's HQ in Baker Street. It looked as if they weren't bluffing. He leaned back in his chair and looked at Keller.

'Why are there asterisks against some names?'

'They are prisoners who are cooperating with us.'

'Can I talk with one of them alone?'

'Who do you have in mind?'

'Mijnheer Maas.'

Keller looked at the young woman and she nodded. Keller looked back at van Kempen.

'If you are satisfied will you cooperate?'

'Maybe.'

Keller nodded. 'I'll arrange for you to talk to him.'

The secretary had accompanied van Kempen on the car journey.

'Are you Dutch?'

The girl laughed. 'Of course I am. Why are you so surprised?'

'I'm surprised that any Dutch person would collaborate with the Germans.'

'It's the only way, Piet.' She smiled. 'I suppose it isn't really Piet is it?'

'What's your name?'

'Maria Koolstra.'

'D'you come from Rotterdam?'

'It's my home. But I was at Leyden, at the university before . . . before the Germans came in.'

'What were you studying?'

'Law and Business Studies.'

'And you end up working for the Krauts?'

She laughed. 'At least they're professionals, not like those people in London. Keller and his people are just playing games with them.'

'How do you know?'

'I have to type out the messages the collaborators send back to London.' She smiled. 'Do you have a security check? A mistake you can put in to show them that you are not under German control?'

When he didn't answer she said, 'Some of your people omitted their security checks without us knowing. Your friend Jan Maas was one of them. London sent a message back pointing out that they were being careless and not using their security checks.' She grinned. 'Ask your friend if you don't believe me.'

'How is he, Jan?'

'He's OK. They don't like doing it, any of them. But it's better than being sent to a concentration camp.'

They turned into a drive towards a long low building and the girl said, 'This used to be a convent but it was turned into a prison.'

'You mean the collaborators are kept in a prison?'

'Of course.'

The car stopped outside the entrance to the building. The armed driver stayed in the car and van Kempen and the girl got out. As they were approaching the building the girl stopped and looked at him.

'When you talk to Jan Maas don't treat him as a collaborator. We can't all be heroes and even heroes don't want to end their lives in a gas oven.'

'Do they really do that if you won't collaborate?'

'They let you rot for a couple of months and then if you don't change your mind you end up in Dachau or Mauthausen – extermination camps.'

'So much for Major Keller's charm.'

She smiled but didn't reply and walked inside the building. There were guards everywhere and when the girl had given her pass and the typed instructions from Keller to the security desk they were shown to a small waiting-room where a picture of Hitler and one of Seyss-Inquart hung side by side on the wall by the door. Seyss-Inquart was *Reichskommissar* of the Netherlands.

When van Kempen turned to speak to the girl she put a finger to her lips and pointed to what looked like a ventilator in the ceiling. A clear warning that the room was bugged.

A civilian came into the room and said to the girl. 'Where do you want him?'

'We'll go outside.'

'I couldn't allow that. It wouldn't be safe.'

'It's what the Major arranged. I'll take full responsibility.'

'I'd better phone Keller.'

'As you wish but I don't know where he is. He's not in Rotterdam until tomorrow.'

The man hesitated. 'All right. But I'll have one of my men out there too.'

'Whatever you want. But the prisoners are to talk in private.'

'Understood. You take your man outside and Maas will be escorted out to you.

They stood under the chestnut trees and van Kempen could see the strain on Jan Maas's face despite his grin.

'I didn't expect our next meeting would be here. By the way what name do you use?'

'Piet de Kruif. How are you?'

'Depressed.'

'Why?'

'It was so easy for them. They knew all about me. Even my real name. I couldn't believe it at first. It was like a bad dream.'

'Go on.'

'They told me that if I didn't cooperate I'd just get sent to one of their bloody camps and that would be the end of me. I thought maybe if I went along with it at least I could omit my security check and London would know that I was controlled by the Germans. You won't believe it but I sent three messages without my security check and the stupid bastards sent a message back that I wasn't using it. I thought the Krauts would shoot me or something. They just laughed. It seemed it had happened many times before. They've got over twenty SOE men in this dump. It's just become a routine, picking up the next idiot who's dropped.'

'How much do they know?'

'The lot. They even showed me sketches of the layout of the rooms at Baker Street. The names of SOE officers and their responsibilities. They know the names of the training staff. And what sort of training we got.'

'How do you think they got this information?'

Maas shrugged. 'I think the Dutch section in London are incompetent. And the Krauts have built up a detailed picture from interrogations. They ferret away at every little detail. They knew more about my controller than I did. They get a bit from one guy and a bit from somebody else and when they drop it on you you realise the game's up.' He shrugged. 'I still bang out the messages and they still respond like everything's OK.' He paused. 'I suppose to you I'm just one more bloody collaborator.'

'No. You didn't have any choice. And you didn't betray anybody.'

Maas sighed. 'Oh but I did.'

'Who?'

Jan Maas looked at his face and said quietly. 'All the SOE people who came after me because London thought everything was OK.'

'That wasn't your fault. That was London for God's sake. You warned them three times and either they ignored it or they were careless.'

Jan Maas smiled the old lop-sided smile. 'Or something.'

'Tell me about Keller. The charmer.'

Maas laughed. 'I think the charm's quite genuine. But he's not soft. There's a lot of steel in that guy.'

'What about the girl? She's a real collaborator. I'm sure they didn't threaten her with a gas-chamber.'

Maas looked at him for a moment, opened his mouth to speak then looked away towards the building. 'You'll have to work that one out for yourself.' He looked back at van Kempen. 'I should go along with them if I were you.'

Then the girl walked over. She looked at her watch. 'Time's up I'm afraid.'

They walked back to the building and Jan Maas was led away by the civilian.

When they were outside the girl said, 'I've got something to tell you.'

Van Kempen looked at her face. 'What?'

'I know who you are. When I first saw you with Keller I felt I'd seen you somewhere before. And when I saw you with Jan Maas I remembered where it was.'

'Go on.'

'If I say Anna van Steen, does that ring a bell?'

'No.'

She smiled. 'Oh but it does. Your name's Paul van Kempen and I once danced a foxtrot with you. It was at Leyden. At a university hop. You'd come down to see Anna and you wished you didn't have to dance with her friends.' She smiled. 'Do you remember now?'

'No. You're quite mistaken.'

'I shan't tell Keller or anyone so don't be worried that anything will happen to Anna.' She sighed softly. 'Can I give you some advice?'

'I'm sure you will whatever I say.'

'*Touché*. Go along with Keller. All this won't last for ever. Better be alive when it's all over.'

'Is that why you go along with Keller?'

She laughed. 'Didn't Jan tell you?'

'Tell me what?'

'I love him. I'm his mistress.'

'Jesus. Why?'

'Why do I love him or why am I his mistress?'

'Both.'

'He's the most interesting man I've ever met. And I sleep with him because that's what men want. He likes young girls.'

'Why do you tell me all this?'

'Because when I saw you and Jan Maas talking under the trees it seemed like it was back in those days. I'd seen you and Jan talking like that when we had all gone for a picnic the Sunday after the hop. And you'd stood there looking over his shoulder, looking for Anna because you were a bit jealous. She was very beautiful and you had a lot of rivals. And then a few weeks later your engagement was in the papers. What happened after that?'

For a moment van Kempen hesitated and then he said bitterly, 'A lot of Dorniers and Heinkels came after that.'

'Have you seen her since?'

'No.'

'She's in Amsterdam now. She works in the library.'

'Don't tell me any more, please.'

'We'd better go. But I haven't given you my advice have I?'

'Haven't you?'

'Don't take all this so seriously. Your life is more important than some phoney sense of honour. You're just a man. Keller's just a man. We're all real. The war is something we have to survive and live through.' She laughed. 'Let's go.'

25

After his meeting with Jan Maas he had been left for two days. In training they had said that they often did that to make a prisoner apprehensive about what was going to happen. To show you that you were so unimportant that you just didn't matter to them any more.

On the third day he had been taken up to Keller's office but the girl wasn't there.

'So what did you find out from our friend Maas?'

'Nothing much. He collaborates – that's all.'

'There was a slip of paper loose in your ID card . . .' He put the slip on the table. 'There's a coded message on it, can you decipher it for me?'

Van Kempen looked at it briefly then shook his head. Keller smiled. 'I've done it for you. It's the address of the safe-house in Amsterdam that they gave you isn't it?'

'If you say so.'

'It's the same address they give to all of you. A butcher's shop in Utrechtstraat.' He smiled. 'We raided it nine months ago and closed it down. It's been empty ever since. But we picked up two SOE people there long after it was closed. They're very careless with people's lives your friends in Baker Street.'

'When do you want me to start?'

'So. You want to collaborate do you?'

'No. But I don't want to end in a gas-oven in one of your extermination camps.'

Keller nodded. 'Very wise too.' He paused. 'I'll have you taken out to the old convent this afternoon. The signals people will show you the ropes and you can make your first transmission the next day.'

Keller stood up, stretching his arms as he looked at van Kempen. 'I'd better warn you that if you try to escape you'll be shot. There's no second chance. And by the way, if you care to give us your real name we are prepared to pass it to the International Red Cross in Geneva. It gives you no protection but they can notify your next of kin that you are a prisoner.'

Van Kempen shook his head. 'No thanks.'

Keller shrugged and pressed the button for the guard to take van Kempen back to his cell.

The next day van Kempen was taken to the prison. It was a far cry from the interviews with Keller. Here he was a prisoner. A prisoner in a cell with no contact with anyone but the guards and the SD signals unit.

The signals team were typical German soldiers whose knowledge of radio and codes had come from civilian jobs and specialist training. The only exceptions were the two SD officers who composed the messages sent back to London. They worked under direct supervision and orders from the RSHA in Berlin. They had the responsibility for making the messages credible, to supply enough information to indicate that the SOE operator was still a free agent. And for the information he gave to have some value to London. Sometimes the information was not only credible but true and to the Germans' short-term disadvantage but more often it was to give a false impression of German troop strengths in Holland, enough to discourage any attempt at invasion.

The signals men obviously despised the collaborators. Not for their collaboration but for the inefficiency of the organisation they worked for.

Van Kempen had thought hard and long about whether to use his security check in his first message. He was angry that all that effort, all that training, had been thrown away as if it didn't matter. But he remembered what Jan Maas

189

had told him – that the Germans had many SOE men inside the prison, either working with the Germans or awaiting their fate as non-collaborators. But like Jan Maas had said, his collaboration would help the Germans capture others who followed. He decided to omit his security check in that first message, so that at least he'd given them the correct indication that he was controlled by the Germans. When he had finished he was taken back to his cell.

Over the next three months van Kempen had been made to send five more messages to London. In all of them he omitted his security check and was shocked that London continued the radio traffic despite him making clear that he was operating under German control.

He was kept like the other prisoners in his cell, with no communication with anyone, apart from the Germans in the radio centre, and they had been instructed to ignore all unnecessary conversation. At the end of the second week he had discovered that Jan Maas was only two cells away and they tapped out short messages in Morse on the water pipes that ran through every cell. Twice in the first month he had heard RAF bombers going over and had seen searchlights sweeping the sky and heard bursts of firing from anti-aircraft batteries. In the third month there were planes going over most nights and the message tapping on the pipes said that Berlin had been bombed a dozen times. But such was the suspicion of prisoners that warnings were tapped out that maybe the Germans had penetrated the crude message system to boost prisoners' morale and then let them discover that any good news wasn't true.

Only the fact that there seemed to be more daylight from the small, barred window high on the wall made him realise that it had been snowing in the night and a few days later the signals operation had closed down for two days except for two men on standby, but there were no messages from London that involved any of the prisoners. And Jan Maas had tapped out on the pipes that it was Christmas.

A week into the New Year was the first daylight raid by US heavy bombers, and the building shook as wave after wave of the big Boeings ploughed through the sky on their way to Germany. The following week van Kempen had to send a signal to London acknowledging that it would be safe for an agent code-named 'Bernard' to be dropped. It was the first time that one of his messages would lead to the capture of another agent.

Another two weeks went by and according to his roughly kept calendar it was the first week in February 1944. And then he was told that he and three other prisoners were to be transferred. The guard refused to say why he was being transferred and said he had no idea where he would be going.

The next day he was taken outside the building and there were three other men there. One of them was Jan Maas. When he spoke to Maas the guard told him to be silent. A Wehrmacht truck drew up and the guard handcuffed each of them before ordering them into the back of the truck. The guard laced up the canvas flaps and they heard him speak to the driver and clatter into the cab beside him.

As the truck turned right at the main gates they heard the air-raid warning start up. But the truck still drove on. They were stopped once by a patrol and then carried on. It was Jan who first heard the planes, pointing up at the canvas roof. They were very low and seconds later they heard machine-gun fire and the thud of rockets and then they were thrown and tossed around as the truck heeled over and ground to a stop. They heard the driver cursing and then more machine-gun fire.

Without thinking van Kempen pushed his head through a gap in the canvas flaps. The truck was on its side in a ditch. He turned quickly to the others.

'The driver's not around nor the guard. Let's go.'

The leather straps came away easily from the worn canvas and van Kempen jumped down into the ditch and the others scrambled down after him. He waited a few moments and then scrambled up to the road and along to the cab. The guard was covered in blood and the windscreen was smashed and there was no sign of the driver.

He stood up slowly and looked around. They were on a narrow country road with no buildings in sight but on the other side of the road was a track that led to a wood about a quarter of a mile away. He asked the others, still crouching in the ditch, if they wanted to make a run for it and when they agreed he insisted that they walk, not run, down the path to the woods.

In ten minutes they were inside the shelter of the woods.

Van Kempen said, 'Anybody got any idea of where we are?'

One of the two he didn't know said, 'I think we're near a village called Bodegraven on a side road to Utrecht.'

'D'you know the area?'

'I did way back. Before the war.'

'How far do those woods go?'

'Quite a way. Up to the village and then round a lake.'

'This is the first place they'll look for us. We'd better split up. Two together. Agreed?'

The others nodded and Jan held up his manacled hands. 'What about these?'

Van Kempen shrugged impatiently. 'Any farmer can get those off. We'll have to take the risk that they're not collaborators.'

The man he didn't know said, 'They may not be collaborators but they'll be shit-scared of the Germans.'

Van Kempen nodded. Impatient to get them on their way. 'We'll have to risk that. We'd better get moving. You two go first.'

'We'll head for Utrecht.' The man shrugged. 'Good luck.'

Maas and van Kempen watched as the other two took a path that appeared to be heading east. When they were

192

out of sight Maas said, 'We can make for Alphen and then Leyden.'

'I'd rather head for Amsterdam.'

'Why?'

'There are people in Leyden who know us from the old days at university. We'd be recognised.'

'Have you got any contacts in Amsterdam?'

'Not that I could contact directly. Anyway we can't do much until we've got rid of the handcuffs.'

Maas nodded. 'I know somebody just this side of Leyden who could get them off for us. We could be there in under two hours.'

'Who is he?'

'It's a girl but her father's got a cycle repair workshop.'

For a moment van Kempen hesitated, then he shrugged and said, 'OK. Let's try it.'

They had left the protection of the woods twenty minutes later and turned westwards skirting the bank of the river. The road was flat and that gave them good warning of oncoming vehicles until they got to a part of the river where the banks gave them no cover at all. And there they rested, lying in the long grass waiting until the right moment. By 4 p.m. they were so cold that they were forced to carry on although it was not yet really dark. But the few vehicles that passed on the main road had their lights on and gave fair warning of their approach. By now they were not only shivering with cold but desperately thirsty. After being confined in a cell for so long they were pathetically out of condition.

It took nearly an hour to get to Lederdorp where Jan's girlfriend lived. There were narrow slits of light at the edges of the window black-outs but the long single street was empty of people. At the corner of an alleyway Maas stopped and pointed. 'It's the place directly opposite the chapel. I'll go first in case there's a problem. If I'm not out in fifteen minutes you go. OK?'

'OK.'

Maas kept close to the wall as he moved cautiously down the narrow alley and then van Kempen heard him knocking, apprehensive as he recognised the Morse V-sign of the resistance. He didn't see the door open or Maas go inside. It was too dark to see anything. A few minutes later he heard a muffled shout, telling him to come on down. He was aware of the door opening and being pulled inside. He blinked in the bright light and saw a young girl in her early twenties and a short but broad-shouldered man in working overalls. He heard Jan Maas say, 'This is my friend.'

The man looked at him carefully and the girl smiled, nervously. Without speaking the father took Maas's hand and led him to a door at the back of the room, beckoning to van Kempen to follow. Through the door was the workshop with bicycles hung from the rafters and bicycles in various stages of repair lined up along the outside wall.

When they were alone the man turned to van Kempen and held out his hand. 'I know your friend already. My name is Drost. Let's get those things off you.'

He led them both over to a wooden bench and took down a massive pair of cutters. Jan Maas was first and they watched the links joining the cuffs snap apart. Then the cutters were carefully adjusted to avoid cutting into flesh and the manacles fell apart one after the other. Drost carried out the same process for van Kempen. When he too was free Drost bent down and gathered up the handcuffs and placed them in a metal pot which he put on a glowing charcoal brazier. With a foot pump the fire was brought to white heat and the handcuffs melted into the molten metal that was already in the pot. Then the fire was allowed to die down.

Drost stood hands on hips. 'There's potato soup for both of you. After you've eaten you sleep up there and you stay there till I tell you otherwise.' He pointed to where a roughly made wooden ladder led up to a gallery edged with cardboard boxes labelled with details of the spares they held. When they turned Drost said,

'You want me to contact the local resistance people for you?'

Van Kempen and Maas looked at each other and then nodded to Drost who just said, 'Might take a couple of days.'

The first night in the loft was uncomfortable but they had a blanket each and they slept fitfully, alerted by every sound in the house. So used to being alone, they found it difficult to think of anything to say to each other.

Drost made clear that he wanted them to stay in the loft except when they needed the toilet and when he asked them down into the workshop to eat.

It was three days before anything happened and then in the evening Drost called them down and there was a man with him. A man in the uniform of the Dutch police. He looked them over and then pointed at Jan Maas.

'You first. Come with me.' He looked at van Kempen. 'And you stay right here. Just sit down and don't move.' He signalled to Jan Maas to follow him into the adjoining room.

After about fifteen minutes van Kempen heard a car start up outside the house. And ten minutes later he heard it come back and the car door slammed to. The policeman came back alone.

'Right,' he said. 'Follow me.'

Van Kempen followed him into the kitchen and the man pointed to the chair at the wooden table. He took a chair himself and sat facing van Kempen.

'Your friend won't be coming back.'

Van Kempen said nothing.

'He tells me your name is van Kempen. Is that so?'
'Yes.'

'And you were an officer in SOE like him.'
'I still am.'

'You were caught by the SD.'
'Yes.'

'And you escaped.'

'Yes.'

'Tell me how you escaped. Everything.'

Van Kempen told him what had happened. And the policeman said, 'What do you want to do?'

'I want to know who you are.'

'Don't worry. I'm a policeman. I work with the Germans when I have to. And I act as a counsellor for a resistance group. They are taking care of your friend but he told me you want to go to Amsterdam, yes?'

'Yes.'

'OK. I'll put you in touch with people there. They will be glad to have a trained man. Especially a radio operator. They have a set and a frequency but nobody who can use it.' He paused. 'They'll help you with permits and clothes and finance.'

'Don't you need to check on me independently?'

The policeman smiled. 'I spoke to your father on the telephone tonight. I had to talk in riddles but the description he gave of his son fitted well. I think he guessed that you're back in Holland from what I said. I tried to make clear that you're OK.'

'How did you persuade him to talk so easily?'

The policeman smiled. 'There were three young men who went to school together and later on they played football for the same team. And they were all crazy about the same girl. I was one of them. Your old man was another. He married the girl. We've only met a couple of times since the old days. Both times by accident.' He paused. 'So sleep tonight and I'll be with you in a few days. It'll mean travelling at night. But I don't have a problem with that.'

'Are you in the resistance?'

'No. I just stand on the side-lines and give advice when it's asked for.'

'Thanks for your help anyway.'

'You still look doubtful, my friend.'

For a moment van Kempen was silent then, looking at the policeman, he said, 'It's how you get after a time. If tomorrow it turns out that you're a collaborator and I'm back in prison, I shall not be shocked. Not even surprised. Nothing surprises me any more. Nothing ever will.'

'How long were you in solitary?'

'I'm not sure. Four – could be five, months.' He shrugged. 'It never mattered.'

The man nodded. 'It'll go, my friend. You'll be back with the rest of us inside a month. Worrying about things that ain't never going to happen.'

26

For a long time van Kempen sat there without speaking and Mallory watched van Kempen's face as he looked towards the window.

Then van Kempen sighed and turned his head to look at Mallory.

'It's Charlie Mallory isn't it?'

'Yes.'

'I think I've had enough for now, Charlie. Maybe we'll talk again some other time.'

'When shall I come back?'

'Are you in a hurry?'

'I'd like to get the assignment over.'

'You tired of hearing old men's stories?'

'No.'

'What else do you want to know?'

'Was that the last you saw of Keller?'

Van Kempen smiled. 'No.'

'Do you think he did things that could be classed as war-crimes?'

Van Kempen shrugged. 'It depends what you call war-crimes.' He smiled. 'Orders are orders.'

'Not if they're illegal.'

Van Kempen laughed softly, 'You're being naïve, Charlie. There was a war on.'

'Is Keller still alive?'

'Oh yes.' He smiled. 'Very much alive.'

'What happened to him when the Allies liberated Holland?'

'He was already back in Germany.'

'Is there any chance I could trace his secretary? The girl.'

'No. I'm afraid not.'

'Did you try to trace her?'

'She joined my resistance group. I didn't need to trace her.'

'What happened to her?'

'She died about five years ago. She had been ill for a long time.' Van Kempen pointed at a photograph on a small table. It was a portrait of a very handsome woman, in a silver frame. 'That was Maria. She was my wife. We married as soon as the war was over.'

'What happened to Jan Maas?'

'He was caught by the Gestapo. He died in a KZ.'

'But you weren't caught?'

'Oh, but I was.' He smiled. 'Two weeks after D-day.'

'But obviously you escaped.'

'In a way. I had help.'

'But you don't want to tell me about your time in the Resistance.'

'Not at the moment.' He smiled. 'It was Commisaris van Steen, Anna's father, who helped me escape.'

'When?'

'You're very pressing. And it really isn't necessary.'

'Why not?'

'Why not?' Van Kempen raised his eyebrows. 'Because your people in London know very well what happened.'

'The people from those days will have all retired long ago. Or maybe they're dead by now.'

'The present people will know too.'

'They wouldn't have given me this assignment if they already knew the facts.'

'You're being naïve again, my friend.'

'I don't understand.'

'You'll have to work it out for yourself.'

'Why is it that everybody from those days says that – you'll have to work it out for yourself?'

'That's because they know the answers. Some of them

don't like the answers.' He shrugged. 'Maybe they hope you don't find out what really happened.'

'Who wouldn't want me to find out what really happened?'

Van Kempen looked towards the silver framed photograph for several moments, and then back at Mallory. 'I think perhaps I'm the only one who doesn't care if you discover the truth.'

'What about my bosses in London?'

'Oh, them. Yes. Well they know the truth. Always have done.'

'Then why should they want to send me out on a wild-goose chase?'

'It's not a wild-goose chase. You're their tracker dog. They want to see what you can uncover. If you don't uncover the truth so much the better. Because if you can't nobody else can.'

'Why should they care one way or another? They weren't involved in any of it.'

Van Kempen smiled. 'You call it "the old boy network". It's part of their job to protect SIS and its image.'

'But if I find evidence and recommend that these men should be arrested and tried – what then?'

Van Kempen shook his head slowly, 'You won't do that, my friend.'

'You mean they're innocent?'

Van Kempen sighed. 'I mean exactly what I said. No more, no less.'

'Does Keller still use that name?'

'No.'

'Would you talk with me again after I've thought about what you've told me?'

Van Kempen shrugged. 'If you really think it's necessary.'

'Could I see you tomorrow afternoon?'

'OK. Let's say four o'clock here.'

Mallory stood up. 'Thanks for giving me so much of your time.'

Van Kempen nodded and walked with Mallory to the street door. When they shook hands van Kempen said, 'Think hard, young man, think hard and long.'

Mallory thought hard – and long. But to no good purpose. He had identified one man who was protected by armed guards, snarling dogs and a lot of influence in high places. And he had no idea what crimes, if any, he was guilty of. He had found out a lot about Keller but nothing that indicated that he had committed anything like a war-crime. And all the time those vague warnings and hints that he was wasting his time. But he was sure now that Keller was the one who mattered. There were only two things he wanted from the Dutchman. A lead to Keller or whatever he called himself now. And some idea of what he had done. The main thing was to get it all wrapped up so that he could get back on a proper assignment. He had come to respect these old men and the things that they had done in the war but they were like some secret society, making it all too clear that he wasn't a member. All of them so sure that he wasn't going to find out anything they didn't want him to know. Ready to talk about what had happened but always drawing a line, beyond which they wouldn't go. It was as if there had been a separate war going on inside the real war, and you had to have been part of it or you would always be an outsider. Those were the rules. But he wasn't part of the club and as far as he was concerned the rules didn't exist.

Mallory had noticed the five fishing rods displayed on the wall in van Kempen's living-room and spent the morning looking in the smaller antique shops. It took him a couple of hours to find what he was looking for. It was a 1918 set of Allcock Spinning lures in beautiful condition. He reckoned that SIS funds could run to a modest sweetener for the Dutchman.

Van Kempen unwrapped the tissue-paper carefully and then folded open the small piece of velvet that covered the lures. He looked at them for several minutes without touching them and then looked at Mallory.

'This is very kind of you. And very thoughtful too.' He smiled. 'They look too beautiful to be used.' He put them carefully on to the couch beside him and then picked up his glass of whisky.

'Cheers.' He smiled amiably. 'I feel I was probably a bit bloody-minded with you yesterday.' He put down his glass, leaning back, folding his arms. 'It's not easy. I don't trust the Brits, especially SIS, but I suppose there comes a time when the past has to be the past. I got the feeling talking to you yesterday that I was being used. Being manipulated. All my experience during the war with SOE tells me that the Brits are really quite ruthless. In war-time a commander has to accept that some of his troops are going to be killed. It's part of war. Some even have to be sacrificed for the sake of others. But your people just threw us to the wolves. SOE was criminally careless and SIS was ruthless.'

'What sort of contact did you have with SIS?'

'When I escaped and joined up with the resistance group in Amsterdam the first thing I did was to radio a message to London to say that all radio traffic to SOE was under German control. And I asked for arrangements to be made for me to be picked up and taken back to London.' He laughed. 'Believe it or not the message that came back just told me to make my own way back. No mention of the radio game. The group I was with were built up around an SIS agent who had been dropped by SIS in 1942. He was a Brit. A good guy. Tough and experienced and a good leader. We did what we were asked, blowing bridges, cutting communications. I guess we weren't more than a nuisance to the Krauts but as it got nearer to D-day the Germans really went for us. SIS were not too pleased with us. They weren't interested in sabotage. They wanted intelligence, order-of-battle stuff, political. And we weren't trained for that.

'I ended up in charge of just a dozen stragglers. The

Gestapo had wiped out the rest. A Kraut named Becker was in charge of the search and destroy squads and anybody they caught was just shot on the spot. They didn't even bury them. Just left their bodies there to rot. I don't know what happened to Becker.'

'He's got a porn empire in Hamburg. And lots of protection.'

'How in character. Somebody should knock him off.' Van Kempen grinned. 'Maybe you can get SIS to do it.'

'What did Keller do?'

'Once the landings had established themselves the SOE radio people were no longer any use to the Germans. Keller signed the order for their execution. Just over fifty were shot. Some Brits, but mostly Hollanders.'

'Who would have a copy of those orders?'

'They'll have been destroyed long ago. Don't waste your time looking for them. Our State Archives have got a list of the victims' names. There was a judicial enquiry after the war but it didn't get very far.' He looked at Mallory. 'And Keller would certainly claim that he was only carrying out orders from above.'

'That wasn't accepted as a defence at the Nuremberg Trials.'

Van Kempen smiled. A grimace as much as a smile. 'Depends on who gave the orders.'

'What does that mean?'

'It means I know who gave Keller the go-ahead. They didn't actually give the order but they could have stopped him from carrying it out.'

'Who could have stopped him?'

'Let's just say his masters could have stopped him.'

'And who were they?'

Van Kempen shook his head. 'I said that the past should be left as the past. But it isn't really so. In this particular case, the past is still with us.' For long moments van Kempen looked at Mallory without speaking, and then he said, 'I am surprised that they sent you on this mission, this assignment.'

'Why?'

'Because you are too young. No matter how many men you speak to from those days you will still not understand. Because if you were told the truth you would not believe it.'

'Try me.'

'No. You must find it out for yourself.'

'How do you know that Keller signed the execution warrant for those SOE men?'

'When the Germans pulled back from Holland, Keller was caught by a detachment of my resistance group, near Venlo on the German border. Maria was with them and she offered to set him free if he told her what had happened to the prisoners. He agreed. When he told her she was bitterly angry but she let him go. She had checked with London on the deal and they agreed. She held Keller after she knew the SOE men had been executed and contacted London again. SIS told her to let him go. She did.'

'How can I find Keller?'

'It won't help you. You'll be walking into a mine-field.'

'I still want to find him.'

'Are you sure?'

'Absolutely.'

'OK. His name now is Kern.'

'Where can I find him?'

Van Kempen shrugged. 'Hollywood, London, Rome – anywhere.'

'You don't mean Kern the film director?'

'I do, my friend.' He stood up. 'That's all the help I can give you. And please God, remember my warning.'

27

The man stood looking out of the tall windows at the people and traffic in the streets below. He wondered if it was time to move. Like a good many others of London's streets Bond Street was no longer special. In fact even Mayfair as a whole was no longer what it had once been. In the old days it was snobbish, but snobbish with style. And now it was going the way of Oxford Street. Fifth Avenue clung to its old image, so did the Faubourg St Honoré. The Kurfürstendamm still kept its style. But the greed and the sharks always won in the end. He had once owned the whole building but as the price of property went up he'd cashed in and now he only rented the two top floors. One for living in, the other for the offices. He'd made a tidy pile out of the sale and lost most of it when he made *Firebird*. But he'd rather lose money on a film than make money as a property owner. There were people who could make money out of money and others who had to earn it by their work and their talents. He had always been one of the latter.

The room was large and he used it as both living-room and work place. The walls and ceiling and woodwork were all painted white. The furniture was a hotch-potch of things that he'd brought back from one place or another where he'd been filming. Everything was either beautiful or interesting but it was an interior decorator's nightmare.

The paintings on the walls were the rewards of a life-time's love of the Impressionists. The largest was a village street by Sisley, a charcoal sketch of a miner by Van Gogh, a farmyard scene that was an early Daubigny and his favourite, a crayon sketch by Berthe Morisot of two young girls.

The man himself was a bear-like figure. Tall, with the heavy sloping shoulders of a boxer. His well-cut suit disguised the inevitable product of years of good eating and drinking. It was a powerful figure crowned by a big head. The jowls and the half-closed observant brown eyes were balanced by the roundness of face that gave an impression of a readiness to smile, an amiability. The face of a man who was ready to listen. Despite the thinning hair there was no attempt to disguise the frontal baldness that became part of the smooth, deep fore-head. The beard was not macho or aggressive, more of the French *savant*. An affectation, neither a chal-lenge nor a disguise. It was a comparatively recent addi-tion.

He turned at a knock on the door. 'Come in.'

'They're here, Erich. I've put them in the dining-room.'

'Thank you, Patty.'

Miss Patterson was in her mid-forties. Tall and hand-some with high cheekbones. A handsomeness that did not come from her having been pretty or beautiful. But a handsomeness that came from good features and the planes of a face that a good lighting man could make look patrician or regal. It was a Katharine Hepburn face. Like a classic wine, improving with the years.

He looked at his watch. 5 p.m. They would be here for at least another two hours. Most of it time wasted. But it had to be gone through.

Connors represented the insurance company that was putting up forty-nine per cent of the film's budget. He was trying hard not to seem Philistine and only concerned with his client's investment.

'I was surprised, Erich, that there was no provision for some market research on audience acceptability.'

The man leaned back in his chair so heavily that it creaked, despite its Edwardian robustness.

206

'You know why, Connors . . .' He shrugged. 'Because we've done it all before. Market research can tell you why the public loved or hated the last film you or somebody else shot, but it can't tell you what they'll think of something that doesn't yet exist.' He paused and leaned forward, his big arms bulging in his jacket. 'It's crystal-ball gazing, Connors. Every film's a gamble. It's got nothing to do with whether it's good or just competent.' He shrugged. 'It can be the weather. Some current event, some public concern about values or whatever. We're gamblers, Connors. You gamble on me and I gamble on what? Thirty years' experience, a feeling for what the public might want and a reputation for delivering inside budget.'

It was Rowe from the Norwegian investors who took up the point. 'My investors have got every confidence in you, Erich, you know that. But it keeps them happy if you indicate your own feelings. Is it the right subject for today?'

'If it was, my friend, we wouldn't be here. I wouldn't anyway. We're talking about two years from now. Maybe two and a half.' He jabbed a thick finger at Rowe. 'Can you tell me what the Dow Jones or the FT index will stand at two years from now? Of course you can't.'

Rowe smiled. 'OK, Erich, don't get worked up. We need you.'

The big man smiled and shrugged. 'They know, my friends. The investors will have looked at my track record inch by inch. They'll know the names of every starlet I've ever had on the couch. No divorces, because I ain't ever been married. I'm not a lush, I don't screw fellas, and I've only once gone over budget; and that was my dough not anyone else's. And any film I've ever made has never done worse than break even. Three have made real big money, five have made everybody very happy and at least ten kept a few chaps in Bull Shots and Bloody Marys.' He paused, eyebrows raised. 'So what next?'

Then it was Kramer's turn. Kramer's people had bought the distribution rights.

'My people think that the script is flawed.'

'In what way, may I ask?'

'Too much improvisation and too much dialogue.'

'Last time we met your people complained that I was paying the two leads far too much.'

'What's that got to do with it?'

'Because – ' the big man's voice was almost a whisper ' – because those two actors are gonna be acting – not repeat not, improvising. That's what they're being paid for, Freddie.'

'All the same . . .'

'All the same nothing. If you chaps want to pull out that's fine by me. The TV rights are sold already in the US of A, the UK, the Commonwealth, France, Germany and Holland. I can go on that and to hell with your *dreck* in LA.'

'We've already bought the distribution rights. All we're suggesting is . . .'

'All you're suggesting is another one eighth of one per cent for publicity. Forget it. The deal's as it stands or not at all.'

'You seem very defensive, Erich, have you got any problems?'

The big man laughed. 'Dozens. But that's what I'm here for. It's waiting around that causes problems. People with nothing to do. As soon as I get the final location reports I'll be pressing the button.' He paused. 'Are we finished, gentlemen?'

There were murmurs of assent and nods and a general relaxation.

'Tell us about it, Erich.'

Erich smiled, jowls quivering, crow's-feet at the corner of his eyes.

'It's going to be another *Zhivago*.'

'For Christ's sake,' said Kramer, 'that was in the cinemas for three months before it even paid for the film stock.'

The big man nodded, smiling. 'You wait, my boys. You're gonna be very happy. All of you.' He looked at his watch, 'I've got to throw you out. Another meeting I'm afraid.'

The bedroom wasn't entirely masculine but it made up for its neutrality by the big double bed with frilly pillows and a second dressing table with triple mirrors and rows of make-up, cosmetics and perfumes. Hundred dollar sizes from Madame Rochas to Obsession and old favourites like Chanel, Guerlain and Rive Gauche.

Somebody had once said at a dinner-party one night that if a man lived out his fantasies, then they were destroyed because they were no longer fantasies. Erich Kern was impressed by the logic even though he knew it wasn't true. All men imagined that every pretty, young starlet got her feet on the ladder via the casting couch and despite articles to the contrary in *Playboy* and *Penthouse* they still felt that if they were film tycoons that's how it would be.

That was how it had always been for Erich Kern. Long before he was a major film director. His pleasure was Marilyn Monroe look-alikes who were rewarded with small parts as soda-fountain girls or cheer-leaders. But Erich Kern played fair and saw that they got at least ten words of dialogue to up the Equity rate.

The girl lying naked on his bed was twenty years old, and she lay back watching him as he stood in his Paisley dressing gown cleaning his teeth.

'How old are you, Erich?'

'Why?'

'Somebody told me they'd read you were sixty-nine.'

'S'right.'

'You're very ardent for sixty-nine.'

'Very what?'

'Ardent.'

'You mean horny.'

'If you insist. Do you want to do it again?'

'We'll see how it goes when we've had a meal, honey.'
'I like it when you call me honey.'
'Why.'
'It makes me feel I'm already in LA.'
'We're gonna be shooting in Spain and Brazil, kid.'
'What are my parts?'
'In one you're a shepherdess but with goats not sheep. And in the second you're a waitress in a night-club. Big smiles and lots of cleavage.'

She laughed. 'Do you like my tits?'

He turned and looked at her as if he needed reminding. 'They're fantastic, honey. Those bastards on the cameras will drag it out to twenty takes when you're on frame. You mark my words.'

He had pushed aside the breakfast tray to the end of the table, reaching for the dailies. Miss Patterson brought in another Thermos of coffee and said, 'There's a young man wants to see you urgently.'

'Oh. Who is he?'

'He gave his name as Mallory.'

'Sounds like a poet but more likely some bloody writer hawking his script of *Son of Jaws*.'

'I don't think so. I think he's a policeman. Got that look about him anyway.'

'OK. Wheel him in.'

Kern stood there in his towelling bath-robe, coffee cup in hand, as Mallory came in. Kern was just like Carter had described him but larger than he had expected. A big man with eyes that seemed to take in everrythiing. Not staring, just observing.

'Well. What is it?'

'My name's Mallory, Mr Kern, I . . .'

'I know that. What is it you want? Patty says you look like a cop. Are you?'

Mallory reached inside his jacket for his SIS ID card and offered it to Kern who looked at it without taking it and then back at Mallory.

'Go on then.'

'I'd like to talk to you about the time you worked for the British in a line-crossing operation in Germany.'

'Who fed you that little concoction?'

'Major Carter.'

'Who's he?'

'He ran the operation. You worked for him.'

'So go talk to him for Christ's sake. I never rewrite other people's scripts.'

'I think it would be to your advantage to talk to me.'

'In what way?'

'There's a question of allegations of war-crimes.'

Kern waved his arm towards a cane armchair. 'You'd better sit down.' He sipped his coffee as he looked at Mallory. 'Who's your boss?'

'My immediate boss is Mike Daley and above him is Toby Young.'

Kern walked bare-footed to the phone, and pressed a button and said, 'Patty, bring your notebook in if you please.'

When Miss Patterson came in with her notebook Kern said, 'This chap's going to give you a couple of names and a telephone number. Get one of them on the phone. I'll take it in the bedroom.'

Without even looking at Mallory, Kern walked slowly to a far door, went in the room and closed the door.

Irritated at Kern's dismissive attitude Mallory nevertheless gave the secretary the names and the telephone number.

He sat looking around the room as he waited. It was almost like an explorer's home. African masks, a miniature Indian head-dress, a pair of red leather boxing gloves that had obviously been used, a classical gguitar and a carved stone miniature of the statue of Jesus at Rio de Janeiro. There were framed photographs in a panel on one wall showing Kern with well-known people, filmstars and politicians.

It was ten minutes before Kern came back, still in his

bath-robe and bare-footed. For a moment or two he stood, towering over the seated Mallory and then he reached for a chair and sat down slowly and carefully.

'Right, my friend. Ask away.'

'How did you get away from Holland?'

'You mean in the end, after the invasion?'

'Yes.'

'There was a young girl. She'd been my secretary at one time but by then she was in the resistance. The Dutch resistance. It was bloody chaos. I was going to try to get over the border at Arnhem but the British made such a cock-up of that I moved down to Nijmegen, but the SS held on to the bridge across the river so I went to ground and made my way down to Venlo. I was asleep in some woods when those people got me. The girl was in charge and she let me go.'

'Can you remember her name?'

'Good God, no. It was a long time ago.'

'Why did she let you go?'

Kern shrugged. 'We had several things in common. And they knew the Allies had won the war.'

'Where did you go when you were freed?'

'I got to Hannover eventually but by that time Montgomery's forces were right on top of me. I got picked up at a small town named Peine and was sent for interrogation at Bad Salzuflen.' He shrugged and smiled. 'It seems you know what happened after that.'

'What happened to you after you brought Major Carter back over the border?'

'I went back to Magdeburg and made a film for the Soviets about the people's army. It went down well and they took me to Berlin. I made several films there and I got a bit of a reputation and they asked me to go to Moscow. And in those days when the Russians asked it was an order. So I went.'

'What happened in Moscow?'

'My God, that would take hours to explain.' He sighed as if the mere thought of explaining would be exhausting.

Mallory smiled. 'It's a big leap from the ruins of Magdeburg to all this.' And he waved his arm at the room.

'Does it really matter in the context of your investigation?'

'Yes it does. I might as well tell you that I'm checking to see if there is any justification for what you did with those SOE prisoners.' He paused. 'The fact that you worked for the British and that you undoubtedly saved the life of Major Carter have to go in the balance on the other side. But you are responsible for the execution of a lot of brave men.'

'I just carried out my orders. I can only assume that the orders were justified in some way.'

'Do you think they were justified?'

Kern shrugged. 'I wondered at the time and I've wondered since.' He shrugged again. 'Who knows? I was told at the time that it was necessary.'

'For what reason?'

'I wasn't told. But I think I can guess why.'

'Why?'

'I'm sorry but I'm not prepared to discuss that. I could be wrong.' Kern looked at his watch and then at Mallory. 'I have to go to Pinewood. I'll have to ask you to leave.'

'Would you be prepared to let us hold your passport?'

Kern looked surprised. 'Are you entitled to do that?'

'I can make it so by applying for a warrant but that would start things that would be hard to stop.'

'You mean legalities?'

'Yes.'

'This is because I have a British passport?'

'Yes.'

'It would be no problem for me. But maybe you should know that I have also a Brazilian passport and an American passport too. Both of them current and valid.'

Mallory half-smiled despite his frustration. 'You've got it all worked out haven't you?'

The big shoulders shrugged. 'That's how it goes, my

boy.' He smiled. 'I had a Soviet passport for about ten years. In the end it was more trouble than it was worth.'

'When can I talk with you again?'

'Is it really necessary?'

'Yes.'

'Let's make it a week from today – here. We'll have a working breakfast, say 10.30, OK?'

'Yes. If I need to speak to you before then can I contact your secretary?'

'By all means. Get the number from her as you go out.'

And to mark Mallory's dismissal Kern walked back into his bedroom and Mallory heard him lock the door and heard a girl laugh.

Mallory took a taxi to the garage and Freddie grinned as he took him over to the Healey.

'New bumper, new offside headlight and a bit of metal bashing and a paint-job on the offside wing.' He laughed. 'Told me she'd hit the post when she went into the driveway of a friend's house.'

'How much, Freddie?'

'She's paid already.'

'How much was it?'

'Hundred and seventy-five.' He laughed. 'I told her it'd have been another hundred at least if you'd been paying. She's a rreal corker that one. Bloody cheeky with it.' He pointed to the dashboard. 'Key's in the ignition. When you've got a bit of spare cash you'd better let me replace the exhaust. Not enough clearance. Gets scraped every bump you go over.'

The nearest parking he could find to the flat was right at the top of Sloane Street behind Harrods and he walked back slowly thinking about Kern. He seemed very sure of himself. But he was an international figure. And was probably a millionaire several times over. Perfect English and despite the tussle with him he was an attractive personality. His mind went to the girl in the silver-framed photograph. Van Kempen's dead wife and Kern's ex-mistress. He wondered what had made her leave Kern and join the resistance. Maybe when things were hotting up she didn't like how the SD were reacting. And if she found Kern attractive what was the attraction of van Kempen, a very different sort of man. No flamboyance there. Maybe the quiet calmness was what she needed.

When he got back to the flat he picked up the post and sat with a cup of tea to go through it, and half an hour later Debbie came in.

'Was the car OK?'

He smiled. 'Better than ever. You needn't have paid for it.'

'Of course I should. It was me who damaged it.'

'I thought you might be here last night.'

She wrinkled her nose. 'I was stuck with a real creep.' She laughed. 'But a generous creep. Took me for late dinner at the Savoy. Then to the Hilton where he had a penthouse suite.'

'Sounds like one of your Saudi friends.'

'No. Greek. Oil tankers and Old Masters.'

'I thought we might go to the theatre tonight.'

She looked doubtful and he said, '*The Phantom*, I've got tickets.'

'Ah that's different. I thought you meant one of those ghastly things about downtrodden workers.'

'But *The Phantom*'s OK?'

'You bet. By the way if you want radios or TVs fixed any time, let me know. I met a chap who does that sort of thing.'

'Great. We'd better leave here about six.'

'Will you drop me back at the club after?'

'Sure. Are you sleeping here tonight or your place?'

She sighed. 'I don't know, Charlie. It all depends.'

'OK. You have first bath.'

She looked disappointed. 'I nicked a bottle of champagne from the club. I thought we'd have it now and celebrate.'

He smiled. 'Celebrate what?'

'I dunno. Anything.' She laughed. 'Let's go to bed. Just for an hour. It's early yet.'

When the phone rang Mike Daley lifted the receiver and listened. Toby Young got up and walked to the window loosening his tie as he stood looking across the London roofscape. Mallory had wondered why Young was at the meeting. He didn't normally involve himself in routine stages of an operation.

He sensed that they didn't believe what he was telling them. Either that or they didn't like what he was reporting.

When he hung up Daley turned to look over his shoulder at Toby Young.

'Mortimer wants to see us both.'

'When?'

'Today, lunch at his club.'

'Is that the Garrick?'

Daley smiled. 'You must be joking. The Reform.'

Toby Young went back to his chair and Daley turned to Mallory.

'Have you got any notes on all this stuff you've been doing?'

'Yes, of course.'

'With you?'

'Yes.'

'Leave them with me and I'll look through them.'

Mallory reached for his brief-case, took out the buff folder and handed it to Daley who put it in one of the drawers in his desk.

'From what you've told me you haven't got anywhere near a case to put before the Director of Public Prosecutions.'

'I'd have thought that signing the death warrant for over fifty prisoners was a pretty good basis.'

'What proof have you got?'

'Van Kempen could testify as to what his wife told him.'

'Oh, for Christ's sake, Charlie. A court wouldn't accept hearsay evidence for a handbag snatch let alone an allegation of war-crimes.'

'So what do we do? Shall I see what else I can find?'

Daley glanced at Young but he didn't respond. Daley thought for a few moments, doodling on his pad, and then he said, 'Just make me out a brief report. Two paragraphs would be ample. You've checked on these people and in no case have you found any evidence that would require – no – hold on – no evidence that would *justify* any further action, legal or otherwise.'

'But that's not true. We know at least what Kern did.'

'We don't. We only know what somebody claims he did. And even then it's hearsay.'

'Let me see if I can get proof.'

'Where? How?'

'I don't know.'

'Forget it, Charlie. We've got problems enough for you to work on without chasing shadows.'

'Will you read my notes before you decide?'

Daley looked at Young who nodded almost imperceptibly.

'OK, Charlie. If you insist. But – ' he wagged his finger at Mallory ' – after I've read them you do what I say.'

'OK.'

When Mallory had left Young said, 'There was no point in refusing to read his notes if it keeps him happy.'

'What do you want me to do?'

'Put them in the shredder and tell him you're even more convinced that we're wasting our time.'

'At least we can be sure that no bloody journalist is going to come up with anything. Not that a paper dared print anyway.'

Daley leaned back in his chair. 'How the hell did those old boys make such cock-ups?'

'They didn't, Mike. What they did was stupid and ruthless but it wasn't a cock-up. It was deliberate.'

'You really think so?'

'I know so. So does Mortimer. That's why we've got to cover up for them. If we didn't we'd get flushed down the toilet with them, Mike. Don't kid yourself about that.'

'We weren't even at school when they were playing those games.' Daley was almost shouting. 'But we're here now. And we're SIS.' He banged his fist on the desk as he stood up. When he got to the door he stopped and said, 'Don't let Mallory play games. We make the rules, not kids like him.'

Mallory drew £200 from his personal account at the bank and used his credit card for the airfare to Amsterdam. He kept receipts for everything so that he could prove that the trip had been at his own expense.

It was 8 p.m. when he got off the airport bus at Amsterdam Central Station where he took a taxi to van Kempen's address. He didn't want to risk a refusal on the telephone.

Van Kempen didn't recognise him at first.

'It's Charlie Mallory, Mr van Kempen. Could you spare me a moment?'

For a moment van Kempen hesitated and then he opened the door wide. 'Of course. You look a little – what's the English word – harassed, isn't it. Let's go in the living-room, you know the way.'

When Mallory was sitting van Kempen said, 'You look as if you've got a problem. Have you?'

Mallory nodded. 'I'm afraid I have.'

'Tell me.'

'Before I tell you can I ask you a question? I need a very straight answer.'

'What's the question?'

'Do you think it would be fair to say that Kern's signing of the death warrants for those prisoners puts him in the category of a war criminal or alternatively guilty of a crime against humanity?'

'Well there's no problem there, Charlie. I don't have any

doubt that by all the standards established at Nuremberg friend Kern was definitely a war-criminal.'

'I think so too. But when I reported my opinion at HQ they told me to close down the operation and write a short report, two paragraphs only, stating that I had investigated the Germans concerned and that I found no evidence that would justify bringing them to trial.'

Van Kempen smiled. 'Are you surprised at their attitude?'

'I was certainly surprised. And when I thought about it afterwards I was angry about it too.'

'I can understand that. But why are you talking to me?'

'I'd better say right now that I'm not here officially. I've come at my own expense. I'm talking to you mainly to make sure that I'm not exaggerating in my own mind what Kern or Keller did.'

'I'm sure you're not.' He smiled. 'Do you suspect that your bosses are doing a white-wash job?'

'It's either that or they're bored with the whole thing.'

'How did you leave it with them? No, go back to when you reported back to them.'

'I told them everything in my notes. Chapter and verse, names – the lot. My immediate boss told me to forget it, there was no proof. Just write the report like I told you.'

'As a matter of interest. Where do you keep your notes? In a safe place?'

'My boss has them.'

'Did you offer them to him or did he ask you for them?'

Mallory closed his eyes, thinking. 'He asked me for them.'

'And then what?'

'I asked him to read the notes and maybe think again and let me pursue it further.'

'And he agreed?'

'Yes.'

'Did you keep a copy of your notes?'

'No. They were handwritten.'

Van Kempen said, 'You won't see those again, Charlie. Did you find Kern?'

'Yes, I found him in London. I had a very brief interview with him. He was very defensive. Asked for the name of my boss and his telephone number and he spoke to one of them.'

'Did you hear the conversation?'

'No, he took the call in his bedroom.'

'And when he came back?'

'He was much the same. Rather arrogant. Maybe that's too strong a word but he was very sure of himself. I threatened to get a warrant for his passport and he obviously didn't give a damn. Said he'd got a Brazilian passport and a United States one too. I said I needed to talk to him further and he said I could see him in a week's time. That's in four days' time now.'

'So how else can I help you?'

'Will you think about if there's somebody or some official record, here in Holland or even in Berlin or Bonn that could prove that he signed those death warrants?'

'But like I said to you before – he would claim that he was just carrying out orders from Berlin. *Befehl ist befehl* and all that stuff.'

'That wasn't acceptable at Nuremberg.'

'The timing was different then. The war was barely over. The world was up in arms about the Germans. The Allies were looking for revenge. And it was a long time ago. Big names. A massive publicity campaign. Goering, Himmler, Hess, Streicher and a whole bunch of generals.'

'Will you think about it all the same?'

'Of course. You staying at the Damrak again?'

Mallory laughed. 'I'm afraid not. I'm paying this time. I'll try and find a pension on one of the canals.'

'You'd better stay here for the night. We can talk again in the morning. I'll show you your room and we'll go out for a snack.' He smiled. 'Good, plain, Dutch food.'

28

They had breakfast together, walked down to the river and then walked back to the house. Van Kempen had put two canvas chairs out on the small patio at the back of the house and they sat there in the sun for a few moments talking about the relaxed Dutch attitude to drugs. Van Kempen had a friend in the police who felt that the new attitude had reduced drug abuse, but wasn't convinced himself.

Then van Kempen said, 'Your problem. I've been thinking about it. I wonder if you'd do something to help me make up my mind?'

'If I can. What is it?'

'You've got a telephone number for Erich Kern haven't you?'

Mallory nodded. 'Yes.'

'And you're due to see him in three days' time?'

'That's what we fixed. His suggestion.'

'OK. Will you phone that number and ask if you could see him tomorrow instead?'

'But . . .'

'Just do what I say.' He smiled. 'Humour me. The phone is in the living-room.'

Puzzled, Mallory walked into the room, checked in his diary for the number and in the local directory for the dialling code to London. And then he dialled the number. After a few rings a woman's voice answered.

'Is that Miss Patterson?'

'It is. Who is that?'

'This is Charles Mallory. I have an appointment with

Mr Kern at 10.30 a.m. on Friday. I wonder if it would be possible to see him tomorrow instead?'

'Mr Kern is in Brazil. He is filming there and then going to India. He won't be in the UK again until next spring.'

'Did he leave a message for me?'

'No.'

'Is there any way I can contact him?'

'You could write to him at this address.'

'When did he leave?'

'He left on Sunday last. He's having a few days' holiday before he starts filming.'

'And you're sure there's no message for me?'

'Quite sure.'

And she hung up.

When van Kempen saw Mallory's face as he walked back on to the patio he smiled. 'He's left the country, yes?'

'Yes. How did you know?'

'From what you told me last night I took it for granted that he'd leave the country. I'm surprised that he didn't leave the same day that you saw him.'

'But he showed no signs of being concerned at anything I said. Not even about the execution of the prisoners. He was cool, calm and dismissive.'

'I'm sure he was. But you're missing the point.'

'So tell me.'

'He was told to leave.'

'By whom?'

Van Kempen smiled. 'Think. Think hard.'

Mallory tried not to show his exasperation. 'You know, I'm sick and tired of people telling me to think hard. If you know the answer just tell me for Christ's sake.'

Van Kempen shook his head, 'Forget it. It doesn't matter. But . . .' he paused, '. . . I can give you the proof that you want if you're really determined to push for him to be tried and exposed.' He shrugged. 'Maria made him sign a confession. I've got it in safe keeping.'

'And you'll let me have it?'

Van Kempen smiled. 'No. That's my insurance. But I'll give you a photocopy. And a notarised statement by my late wife confirming the circumstances of the confession.' Van Kempen reached inside his jacket and brought out a sheet of paper and handed it to Mallory, who opened it and read it carefully.

> Het Grubbenvorst,
> Venlo,
> Nederland
> February 9, 1945

I, Erich Ludwig Keller, hereby confirm that in the course of my duties I signed the order to execute 51 Dutch and British captured agents on instructions from the appropriate authorities.

Signed Erich Ludwig Keller (Oberst) Abwehr/SD

> May 10, 1957
> c/o Bank of America,
> Keizersgracht 617,
> Amsterdam

I, Maria van Kempen (formerly Koolstra) confirm that I witnessed the signing of the above statement. I was for a period secretary to Oberst Keller before the Abwehr was incorporated in the SD.

Maria van Kempen

He read the page several times and then looked at van Kempen.

'Thanks. This will be enough to force them to do something.'

Van Kempen said quietly, 'What they do may not be what you want, my friend.'

'Why do you say that?'

'I told you. I don't trust SIS.'

'But they were different people in your time during the war.'

'Makes no difference, Charlie. They're still SIS and I still don't trust them.'

'Does anyone else know about these statements?'

'Only one. My bank manager. He was in the resistance too, and he doesn't trust your people either. If anything abnormal happened to me copies of that document would go to all the media right away.'

'You think that even today you could be harassed by SIS?'

'At this stage they don't harass, Charlie, they kill.'

'I don't believe it.'

'Not you, Charlie. But there are lots of layers in their cake. All intelligence services have "dirty tricks" men. SIS are no exception.'

'Can I take this copy back with me?'

'Of course. If you want to.'

Mallory smiled. 'They're going to get a shock when I produce this.'

'They know already. You'll just be rubbing their faces in the dirt.'

'You really think they know?'

Van Kempen stood up and said, 'You want me to run you out to Schipol?'

'No. It's OK. I'll get the bus. But thanks for the offer.'

Mallory phoned Daley but his secretary said that he wouldn't be back until the next day. He asked her to pencil in an appointment for him and she gave him half an hour from 10.30 to 11.00.

When he phoned Debbie's number the answering machine was on and he smiled as he listened to her putting on her bedroom voice. 'This is Debbie. I'm not available at the moment. But I'll be back shortly. Please leave me a message after the tone. I'm looking forward to hearing from you. Bye.' He waited for the tone and said, 'This is Burt Lancaster. Warren

Beatty told me about you. How about you give me a call at the Park Lane Hilton. Room 504. Bye, honey.'

He walked down to Sloane Square and made six copies of van Kempen's document and then called his father.

They had dinner together at his father's place. Lamb's liver and mashed potatoes followed by an Ogen melon with lots of brown sugar.

When they were alone he told his father a much curtailed version of what he had been doing.

'Tell me about the legal bits on war-crimes.'

'In which country?'

'Here. In the UK.'

'But you said this man committed the alleged crimes in Holland. If that's the case the Dutch government would have to try him.'

'But he's got a British passport.'

'That makes no difference and you say he's got a Brazilian and an American passport too.' His father paused. 'Anyway there was an international agreement that there was a time limit to war-crime prosecutions and that's long gone by. Maybe the DPP could consider a case of crimes against humanity. But it would still have to be the Dutch who brought the case. They'd have to ask for his extradition from wherever he was living. And extradition's not easy.'

'But if he uses a British passport we could arrest him and pass him over to the Dutch. Like the Barbie case.'

'I suppose if your people really wanted him brought to justice they could probably cut a few corners.'

'If it's all so impossible why do the newspapers keep on about prosecuting these people?'

'You know newspapers as well as I do. They print first and think afterwards.'

'But if they were given a copy of the document they could expose Kern.'

'I suppose so. Tell me. Why didn't your Dutch friend pass this material to the Dutch authorities long ago?'

'I don't know.'

'I should ask him some time.'

'I'll see what my people say. At least they can't ignore it.'

His father smiled. 'Remember what I've always told you, my boy. Keep your powder dry when you're dealing with those chaps.'

Mallory laughed. 'I will.'

When Mallory handed Daley the photocopy of Keller's confession and Maria van Kempen's note, Daley read it carefully and it seemed a long time before he looked back at Mallory.

'You got this from van Kempen, yes?'

'Yes.'

'What did you have to do to squeeze this out of him?'

'Just talk.'

It was only then that he saw the anger in Daley's eyes. Daley leant back in his chair. 'OK. Something else for the files.'

'What shall we do about it? What's our next move?'

'I think we've done enough, Charlie. Whatever he did or didn't do, it was done in Holland.'

'We can't just let this man get away with it. He had those prisoners executed. Some were British, and all of them were SOE.'

'The DPP wouldn't touch it, Charlie.'

'So let's feed the story to the press. At least let people know what the bastard did. By anybody's standards he's a war-criminal.'

Daley shook his head slowly, 'Forget it, Charlie. We've got more important things to worry about.'

'But this man ordered the deaths of over fifty men and doesn't give a damn. A millionaire. World famous and made his reputation with films about the repression of the under-dogs.'

Daley said harshly, 'Forget it. And that's an order.'

For a moment Mallory wasn't sure what he should do

and then, making up his mind, he said, 'Can I ask for an interview with the DG, sir?'

'No.'

Daley's eyes were hard and there was a pulse beating by his eye, and his anger now was open and unmistakable.

'In that case, Mr Daley, I resign.'

Daley exploded. 'You must be out of your fucking mind, Mallory. You – a responsible officer, resign because we won't do something that would make us laughing-stocks at the DPP's office.'

'That's not why I'm resigning.'

'Go on then, enlighten me. What's the reason?'

'The reason is that I'm bloody sure that SIS is covering up for a war-criminal. Why, I don't know, but I want no part of it.'

And Mallory saw Daley change in seconds from an angry man to a very shrewd executive who wanted to put down a rebellion by charm and persuasion.

'How long since you had a proper leave, Charlie?'

'A couple of years.'

'And how long have you been working for me?'

'Just over five years.'

'Have I ever let you down on a job?'

'No.'

'Well. Let's calm down. Let me do a bit of thinking about this chap. Toby Young might come up with something. I can't promise anything.' He shrugged. 'You know how it is as well as I do. There are politicians poncing around in Westminster who ought to be strung from the lampposts, but there's nothing we can do about 'em. That's politics, Charlie. The CIA and the FBI will tell you the same. They can catch him with both hands in the cookie jar but they, in their turn, have got something on somebody else. Sink me and I'll bring down the bloody roof. So. Do me a favour. Have a week off. I'll ferret around a bit and then we'll get together and see what we can do. OK?'

Mallory nodded. 'OK. I'll be at the flat if you want me.'

'OK. Leave it to me.'

Toby Young tossed the photocopy on to his desk and looked at Daley.

'What are you going to do about him?'

'Squeeze the bugger.'

Young sighed, a deep, slow sigh. 'No grievous bodily harm, Mike. He's obviously naïve or he'd have taken the hint long ago.' He smiled. 'Let's say give a little warning of how things can get out of hand.'

Daley smiled. 'I thought I'd . . .'

Young held up his hand. 'I don't want to know, Mike. I don't want to know. But when the music stops make sure there's a chair for the stupid little man to sit on.' He smiled. 'And maybe a lollipop. A year in Rio maybe.'

'I get the message. Leave it to me.'

Mallory stood with his hands on his hips looking around the flat. It looked a real mess. Unwashed crockery in the sink, tattered curtains and lop-sided lamp-shades. It might be October but the place needed a spring-clean. And as always there was no washing-up liquid, no Flash, no Windolene and no sponges or dusters.

He went down to Safeway and came back with a cardboard box with the things he needed. By mid-afternoon the next day it all looked so good that he wanted Debbie to see it. But when he phoned it was still the answering machine.

It was late in the evening when the door-bell rang. It was both too early and too late for it to be Debbie and he switched off the radio and walked to the door.

The two men who were standing there when he opened the door were both in their forties, one in a suit and the other in sports coat and chinos. And he was the one who smiled and said, 'Mr Mallory? Charles Mallory?'

'That's me.'

'Sergeant Tucker and my colleague Sergeant Adams.' He held up a Metropolitan Police ID card. 'Could we have a word with you?'

Mallory nodded. 'Sure. Come in.'

The two policemen stood there until Mallory pointed to the armchairs. 'Please sit down. Would you like a drink?'

Sergeant Tucker smiled. An amiable, friendly smile. 'Maybe later, sir.' He looked around the flat. Casually but professionally.

'How long have you had this flat, Mr Mallory?'

'About four years. Why? Is there some problem?'

'I think I ought to tell you at this point that we're here officially and – ' he smiled ' – I have to caution you that anything you say can be used as evidence in court.'

'I don't understand, Sergeant. What's it all about?'

'We're from the Vice Squad at Savile Row and we have reason to believe that you are living on the immoral earnings of a girl named Deborah Primrose Harper.'

'You're kidding,' Mallory said, but at the moment all he could think of was that she'd never told him that her second name was Primrose.

'I'm afraid not. Under the Sexual Offences Act 1956 and amended by the 1967 Act, a man is guilty of an offence if he knowingly lives wholly or in part on the earnings of prostitution.'

'This is crazy. You must have made some mistake. I'm an officer in SIS.'

'We know that, sir. The Chief Super at Savile Row has been in touch with Century House.'

'Who was he in touch with?'

'A Mr Faraday in the Legal Department, sir.'

'Jesus. What did he say?'

Sergeant Tucker shrugged. 'He just asked to be kept in touch.' He reached in his pocket and slid the rubber band off his note-pad and turned several pages. When he looked back at Mallory he said, 'You're entitled to call your solicitor, Mr Mallory, before I ask you any questions.'

'Just carry on.'

'Right, sir. Is it correct to say that you knew that Miss Harper is a prostitute?'

'It depends on what you call a prostitute. She may be a bit wild but I'd certainly never describe her as a prostitute.'

'The legal definition is – and I quote the Street Offences Act 1959 – "a woman who offers her body commonly for sexual intercourse or acts of lewdness for reward".' He smiled. 'A bit Dickensian the wording, but that's the definition.'

'What the hell is lewdness?'

'It covers a variety of things. An exhibition of sexual intercourse. Fellatio. Cunnilingus – that sort of thing.'

'But Debbie's just a party-girl. Like I said – a bit wild but it was never a business.'

Sergeant Tucker smiled. 'They like to call themselves fancy names. Hostesses, models, escorts – party-girls. You name it. But if they screw for money they're prostitutes in the eyes of the law.'

'Have you spoken to Debbie about all this?'

'Yes. She was most of the day at Savile Row. She's out on police bail. Goes in front of the magistrate tomorrow at Marlborough Street Court.'

'She must have been shattered.'

'She seemed quite cheerful. It isn't the first time she's been to court.'

'Did you talk to her about me and our relationship?'

'Of course. Thinks a lot of you, sir. Denied everything concerning you.'

'So why are you here?'

'We took out a warrant, sir. Yesterday morning. To look at your bank account and hers.'

For the first time, Mallory smiled. 'You won't find a rich haul of immoral earnings in my account.'

'That's not quite true, sir. We found fourteen payments by the girl, to you or on your behalf.' He paused. 'Do you own a Healey 3000 URE 390P?'

'Yes.'

'And it was repaired following a damage only accident at – ' he looked at his notes ' – at Fellowes Auto Services three weeks ago. The cost was £175?'

'Yes.'

'A bill that was paid by Miss Harper?'

'Yes. But that was because she'd borrowed my car and caused the damage.'

'So she said, but when we asked her where she had the accident she hadn't a clue.' Looking back at his notes he said, 'There are a number of payments to you on her cheque-book in your name.'

'Well she paid sometimes for various things. I can remember her paying me for some very long and expensive overseas telephone calls. Calls to Australia and Canada.' He smiled. 'They were just friends of hers.'

'Male friends?'

'Probably.'

'Clients of hers?'

'You're trying to put words in my mouth, sergeant.'

'I assure you I'm not, Mr Mallory. There's another point I should mention. She admits that on several occasions she had sex with various men here in your flat. I assume you agreed to that?'

'I allowed her to stay here if she wanted to. Her place is pretty awful.'

'But you allowed her to use this flat when you were absent?'

'Yes. I often have to go away at very short notice.'

'She has a key to the flat here?'

'I gave her one some time ago. I can't remember if she's still got it.'

'Well, back to the present. Miss Harper will probably be fined twenty quid. But in your case the law takes the matter more seriously. If you are tried summarily it would mean six months but if you're tried on indictment it could be as much as seven years.'

'What's the difference between an indictment and summary trial?'

231

'A serious offence is tried on indictment at a Crown Court with a jury. But because the courts are so busy cases are sometimes sent to lower courts, Magistrates Courts, where the accused consents to forgo his constitutional right to be tried by a jury.' Sergeant Tucker smiled. 'Some people feel that being tried by twelve of their fellows might give them a better chance of being found not guilty.'

'Who decides which court it goes to?'

'The police legal department usually.'

'And in this case?'

'I guess it depends on what cooperation you give us.'

'Does this get in the press?'

'I'm afraid so. But not until we formally charge you.'

'Are you charging me now?'

'Good Lord, no. We'll come back in a couple of days and talk to you again. But I have to warn you not to have any contact with Miss Harper. But feel free to consult a lawyer if you wish to.' As he stood up he said, 'Your father's a barrister if I remember rightly isn't he?'

'He is.'

'A nice man. He acted for my wife when we were divorced. Didn't try and bankrupt me. Played it right down the middle. Well. I'll get on my way.' He looked at Sergeant Adams who nodded and with one last quick glance around the flat the two of them left.

When he was alone he sat down trying to collect his thoughts. At first it had seemed no more than a crazy mistake but as the sergeant had slowly recited the items that they saw as evidence he had realised that mistake or not it was going to look as if there was evidence that a prosecution could make sound pretty damning in court. God knows what Mike Daley and Toby Young would think. And God knows what the press would make of it. He could imagine the headlines – 'Secret Service man in sex scandal' and there would be plenty more, worse than that. He thought of contacting his father but felt too embarrassed to tell him the details. The longer he thought about it the more bizarre it seemed to be. Even the policeman's attitude was ominous. Amiable and easy-going because he felt that he'd got it all wrapped up. He knew the feeling. He'd often had it himself. When weeks of surveillance finally nailed the suspect. And then there was no need to be aggressive. It was in the bag. Sgt Tucker had made it seem so run-of-the-mill. All boys together and one of you just happened to live off the immoral earnings of Debbie Harper. Debbie Harper – prostitute. Or Debbie Harper – silly, happy-go-lucky Debbie who had never done anyone any harm in all her life.

He wondered what his father's reactions would be when it came out. 'Prominent lawyer's son a pimp.' He realised he didn't even know the difference between a pimp and a ponce. Maybe they were the same thing. There was nothing the press liked better than visiting the sins of children on their parents. It made some people feel good that the rich or the successful were brought down by their children taking drugs, or some other minor criminal activity.

Then the phone rang. He looked at his watch. It was nearly midnight. He hoped it wasn't Debbie. He picked up the phone and gave his number not his name.

'Mike Daley here, Charlie. What's going on? I had that idiot Faraday from legal dithering away. What's it all about?'

'Two cops came round. Said they were from the Vice Squad. Accused me of living off immoral earnings.'

There was a long pause. 'I don't believe it. Did you get it all cleared up?'

'No way. They say they have enough evidence to prosecute me. Suggested I could get up to seven years if I didn't cooperate.'

'The cheeky bastards. Listen. How long will it take you to get your kit together?'

'About twenty minutes.'

'Just grab the essentials and come round to my place.

Meantime I'll speak to Toby. And don't you worry. We'll fix those bastards, believe you me. Now get cracking.'

And the phone went dead. Half an hour later he found a taxi in Sloane Square which took him to Daley's place at the far end of Fulham Road.

Mike Daley answered the door himself and took him up to the room he called his study. A small comfortable room, its walls covered with photographs of boxers and footballers and a group photograph of Fulham FC when Jimmy Hill was captain.

'Sit down, fella.' Daley pointed at the only comfortable chair and pulled up a leather pouffe for himself.

'I've spoken to Toby and he agrees with me one hundred per cent.' He grinned. 'I take it that it ain't true what those guys came up with?'

'Of course it wasn't. She banged up my Healey and paid for the repair as it was her fault. To them it's my pay-off from immoral earnings. The other things were payments for long-distance phone calls she made. But the way they said it made it sound like it would be pretty damning in a court.'

'Well, it ain't gonna get in no court. You can count on that.' He paused. 'Do you remember their names – the two cops?'

'The one who did all the talking was a Sergeant Tucker. The other just listened and made notes. His name was Adams. Sergeant Adams. They said they came from Savile Row nick.'

'D'you speak Spanish?'

Mallory looked surprised. 'No. I'm afraid not.'

'Well now's your chance to learn. We're cooperating with a special Spanish police squad based in Malaga. Anti-terrorist stuff. You'll be our liaison man.'

'How long will I be there?'

'Until we've clobbered your friends at Savile Row.'

'What if they won't play?'

'They'll play all right. Never fear. Those bastards know which side their bread's buttered. They didn't even have

234

the decency to notify us before they jumped you. Now you get a good night's sleep. Forget this farce like it never happened and I'll run you to the airport myself. Take-off time eleven oh five so we'll leave here just after nine. Facilities can get you fixed up with a seat on the plane and accommodation in Malaga.' He grinned. 'OK, Charlie?'

'Thanks a lot, Mike. It was a real nightmare.'

'Like I said, forget it. You've got a bathroom next door. I'll take you to your kip.'

Fifteen minutes later, in the dining-room Daley dialled a number and when he heard the familiar voice he said quietly, 'OK. Like a lamb.' And hung up.

Packard who was also working with the Spanish security police met him in at Malaga airport and drove him out to a pleasant villa on the hills behind El Palo. He stayed for a couple of hours and explained the set-up. It was a complex operation of surveillance by undercover officers using radio, telephone taps and all the usual techniques. Included in the operation was surveillance of several British ex-pats who had moved to Spain with the proceeds of major robberies. These were suspected of playing some sort of role in drug-running, much of which found its way eventually to the UK. It would be that part of the operation that he was to be mainly concerned with. Packard had brought him a dozen files to read. An elderly Spanish lady was going to be his full-time housekeeper and a car and driver would be provided to take him back and forth between the villa and the operational HQ based in a large mansion on the outskirts of Malaga.

The third day after he arrived in Spain, Daley had phoned him from London. The police had been persuaded to drop the case but they'd refused to destroy their records. But Daley was hoping to work on that. Anyway there was nothing for him to worry about. When he asked what had happened to Debbie Harper, Daley said he didn't know.

He had tried to put the war-crimes thing out of his mind. But it still angered him that Kern had got away with it. And he kept remembering what his father had asked. Why didn't the Dutch authorities do anything about Kern? His crimes were committed in Holland so they would be justified in asking for his extradition. They had extradition treaties with most countries. Finally, he decided to contact van Kempen and suggest it to him.

He phoned van Kempen's number several times and eventually the Dutch operator told him that the number was no longer in use. So he wrote a brief note to the Dutchman and made the point about extradition. And then more or less forgot the whole issue. He'd done what he could and it was no longer his concern.

29

With Mallory's involvement in a new operation, as the days went by the doubts and resentments of the last few weeks had gradually receded. He wasn't sure what he would eventually do, but for the moment he was in neutral, coasting along in a situation where the daily details of the Spanish operation could occupy his mind.

There was still an hour of sunshine left when he took his coffee and the portable radio out on to the paved patio at the front of the villa. It had become a pleasant routine with the theatrical view out to the sea, the steep hill and the masses of bougainvillea, sprawling clumps of geraniums and a stillness and quiet that was balm to a troubled mind.

He saw the car in the distance coming slowly up the pot-holed road that led up the mountain-side to Olias, weaving its way around the deep ruts that had been cut by the torrents that rushed down to the coast road when the rains came. Then, to his surprise, he saw the car turn off on to the track that led past the villa to the group of cottages perched on the jutting headland that led to a sports club.

The car stopped for a few moments and then turned into the sloping drive that led up to the car-port beside his villa. Half-way up the steep slope the car stopped and a few moments later a man got out of the car. He stood for a moment, putting on his jacket, peering up towards the patio. He was tall, and Mallory guessed that he must be in his late sixties. As the man came slowly up the drive Mallory noticed that he had a slight limp and when he reached the half dozen steps that led up to the patio itself he came up slowly and cautiously step by step.

Mallory stood up and walked towards the man. 'I'm sorry but I don't speak Spanish. Can I help you?'

The man straightened up, slightly breathless as he said in English, with a smile, 'I don't speak Spanish either.' He paused for breath then said, 'I think you must be Mr Mallory. Charles Mallory.'

'Yes.' He pointed to one of the cane armchairs. 'Do sit down. It's a steep slope up to the villa.' He smiled. 'Not all that easy even in a car.'

'You're right. But it would be easier if I didn't smoke.' He put the brief-case that he had been carrying against the leg of the chair. 'Would you mind if we had a chat, Mr Mallory?'

'Please go ahead.'

'My name is Verwoord. Frank Verwoord. I'm the manager of the Bank of America branch in Amsterdam. Paul van Kempen is a very old friend of mine. He told me about his talks with you. I knew his wife, Maria, too.' He smiled and shrugged. 'We were all in the resistance together. That's why I've come to see you.' He paused. 'You wrote him a letter didn't you? Asking why the Dutch government hadn't taken any action against the man we all knew as Keller.'

'So he got it all right.'

'I'm afraid he didn't. It came into my hands because I'm the executor of his will.'

'I don't understand.'

'I'm afraid Paul van Kempen is dead, Mr Mallory.'

'Good God. I can't believe it. What happened? He seemed so fit.'

'He was knocked down by a car. A hit-and-run driver. Paul was killed instantly.' He paused. 'Because of your note and what he had told me about your talks I felt I ought to get in touch with you. He had a telephone number for you in his diary. I phoned several times on successive days and in the end the operator cut in and told me the number was no longer in use. That worried me. So I contacted Century House.' He paused, significantly. 'They said they'd never heard of you. And that worried me even more.'

'How did you find out that I was here?'

'There were people in SIS who owed me favours. One man in particular. I told him I wanted to talk to you and he did a bit of checking – and here I am.'

'But why was it so important to contact me?'

Verwoord sighed. 'Because I was sure you didn't realise what you'd got yourself into. Van Kempen told me that he was thinking of contacting you because he thought that you didn't realise how precarious, maybe dangerous, was your position.'

'I don't understand, Mr Verwoord.'

'Tell me what happened after you got back from Amsterdam and reported what you'd found out?'

For several moments Mallory hesitated and then he decided to tell Verwoord what had happened. After he had finished Verwoord sat for a long time without speaking. Then he said, 'You realise that what happened to you with the police and what happened to Paul van Kempen both happened because of what you'd found out. And your people were determined to stop you.' He paused. 'You realise that what happened to Paul is not unusual for people who get in the way of intelligence organisations, whether it's the KGB, the CIA, or SIS.'

'You mean SIS could have been responsible for his death?'

'I'm quite sure they were. But I couldn't prove it. There are people killed by cars every day in every country. And there are hit-and-run drivers in every country. That's why dirty-tricks squads use them as a way of killing people who they want out of the way. They all do it, Mr Mallory. It's all part of the games they play. Like your visit from the police.'

'What do you mean?'

'Well let's just look at the facts. Van Kempen told you that Keller was Kern. You go to see him. He phones SIS.

239

Two days later he leaves the country. You report to your bosses what you have found out from van Kempen on your second visit. Two days after that you get a visit from the Vice police on a trumped-up charge. They don't charge you. They just leave the threat there. Scandal, disgrace. You have to resign. Who's going to believe anything you say after all that? Just a delinquent officer of SIS who is justly dismissed and is now trying to revenge himself on his old organisation.

'And then your friends come in like the Fifth Cavalry. Leave it to them. No problem. Let's get you out of the country. Out of the way. No threats of resignation when they've so obviously been your saviours. And just as a piece of insurance they mention that the charges are dropped but the police won't destroy the records. They are always there if they're needed. In case you get any silly ideas about talking to the press.' And then, very quietly, Verwoord said, 'And the only other man who can stop the cover-up is van Kempen. He must have been wiped out on the same day you got your visit from the police.' He looked at Mallory, 'Do you believe me?'

Mallory nodded. 'I'm afraid I do. I've been a fool. But I still don't understand why what I found out is so important.'

'That would take a long time to explain.'

'Does that mean that you know why?'

'Yes.'

'Tell me then.'

'Could I be rude and suggest that we go somewhere for a meal. I haven't eaten today. It was an early start to my journey.'

'I'm sorry. Of course. There's a pleasant little restaurant right at the bottom of the hill. It's not very grand but the food is good.'

'That would be fine.'

They had eaten a good meal and were on the coffee and there had been no talk of recent events.

'Do you like being a bank manager?' Mallory asked.

Verwoord smiled. 'Yes. In fact I do. It's not as boring as most people assume.' He took a sip of his coffee. 'And apart from that I have a theory about work and life that makes it all quite civilised.'

'What's the theory?'

'I think that people waste their lives. Their work becomes the whole of their lives. For me, I believe that when work is over I've got another life from 6 p.m. To midnight. Six hours to do whatever I want. And I firmly believe that anyone can do anything they want if they want to enough.'

'And what do you do?'

Verwoord smiled. 'Well, there are certain limits that time and age make. I know that I'm never going to lead Ajax on to the field for the final of the world cup. And I'm pretty sure I'm never going to conduct the Concertgebouw in an evening of Beethoven. But apart from things like that - well, I play the cello. Badly, I'm afraid. But at least I can now appreciate the playing of Fournier or Casals. I also collect stamps.' He smiled. 'British colonials as a matter of fact. And like our friend Paul, I'm a licensed radio ham and can chat with others all over the world. There's something very satisfying about listening to a guy in Canada talking about going out to clear the snow to his truck with a ham in South Africa complaining about the mosquitoes.' He paused. 'And what do you do, my friend?'

'I'm afraid I waste my time.'

'Well it's not easy with your job. You spend too many evenings in strange hotels in other countries. Bored and a bit lonely and then feeling that a night-club bar and a pretty girl would be the ideal antidote.'

Mallory laughed. 'I'm afraid you're right.' He paused. 'Can I suggest you stay with me at the villa tonight?'

'That would be very nice if you have room enough.'

'There are a couple of spare bedrooms. Are you ready to go?'

'Will you allow me to pay the bill?'

'Certainly not. Apart from your concern for me I have an account here on my subsistence allowance.' He smiled. 'Century House will be picking up the bill.'

There was summer lightning flickering in the sky as they drove back to the villa in Verwoord's hire-car and by the time they were making their way up the steep steps to the patio the first drops of rain were cooling the air.

Mallory had made more coffee and put the Cona and cups with a sugar-bowl and cream on the low table between them.

He smiled as he looked across at the elderly Dutchman.

'Would you rather leave the rest until tomorrow?'

'I'd like to go back mid-day, tomorrow. Are you tired?'

'No. I'm fine.'

'Well let me start at the end, rather than the beginning.' He took a deep breath. 'Erich Kern was an SIS man and had been all his life since he was about nineteen or twenty. He worked as an assistant stage manager, a dogsbody, at one of those typically small pre-war Berlin theatres that specialised in political satire. Poking fun at the government and exposing the peccadilloes of politicians. A bit like *Le Canard Enchaîné* or your *Private Eye*. And of course that meant that the politicians and high society loved it. The place was full of them every night. You can imagine that a place like that was an intelligence agent's dream. The gossip of all the inner circles gave an insight into every ministry, the armed forces and top industrialists.'

'How was he recruited in the first place?'

'I'll tell you later. Just let me lay out the scenario for you.' He paused. 'Now I'd better explain something else. SIS was a professional organisation and its role was the collecting of intelligence all over the world. Friends as well as enemies. But obviously in those last few years before the war Berlin was the prime target. And I'd guess that Erich Kern, despite his youth, was one of the best listening posts that SIS had in all Germany.

'So. The war comes and eventually SOE is formed, as Churchill said – "to set Europe ablaze". And setting Europe ablaze meant that the Gestapo, the Sicherheitsdienst and the Abwehr were all given orders to smash the resistance at all costs. And that made the previously quiet lives of well-placed SIS men suddenly come under the same pressure. You can imagine what SIS felt about SOE and its wild amateur cowboys.'

'Van Kempen was SOE wasn't he?'

'He started in SOE but the group he joined after he escaped was run by SIS. It was a bit of a mixture. By then the resistance was doing its own thing and SIS groups were doing sabotage because communications with any organisations in London were a shambles. Especially after D-day. Anyway, back to Keller. In December 1939 he was called up and because of his languages and background he was recruited into the SD, the Sicherheitsdienst. London could hardly believe their luck.

'When the Dutch royal family left for England I was a young reserve soldier and I was part of their escort. I joined SIS . . . thank God . . . did my training and was dropped back in Holland as a radio operator. About eighteen months later Erich Keller was posted to Holland by the SD to head up a complicated signals detection unit in the Hague. SIS put him in touch with me and I acted as his radio operator to SIS in London.

'We didn't meet more often than once in two weeks unless there was some emergency. He told me about the radio game they were playing against SOE. He said that the signals security in London was so bad that they were picking up every SOE man as he landed. But what matters now is that he told me that they were only so successful because SOE in London seemed to ignore all the standard signals security procedures. Most of the captured men had made clear in their signals traffic for the Germans that they were operating under duress.' He paused. 'And London ignored the warnings.'

'Why did they do that?'

'Keller told me that at first he'd thought that it was just carelessness. But in the end it was so incredibly bad that he came to the conclusion that somebody in SIS had planted a man inside SOE who over-rode the security checks from the captured operators.'

'But who the hell would do that?'

'There was a man very near the top of SIS who had a pathological hatred for SOE and the problems they caused to SIS. I believe others had the same suspicions. The man died a few years ago.'

'It seems incredible.'

'I know. But the one thing I learned about SIS while I was part of it, was that nothing, however far-fetched, is impossible where they are concerned. And that still applies today in my reckoning.

'Anyway. The allies have landed. They're heading for Holland and Keller gets an order from Berlin, from the RSHA, that all the SOE prisoners are to be executed. Keller uses me to send a signal to SIS in London asking what he should do. A signal came back which was in a personal code that only Keller could decipher, and I passed it on to him. I don't know what it said but we both know what happened to those men.'

'What happened then to Keller?'

'He was trying to get over the border into Germany when the British army was closing in. Van Kempen's late wife had been Keller's mistress for a short time but she'd long ago left Keller and joined the resistance. The group she was with happened to get Keller in some woods near Venlo. For various reasons they let him go. He was picked up by the British near Hannover and once they found out who he was his controller from the days in Berlin took him over. He volunteered to go on working for SIS until things settled down and he joined the line-crossing organisation. I think you know the rest.'

'You think my bosses in London know all this?'

'I'm sure they do.'

'So why send me off on a wild-goose chase?'

'It isn't a wild-goose chase. It's that old army motto – "time spent in reconnaissance is seldom wasted." '

'I don't get it.'

'You're young and competent with a lot of resources behind you. You couldn't have found out what it was all about without several coincidences. If *you* can't then some crummy journalist from a gutter tabloid wouldn't find out.'

'What were the coincidences?'

'The first was your previous connection with the police in Hamburg. That led you to van Kempen – and I suppose that led you to me. Or me to you. Your people are protecting Erich Kern. They certainly owe him that, and far more. If somebody gets killed in the process they'd count that as part of the cost.'

'Who was it pulled the strings at Century House to tell you where I was?'

'He was the man who originally recruited Kern in Berlin, and was his case-officer ever since. And it was he who got Kern into the line-crossing operations.' Verwoord smiled. 'You met him briefly. His name's Stafford. Brigadier General Stafford – retired.'

'I thought he was a real old blimp. I was obviously very wrong.'

'It's his cover, my friend. Suits him too. Like all good covers.'

'What the hell do I do about all this?'

'Nothing. Absolutely nothing. You forget all about it. Wipe it out of your mind. It never happened. And you don't resign, you just carry on.'

'They'll know that I know what they've been covering up.'

'They won't. They don't know I've come to see you. They don't even know what I know. Neither would you if Paul van Kempen hadn't made me his executor a long time ago.'

'Why did you go to all this trouble about me?'

'For much the same reason that your bosses protect Kern.' He smiled. 'Paul told me that you said that all the old men from the war days seemed to belong to a club. Covering up for one another. You're in the same club, my friend. A different war admittedly. A cold war. But you're in it, whether you acknowledge it or not. There is no single good reason why you should pursue this business any further. So forget it and get on with your life. OK?'

Mallory smiled. 'Yes. And thanks for your help.' He hesitated and then he said, 'What about the police business?'

'You mean the charges still on file?'

'Yes.'

Verwoord laughed, softly, 'There are no charges, boy. There never were any. And those two Joes weren't cops either. They were from SIS's dirty-tricks brigade.'

'Are you sure?'

'Of course I am. The timing was too good to be true. I must get some sleep, Charlie.'

'Me too. Thanks again.'

It was 11 a.m. when Mallory woke up the next morning and Verwoord had already gone. As he stood in his bathrobe in the morning sunshine he realised that it was a long time since he had slept so soundly. He'd been dragged down slowly, day by day, by all those old men, and somehow Verwoord had cleared his mind and charged his drained batteries again. And suddenly he had a thought, walking back into the villa, taking out his diary and checking the number. Then dialling it slowly and carefully. It only rang twice before the phone was picked up at the other end.

'Hi. Who's that?'

'It's me, Debbie, Charlie.'

'Charlie. Where the hell have you been? I've been ringing casualty wards at every hospital in London. What have you been doing? And where are you?'

'I've been working, honey. How are you?'

'I'm fine. You know me. I'm always fine. So where are you?'

'I'm in Spain.'

'You crafty bastard. Lying in the sun on topless beaches I bet.'

'They don't have topless beaches in Spain.'

'You wanna bet?'

'I should be back next week. Will you phone my old man and tell him.'

'I phoned him once and he phoned me once. He said not to worry, you were just a lazy bastard, too idle to phone.'

'And you've had no problems since I saw you last.'

'No. What do you mean problems? D'you think I sound preggers or something?'

'No. You sound wonderful.'

'You gonna bring me something back?'

'Like what?'

'Like Julio Iglesias. By the way, was that you left that cheeky message on my answerphone?'

'Of course not.'

'You're lying. If it wasn't you you'd have asked me what cheeky message.'

'I think maybe you ought to have my job instead of me.'

She laughed. 'Got to go, sweetie. *Arrivederci* or whatever Spaniards say.'

Toby Young was standing at his desk checking papers before he put them in his black brief-case.

'Do you think Mallory rumbled what was going on?'

Daley shrugged. 'I hope so. All part of the learning process.'

'What are you going to do with him when he's back?'

'A week's leave. A bit of nannying and then I've got a surveillance job for him in Newcastle.'

Young looked up from his papers, smiling. 'Is that the Czech consulate thing?'

'Yeah.'

Young pressed the catches closed on his brief-case, picked it up and walked slowly to the door, looking back at Daley as he said, 'I'd like to vet your report before it goes to the DG, Mike.'

Daley grinned. 'Of course. The Authorised Version.'